"He's not dead. I'r

"Are you? Maybe you c   e a huge favor and
convince the townspeople of that." Holly's voice
sounded bitter.

"What are you saying?" Jeremy asked.

"Rumor has it that Russell was murdered. And that I
was the one who killed him."

"Did you?"

"No. I didn't."

Oddly enough, he believed her.

"Okay. Then we can work together to find my
brother."

"I've tried. It seems Russell has disappeared without
a trace."

"We'll see about that. One other thing. Since this is
my brother's house, I'm going to have to stay here."

"That's not a good idea. Everyone around here already
thinks I'm a horrible person. It wouldn't look good for
me to live with my missing ex-fiancé's brother."

"In that case, since I'm going to stay here, I hope you
have somewhere else you can go."

"You can't be serious. You expect me to leave my
own home?"

"I expect nothing. The decision's yours. I'm staying
here until Russell turns up and says otherwise."

Though she narrowed her gaze, she didn't protest.

"Follow me. I'll show you your room."

Dear Reader,

Once again, I got to return to my fictional Alaskan town of Blake. Though I've visited the state only once during a weeklong cruise, I love the self-sufficiency of its residents and the awe-inspiring beauty of the landscape.

In this story, meet Holly Davis, an artist who makes a living selling her work online. She left everything in the Lower 48 to move to Alaska for love, only to learn nothing is as it seems.

And in comes Jeremy Elliot, a former bad boy who left town at the age of sixteen to make it on his own in Seattle. He was wrongfully convicted and sent to prison, but is released and exonerated and paid restitution. He's returned to Blake to reconcile with his brother, Russell, only to learn Russell has been missing for eighteen months and a beautiful woman named Holly is living in Russell's house.

Together they must not only fight off their intense attraction to each other but also the swirling rumors and judgment of a small town as they attempt to find Russell. The more they look, the more it seems someone wants to stop them.

I hope you enjoy reading about their journey, both to love and discovering exactly what happened to Russell and how to make things right.

Karen Whiddon

ALASKAN DISAPPEARANCE

KAREN WHIDDON

Harlequin

ROMANTIC SUSPENSE

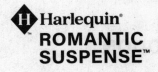

Harlequin®
ROMANTIC SUSPENSE™

ISBN-13: 978-1-335-50264-3

Alaskan Disappearance

Copyright © 2024 by Karen Whiddon

Harlequin Enterprises ULC
22 Adelaide St. West, 41st Floor
Toronto, Ontario M5H 4E3, Canada
www.Harlequin.com

Printed in Lithuania

MIX
Paper | Supporting responsible forestry
FSC® C021394

Karen Whiddon started weaving fanciful tales for her younger brothers at the age of eleven. Amid the gorgeous Catskill Mountains, then the majestic Rocky Mountains, she fueled her imagination with the natural beauty surrounding her. Karen now lives in north Texas, writes full-time and volunteers for a boxer dog rescue. She shares her life with her hero of a husband and four to five dogs, depending on if she is fostering. You can email Karen at kwhiddon1@aol.com. Fans can also check out her website, karenwhiddon.com.

Books by Karen Whiddon

Harlequin Romantic Suspense

Texas Sheriff's Deadly Mission
Texas Rancher's Hidden Danger
Finding the Rancher's Son
The Spy Switch
Protected by the Texas Rancher
Secret Alaskan Hideaway
Saved by the Texas Cowboy
Missing in Texas
Murder at the Alaskan Lodge
Vanished in Texas
Alaskan Disappearance

The Coltons of Owl Creek

Colton Mountain Search

Visit the Author Profile page
at Harlequin.com for more titles.

To my tribe of volunteers who rescue dogs.
Working tirelessly behind the scenes to save
creatures who depend on us so much.

Chapter 1

When the shaggy-haired, muscular man with the intricate bicep tattoo showed up on her doorstep, Holly Davis thought he might be a ghost. Naturally, logic prevailed, but not until she'd taken a step back in surprise and gasped out loud. This man, whoever he was, looked like a younger and rougher and much more handsome version of her missing ex-fiancé, Russell Elliot. But eyeing him again, maybe not. This guy was a lot taller, at least six feet two to Russell's five feet ten. And definitely sexier, for sure.

Even Thor, her giant Tibetan mastiff who'd barely tolerated Russell, didn't bark. Instead, he stayed by Holly's side, seemingly happy to meet this man, wagging his feathery tail.

The stranger glanced at the dog. His steely expression briefly softened before he returned his intense gaze to Holly.

"Can I help you?" she managed to ask, her mouth suddenly dry.

"I'm looking for Russell," he replied, his piercing brown eyes cutting straight to her soul. "Russell Elliot."

Momentarily flabbergasted, she wasn't sure how to respond. He must be an outsider. Everyone around here knew

Russell had been missing for over eighteen months. "And you are?" she asked.

"I'm Jeremy. Jeremy Elliot, Russell's younger brother."

Blinking, it took a few seconds for her to digest his words. Now she understood why this man looked so familiar. Russell had mentioned his younger brother, of course, but only to say Jeremy had chosen the wrong path and was serving time in prison.

Clearly that was no longer the case.

Weighing the potential for danger had become something she'd unfortunately gotten used to doing. This man, who she believed spoke the truth, didn't appear to be a threat. At least, not yet. And since she was about to deliver bad news, she figured he'd be okay. At least until he got over the shock.

"I think you should come in," she said, stepping aside and motioning him to go past her. "We have a lot we need to discuss."

He followed her inside without commenting. She left the door open, just in case. While she felt confident her giant dog would protect her, it didn't hurt to have an easy route to escape.

As she led the way to her small living room, the sheer size of him seemed overly intimidating. If not for her equally massive dog, she might have been worried. When she gestured toward a chair, he dropped into it. Crossing his massive arms in front of him, he stared, apparently waiting for her to explain.

Again, the possibility that she might be in danger crossed her mind. She'd certainly faced enough rancor and threats from the townspeople of Blake, Alaska. For whatever reason, without any actual evidence, a lot of them seemed convinced she'd done something to Russell. No doubt his younger brother would think the same. After all, she was the outsider around here.

Trying to decide if she should text her boss, Kip, she took a deep breath and retrieved her phone from the coffee table. Without commenting, she fired off a quick message, simply stating that a man claiming to be Russell's younger brother had arrived and that she was home alone. Kip managed the general store in downtown Blake and had been the only one to offer her a job once Russell left her high and dry. He'd also told her to let him know if she felt in danger. So far, she hadn't had to. Until today. Better to be safe than sorry.

Hoping that her face revealed none of her thoughts, she sat on the couch across from him. Their gazes met, and she swallowed, trying to figure out what to say, where to begin. Finally, she decided to simply tell him the truth outright. "Russell is missing," she said, her voice slightly unsteady. "He hasn't been seen around here for well over eighteen months."

To his credit, Jeremy digested her words without outwardly reacting. She wasn't sure what she'd expected. Denial, maybe? Definitely accusations. Those were sure to come. After all, she'd been dealing with them off and on for the last year and a half.

"And you are?" he asked, his tone remaining cordial. "After all, this is my brother's house, correct? If he's missing, why are you staying in his home?"

Again, she felt a slight shiver. Awareness, danger, she really couldn't tell which. At least the knowledge that Kip would be rushing over brought her a small measure of comfort.

"I'm Holly Davis. This house is half mine. And I'm Russell's ex-fiancée," she explained. "We've been living together, up until shortly before he took off without even saying goodbye." She left out the rest, all the reasons everyone in town believed she'd had motive to do away with Russell.

Some of her turmoil must have shown in her face, because his hard expression softened. "I didn't even know he was engaged," he said. "Obviously. But the two of us haven't spoken in a lot of years." He tilted his great shaggy head and studied her. The directness of his gaze had her feeling like he could see all of her secrets. Yet she couldn't seem to make herself look away.

"Tell me what happened," he said. "Do you have any idea where he went? Or why he took off like that?"

The gentleness in his husky voice almost did her in. He had no idea what she'd endured, both at his brother's hands and then in the months after his disappearance.

But she knew better than to say any of that to him. Though maybe she should. He'd find out anyway.

"Russell began acting different a few months before he left," she said, wondering how many details to share. "It almost felt like once he'd finally talked me into moving up here, he no longer had to pretend to be someone he wasn't."

His gaze never left her face. "Different how? Can you elaborate?"

Oh, she could. But she barely knew this man. No doubt he wouldn't like hearing what a monster his older brother had become.

Luckily, the sound of tires on the gravel driveway saved her from answering.

"One of my friends is here to check on me," she said, not bothering to hide her relief. She hurried to the door, peering out just as Kip Roberts came up on the front porch.

"Are you okay?" he asked, his concerned gaze searching her face.

"Yes, thank you. I wasn't sure what to think when this man showed up. I'm grateful you were able to leave the store."

Kip dipped his bald head in a gruff nod. "Is he still here?"

"Yes," she started to say. Before she could step aside to show Kip in, she felt the large stranger move up behind her.

"Kip?" he asked. "Is that really you? It's been a long time, man."

"Jeremy! I almost didn't believe it when Holly said Russell's brother showed up." Kip grinned.

Holly barely managed to move out of the way before the two men shook hands and did that guy hug thing. "Come on inside," she said. Once they had, she closed the door and returned to her seat on the couch. She listened as Jeremy told her boss that he'd recently been released from prison.

"When'd you get out?" Kip asked Jeremy.

"Just a couple days ago." Looking down, Jeremy shook his head. "I couldn't go back to my old life, and Russell is my only family. Despite everything, I came here hoping he'd give me a second chance. I wanted to show him how I've turned my life around."

Kip nodded, then looked past Jeremy to Holly. "Maybe we should all sit down and talk. A lot has happened since you left town."

But before he could move to a chair, his phone rang. Glancing at it, he frowned. "Sorry, I need to take this."

After answering, Kip listened for a moment. "I'm on my way," he said and ended the call. "I hate to do this, but I've got to head back to the store." He glanced at Holly. "You'll have to catch Jeremy up. Go ahead and tell him everything.

I've known him since he was knee-high. He's a good guy. Yeah, he's made some mistakes, but haven't we all?"

Sticking out his hand, the two men shook again. "I'm sure I'll see you around," Kip said. "Stop by the store and we can head over to Mikki's and grab a beer."

"I'll do that, except it'll have to be nonalcoholic since I no longer drink." Jeremy followed him to the door, leaving Holly to trail behind. "It was good to see you. Thank you for vouching for me."

"No problem." Kip waved and climbed into his truck. Once he drove off, Jeremy closed the door himself and turned to face Holly.

Again she felt that shiver of awareness. To hide it, she tried to summon up a smile, but she failed miserably. "Come on and sit down," she said, resigned. "I've got a lot of ground to cover, and sadly, most of it isn't good."

Though his mouth tightened at her words, he simply nodded and made his way to the living room.

She waited until he'd once again gotten settled in the chair before asking him if he wanted something to drink. "I still have some coffee left," she said.

"Water's just fine."

Keeping her back straight, she brought them both a glass of water. His fingers brushed against hers as he accepted it, and she had to forcibly keep herself from jerking away.

Jumpy? Certainly. But then she'd earned the right to be.

With slow, deliberate movements, she lowered herself into the couch opposite him, placing her glass of water on the flamingo coaster she kept on her end table.

Thor, panting happily, jumped up next to her, turned a circle and laid down. He placed his big head on his large paws and watched Jeremy intently.

She tangled her fingers in the dog's long and luxurious

fur, glad for his presence. In the eighteen months she'd lived with him, she'd learned to trust his judgment implicitly. If Thor didn't like someone, it always turned out that he had good reason. Right now, the huge black mastiff didn't seem to have any issues with this man. Which definitely wouldn't be because Jeremy reminded him of Russell. Thor had barely tolerated her former fiancé. Either way, for now she'd consider it a good sign.

When she looked up, she realized Jeremy and Thor had locked gazes. She braced herself, aware that Thor might not like this. Instead, the dog began wagging his huge, feathery tail.

"What's his name?" Jeremy asked. "He's sure a good-looking dog."

This made her smile. She'd learned Thor's breed appeared to be an acquired taste. "Thor," she replied. "Russell gifted him to me as a puppy right after I moved here."

Slowly, he nodded. "Tibetan mastiffs are stubborn, but once you learn to work with that, they're great dogs."

Unsure how to reply, she simply smiled. "He's my best friend," she said, not caring if he thought her weird.

An awkward kind of silence fell. Two total strangers and a massive dog, all eyeing each other awkwardly.

"Tell me about my brother," Jeremy finally said. "He stopped communicating with me years ago. I wrote him several times when I was in prison, but he never responded."

Unsure where to start, she sighed. "I might as well go back to the beginning. Russell and I met when he purchased one of my paintings a couple of years ago."

Pointing toward the piece, which hung in a place of honor over the fireplace, even now she could still smile at the memory. "I usually ship them to the buyers, but Russell insisted on flying down to Texas to get it personally instead."

"You're an artist," Jeremy said, his flat voice not revealing his thoughts. "Very nice."

"I am and thank you." She paused for a moment to collect her thoughts. "Long story short, we went out to dinner. Russell was funny and charming. After he got back to Alaska, he continued contacting me, and we began a long-distance relationship."

It had been a friendship at first, though she didn't feel the need to share that information. "Over several months, we got to know each other very well. He flew down a couple more times for the weekend, things like that."

"And then he proposed?" Jeremy asked, frowning. "That seems sudden."

"A whirlwind," she agreed. "But no, he didn't propose at first. Instead, he invited me to move up to Alaska to live with him. Now, I don't know about you, but I wasn't keen on the idea of leaving everything and everyone I cared about and traveling to the wilderness of Alaska with a man I'd only known a few months."

"Yet you did," he said, his gaze steady. "Why?"

Now it was her turn to frown. "I'm not sure how to explain it. He said he loved me, couldn't live without me. When I still resisted, he showed up on my doorstep with an engagement ring." Which she'd long ago stopped wearing, instead storing it at the bottom of her underwear drawer.

"So, you came here."

"Yes." She nodded. "A little over eighteen months ago. I sold my furniture, had all my unsold art shipped, along with my clothes, and traveled to Blake, Alaska, to live out what I thought was a fairy-tale love story. He talked me into buying this house, and I used my inheritance to pay for my half."

Too late, she heard the bitterness in her voice. Realizing she'd need to take a break if she wanted to attempt to tell the rest, she excused herself and headed to the bathroom. Thor jumped off the couch and padded after her.

Once there, she closed the door and stood, staring at herself in the mirror. Her flushed face and wide eyes testified to her tumultuous emotions. Thor leaned against her leg, offering comfort the only way he knew how.

Thankful for her dog, she bent down and kissed his head. Then she washed her hands and began applying lotion. A simple act that she always found calming. She'd take a few minutes to regain her composure before going out and facing Russell's brother once again.

After Holly and her dog left the room, Jeremy tried to digest what he'd learned so far. Cute story, but something wasn't right, though he didn't have enough information yet to put his finger on exactly what. He had to admit that he found Russell's fiancée strikingly beautiful. With her huge blue eyes, shock of wild platinum hair and petite yet curvy figure, he could see why Russell had been drawn to her. Hell, any man would be.

But he sensed something was off. Her nervousness bordered on evasion. Which was weird. Unlike Jeremy, Russell had been a model citizen. He'd always walked the straight and narrow path of respectability, taking care to treat everyone fairly. Everyone except his younger brother, that is. Maybe because their father had died when Russell had been sixteen and Jeremy twelve, the burden of raising them falling on the older boy's shoulders. He'd done the best he could, and done a damn fine job of it.

Jeremy had always looked up to him. Which is why when he'd done some rebelling in his teenage years and Russell had thrown him out and refused to take his calls, the abandonment had cut like a serrated knife thrust into his heart and twisted.

He'd never understood how his brother could decide to simply cease being family. For Jeremy, he couldn't believe Russell no longer loved him.

Which was part of the reason the instant a reformed Jeremy had done his time, he'd hightailed it back home, ready to make amends. That and the fact he had nowhere else to go. He hadn't known what he'd do if Russell refused to see him or allow him to stay.

He'd gone over this scenario in his mind a hundred times, rehearsing, preparing himself for any response. Except there'd been no way to anticipate this. Russell had gone missing. And not even recently. Well over a year ago. While a beautiful woman claiming to be his fiancée lived in Russell's house.

The very same house Jeremy had intended to stay in.

Finally, the bathroom door opened and Holly emerged. Once again, her beauty knocked the breath from his lungs. Her giant dog padded after her, sticking close to her side.

When her bright blue eyes met his, he leaned forward. "Are you okay?" he asked, noting the pulse beating wildly at the base of her throat.

"There's a lot I need to tell you," she said, dropping into her chair. "All I ask is that you let me speak without interrupting. I promise to answer questions when I'm done, but this is going to be hard enough to get through as it is."

Slowly, he nodded.

She moistened her lips, drawing his gaze to her mouth. "At first, things were amazing. Once I got all my stuff unpacked, he showed me how he'd fixed up one of the storage closets for me to use as my studio." Her slow smile barely touched her eyes, but he saw a fleeting glimmer of the happiness she'd clearly once felt.

"Anyway, fast-forward a couple of months. Russell changed. Not all at once. He started pulling away from me, acting secretive. He'd go to town to have a drink at Mikki's, but when he finally showed up five hours later, he'd be drunk and angry, ready to pick a fight."

Though Jeremy had agreed not to interrupt, he nearly did then. Russell didn't drink. He'd always held his abstinence up like a shining trophy, brandishing it every time Jeremy had messed up. Which had been pretty damn often back in the day.

Swallowing back his words, Jeremy managed to nod.

"It got worse," she continued, her voice breaking. "Russell changed. I'll spare you the details." Her one shoulder shrug somehow made her seem more fragile. "I'm sure you'll hear all about it in town."

Because he wasn't sure if she'd finished or not, he waited, pretending a patience he didn't feel.

"Anyway, to make a long story short, one night Russell went to town and never came home. No one knew anything. He'd gone to Mikki's to drink, left right after last call, and I never saw him again." She sighed. "They found his phone where he'd left it on the bar."

"His truck?" he asked, unable to help himself. "Did he take it?"

"Yes." Her lips tightened. "And apparently since Alaska is so big and so wild, there are tons of places someone who doesn't want to be found can hide."

"Is that what you think? That Russell is hiding out somewhere?"

"He has to be." Lifting her chin, she met and held his gaze. "Because it's better than the alternative."

Jeremy could barely bring himself to put that into words. But he had to, before she did. "He's not dead," he said. "I'm certain of that."

"Are you? Maybe you could do me a huge favor and convince the townspeople of that." The bitterness in her voice seemed at odds with her steady gaze.

"What are you saying?" he asked. "I'm not sure I understand."

"Rumor has it that Russell was murdered. And that I was the one who killed him."

For a second her words didn't register. He stared at her, trying to decide if she meant it.

"Did you?" he finally managed to ask.

"No. I didn't."

Oddly enough, he believed her. During the time he'd spent incarcerated, Jeremy had become an expert judge of character. Most of the men he'd met were accomplished liars; it came with the territory. Somehow, he'd developed what he liked to think of as a sixth sense. Time and time again, he'd been proven right.

Listening to Holly Davis right now, he felt certain she was telling the truth.

"Okay," he replied. "Then we can work together to find my brother."

Astonishment flashed across her face, before she caught herself and steadied her expression. "I've tried. The state police claim they performed an exhaustive investigation. They found no evidence of foul play. It would seem that Russell has disappeared without a trace."

"We'll see about that." He took a deep breath, bracing himself for her reaction. "One other thing. Since this is my brother's house, I'm going to have to ask you to let me stay here." He didn't tell her he had nowhere else to go.

She blanched. "I don't think that's a good idea. Everyone around here already thinks I'm a horrible person. It wouldn't look good for me to live with my missing ex-fiancé's brother."

"I understand," he replied. "In that case, since I am going to stay here, I hope you have somewhere else you can go."

Momentarily, her mouth fell open as she stared at him. "You can't be serious," she finally said. "You expect me to leave my own home?"

"I expect nothing. I'll leave that decision completely up to you. I'm staying here until Russell turns up and says otherwise." Which he would if he were here, though Jeremy kept that to himself.

Though she narrowed her gaze, she didn't protest.

"I'd like a spare key if you have one," he continued.

Instead, she turned on her heel and marched toward the hallway. "Follow me," she ordered. "I'll show you to your room."

Slightly surprised that she'd given in so quickly, he hurried after her. When they reached the middle bedroom, she stopped. "You can stay here," she said, pointing.

To his dismay, his throat closed up. She'd given him his childhood room, the one he'd slept in until Russell had thrown him out.

Stepping inside, he realized only the furniture remained from those days. Everything else, any hint that Jeremy Elliot had ever existed, had been purged from the room. Likely years ago, after his older brother had cut off all contact.

"This is the guest room," Holly said from the doorway. "Since we rarely have guests, it's never used. I'll bring you some clean sheets to put on the bed."

"Thanks." The word came out strangled, the rust in his

voice a testament to his tangled emotions. His brother had not only stopped communicating with him, but he'd also apparently done his best to erase all reminders of Jeremy's existence.

Learning this hurt far more than it should have.

Holly must have gone after the sheets, because the next thing he knew she'd returned and thrust them at him. "Here you go," she said, her grim tone matching her expression. "And since you're determined to stay here, I think we need to establish some ground rules."

Accepting the linens, he simply nodded.

"First up, I need you to respect my boundaries. Do you understand what that means?"

"Yes," he answered immediately. "And I can assure you that I have zero intention of behaving in any way inappropriately."

"Good. Because I won't stand for it." She took a deep breath, her gaze direct. "The second thing I need to ask is that if anyone in Blake implies our situation is anything but platonic, you promise to set them straight. I'm already an outcast around here. I don't need you to make things worse."

Slowly, he nodded. "I can do that. But I doubt anyone is going to make something out of nothing. You're my brother's fiancée. They'd be insulting me if they insinuated something was going on between us."

"Former," she corrected. "Former fiancée. That's why I said he's my ex. Russell and I broke things off shortly before he disappeared."

This caught him completely off guard. Yet, he realized she'd actually tried to tell him this. Hearing only what he wanted to hear, he hadn't truly been listening.

"Why?" he asked, surprising himself. "Why'd you break it off?"

"That's personal."

"You're right," he replied, accepting her statement. "But can you tell me this? Who broke up with who?"

For the space of a few heartbeats, she simply stared at him. When she finally spoke, she lifted her chin and squared her shoulders. "I no longer wear his ring," she said. "Here. A spare house key." She placed it on the dresser. Then, before he could ask any more questions, she left the room.

Something wasn't right here. But Jeremy knew better than to pursue any other answers now. The truth would come out with time. It always did.

For now, he'd unpack his meager belongings and try to get situated. Luckily, he had a substantial amount of money in the bank from his wrongful imprisonment settlement. This would have to tide him over until he could figure out what he could do for work. He still wanted to explore the possibility of starting his own business. In prison, he'd taken part in a dog training program and learned, to his surprise, that he had a knack for it. He'd done so well in fact that he'd been promoted to being in charge of the other inmates. And eventually, the warden had allowed him to participate in more specialized training. He'd worked with three drug and weapon detection canines and one cadaver dog before his release had come through.

As if thinking about dogs had summoned him, the huge black Tibetan mastiff ambled over and shoved his nose at Jeremy's hand. Jeremy obliged by crouching down on his haunches and using his fingers to massage the massive dog's fur. Thor groaned, low in his throat, and rolled his eyes.

At least this part of the situation was going to work out fine, Jeremy thought, grinning. Dogs always made things better.

Chapter 2

That had been…brutal. Hurrying to her room, the bedroom vacated by Russell months before he'd left, Holly closed and locked the door behind her. This time, Thor chose not to go with her, remaining behind with Jeremy. Which stung. Even her dog appeared to be abandoning her, which was silly. No doubt he wanted to check out the stranger on his own.

The stranger, now unwanted guest. She hated that she no longer had any privacy living in her own home.

Except it wasn't all hers. It never had been. She and Russell had each purchased equal shares in the house. She only owned half.

And being the closest relative to the missing homeowner, Jeremy had as much right to live on the property as she did. Actually, it seemed to be a gray area. She guessed he'd be within his legal rights to toss her out on her ear if he wanted. Thankfully, so far he hadn't appeared inclined to do so. Yet.

She'd have to figure out something to ensure he'd let her stay. Not only did she truly have nowhere to go, but even with her part-time job working at the general store and selling her art online, she didn't make enough to afford someplace else. At least, not around here. Pickings were slim in the small town of Blake. Real estate only moved during the warmer months because no one wanted to move in three feet of snow. And rentals tended to go to family members or friends. With her less than stellar reputation, she doubted anyone would be willing to rent to her, even if she could afford it.

As much as she'd come to love Alaska, she really should leave. Actually, she'd been halfheartedly saving up to make her way back to the lower forty-eight. Someplace less expensive, though she wasn't sure where. But if she wanted to sell the house, she'd have to get Russell to sign off since he owned half. Getting that money back would allow her to purchase another place of her own. Except she honestly adored this home.

Truthfully, now that Russell hadn't returned, she kind of wanted to stay here. The small house suited her fine and she didn't have to pay rent. She had her painting room where she could make art without interruption. And since Kip had hired her to work stocking the back room at the general store, she felt she'd forged a kind of stalemate with those in town. No one went out of their way to socialize with her, but that was okay since she'd always been kind of an introverted loner.

Her life had become settled. Quiet. Not perfect, not by a long shot. But comfortable, which was a huge relief after dealing with Russell's mercurial mood swings and vicious, violent temper. Her initial worries that Russell would return and hurt her had faded. Where at first, she'd jumped at every sound and every shadow, she thought less and less about that these days. Having a giant and devoted guard dog helped too. She actually felt...safe. Even from Russell's side chick, Tanya, who'd tried to make Holly's life a living hell. Tanya had called and made threats wanting Holly to go back where she came from. When Holly had changed the number for the landline, Tanya had started driving by and leaving hateful notes taped to the front door. She'd spread terrible rumors around town, though the only ones who seemed to believe them were her gal pals.

Since Holly refused to react, Tanya's stalking had gradually tapered off. Holly no longer felt threatened by her, though she did still keep a watchful eye on her surroundings, just in case.

Holly would say she considered her current life unremarkable. Until now. Russell's younger brother, a man who'd just gotten released from *prison*, for Pete's sake, would be staying here. And while she wasn't sure, she believed she'd read that violent tendencies ran in families. Which meant she'd need to be extremely careful around him. Back to startling at every sound and walking on eggshells.

A shudder snaked down her spine. She didn't like this situation. Not one bit. Yet she'd be damned if she'd let this stranger chase her out of the place she'd come to consider her home. Especially since she had no place else to go.

Squaring her shoulders, she took a deep breath and opened her door. When she walked back into the living room, she stopped short. Thor, her loyal fur kid, lay on his back, all four legs up in the air while Jeremy rubbed his belly. Holly swore Thor's eyes appeared to have rolled back into his head. And the dog, with his tongue hanging out one side of his open mouth, actually appeared to be smiling. Neither dog nor man even noticed her arrival.

After her initial jolt of irrational betrayal, she couldn't help but laugh. Thor looked so goofy, and the fact that Jeremy took the time to love on her dog made her more inclined to like him. At least a little.

Her laughter got their attention. Thor lazily turned his

head toward her, though he made no move to get up. Jeremy slowly got to his feet, smiled a sheepish smile and shrugged. "What can I say? I like dogs and dogs like me."

"Clearly," she agreed. "Since we're going to be sharing space for a while, do you mind if I ask you a few questions?"

"Not at all." Gesturing toward the chair, he took a seat on the sofa. "Go ahead. Then after I answer yours, I've got a few of my own."

"Fair enough." She sat and crossed her legs. Thor grunted and took himself off to the kitchen. A moment later, she heard him drinking water. Bracing herself, she decided to get the hardest part out of the way first. "You said you'd just gotten out of prison. What crime exactly were you imprisoned for?"

His casual posture disappeared.

"Right to the chase. I don't blame you." Visibly tense, he swallowed hard before continuing. "I was found guilty of distribution of a controlled substance that resulted in three fentanyl overdose deaths."

She gasped, unable to help herself. "You're a drug dealer?"

"No. I never was." He shifted in his seat, clearly uncomfortable. "Unfortunately, I once had an addiction problem. I got myself clean and had actively started to try and help others do the same. One of my friends had actually gone to make a purchase. I found out and went there to stop him. As bad luck would have it, I arrived right when a DEA sting was going down. I was arrested along with my friend and the actual dealers. And worse, several people had already died from the tainted drugs. The dealer remembered me from before and thought I'd informed on him, so he lied and said I was a dealer too. They pinned the murders on me."

"Wow." She didn't know what else to say. "I'm sorry that people lost their lives. Did they ever find the person who actually killed them?"

He shrugged. "I don't know."

As usual, she tried to find the good in all the bad. "Part of that sounds like it was a good thing though. If you'd actually taken the drugs, you likely would have overdosed too."

"There is that," he agreed. "And while I eventually felt grateful that my life had been spared, being railroaded into a conviction and prison sentence…"

Though he let the words trail off, she understood what he was trying to say. Even though she barely knew him, she couldn't help but sympathize.

"How long were you locked up?"

His jaw worked. "Too long," he said. "Nearly three years. But my court-appointed lawyer actually believed me. He worked hard, and we finally got my case to appeal. Everything the prosecution did—and didn't do—came to light. The conviction was thrown out, and I was exonerated."

Something about the way he straightened his shoulders and lifted his chin touched her. "I hope they also made restitution."

"They did."

Slowly, she exhaled. "I'm sorry that happened to you," she said, her voice soft.

"Me too. Now it's my turn."

Though she wasn't finished, she agreed. "Go ahead."

"Did you love my brother?"

The simple question took her aback. "That's kind of personal," she said, stalling.

"Nope, you can't dodge the question. This is all personal." He held her gaze and repeated his question. "Did you love Russell?"

"I did," she answered. "Once. Obviously. I completely uprooted my life and traveled thousands of miles from my home to be with him."

Naturally he latched on to her prevarication. "Once? What do you mean?"

"I'm not sure Russell would want me discussing our relationship with you," she said, hoping he'd accept that and move on.

"I need to know. Tell me what was going on with him prior to his disappearance. Any insight you can share could help."

Though she seriously doubted that, she decided he might as well know the truth. "Your brother changed," she said, her words clipped. "Quite a bit. At first, I thought it was the alcohol. And that definitely played a part in his behavior. But I began to suspect there might be something more."

"Like what?" Clearly impatient, he shifted in his seat.

"I'm thinking some kind of drugs."

"No. Not possible. My brother hated drugs. He couldn't forgive my use of them," he said. "He threw me out when I was only sixteen. That's how I know without a shadow of doubt that Russell would never use."

Though she hated to burst his bubble, she'd already gone this far, so she might as well tell him everything. "He hurt his back. The doctor prescribed pain pills. I think he got addicted to them."

"You think?" His eyes blazed. "You can't speculate about this kind of thing. What evidence did you have?"

Suddenly weary, she found herself blinking back tears. "You weren't here. You didn't see the changes. And you know what? I don't care what you believe. You asked me to give you the truth, and that's what I've done."

"Your truth," he pointed out.

"My truth," she agreed. "But that's all I have. I think we can agree to maybe pick up this discussion another time. You just got here, and I know you're tired. And you must be hungry. I've got the stir fry all prepped and ready to cook. Would you like to eat early, so you can get some rest?"

Though he continued to glare at her, thankfully he dropped the subject for now.

"I could eat," he finally admitted. "And thank you for offering to cook for me. Is there anything I can do to help?"

That was new, though she managed to hide her surprise. Not once had Russell ever offered to assist her. He'd never even given a reason, instead choosing to make himself scarce the moment she started cooking.

"Not this time," she replied, smiling. "I've got everything ready. All I need to do is cook it."

Since chicken stir fry was one of her favorite meals and she made it often, it turned out just the way she liked it. The freshly cut vegetables were crisp and flavorful and the chicken tender. She served it over jasmine rice.

When she brought their plates to the table, his eyes widened. "That looks amazing."

Thor, watching them both intently, thumped his tail in agreement.

"Thanks," she said, putting his food in front of him.

Once she'd taken her seat across from him, he dug in. He devoured his food with a single-minded intensity, as if he worried this meal might be his last. She couldn't help but watch him through her lashes as she ate.

He finished before she'd made it halfway through hers. "There's more in the wok," she told him, guessing he might want seconds.

Shooting her a grateful look, he went and refilled his

plate. This time, he ate a little more slowly, finishing up about the same time as she did.

"You're an excellent cook," he said. The compliment startled her, since Russell had taken to disparaging everything she made. She'd eventually stopped trying to please him, and once he started eating his evening meal in town at the bar, she'd simply made whatever she wanted.

"I'll clean up," Jeremy said, gathering up the plates and carrying them to the sink.

Mildly amazed, she sat back and let him. Russell had put in a dishwasher when he'd renovated the kitchen, so it didn't take long at all for Jeremy to rinse everything off and load it up.

"Thanks again," he said, returning to the table.

"You're welcome." She took a sip of her tea. "Do you mind me asking you if you have a plan?"

He eyed her. "You mean how I'm going to go about finding Russell?"

"That too, but I meant beyond that. Whether or not you're able to locate your brother, what are you planning to do with your life now that you're free?"

She could tell by the sudden tension in his jaw that he had to bite back down on his knee-jerk response. Neither of them could claim the other's questions were too personal, as long as they didn't cross a line. He knew it as well as she.

"I'm still thinking about it," he said, his nonanswer making her sigh.

"Well, if you ever want to bounce some ideas off me, just let me know," she offered, meaning it.

His hard expression softened somewhat. "Thanks. I appreciate it."

The sudden jolt of attraction startled her. Flustered, she

reached for her phone and made a show of scrolling social media.

"You have Wi-Fi here?" he asked. "That's pretty amazing. I remember when only the places downtown had access."

She barely looked up, still battling her racing heart. "Anything is available for a price. Russell was willing to pay whatever it took. He ran his business from here, so he deemed having good internet crucial."

"Sounds like Russell," he said.

When she looked up, the warmth in his brown eyes made her mouth go dry. What the heck was wrong with her? How could she possibly be attracted to the brother of the man who'd once tried to kill her?

Shaken, she mumbled some lame excuse and hurried to her room.

Once Holly left, Jeremy let out a breath he hadn't even realized he'd been holding. Granted, he'd been a long time without access to a woman, but he shouldn't be constantly battling arousal by simply being in the same room with his brother's fiancée. Or ex-fiancée, whichever the case might be.

He supposed he should be glad he clearly didn't affect her the same way. That would definitely be asking for trouble.

Getting up, he decided to check out the house. While Holly had obviously added her stamp on the decor, he could spot his brother's personality all over the place.

Checking out the books in the bookshelf near the fireplace, he saw Russell's reading habits hadn't changed. Thrillers and horror, the newest bestsellers side by side with older novels. Several framed photographs also sat on the shelves. He picked up one of his brother and Holly, both holding up large salmon and beaming at the camera.

They looked happy, he mused. Though he had no idea how long ago that might have been taken, he liked how relaxed Russell appeared.

There were a few more photos, some of Russell alone, some of Holly. Finally, on the bottom shelf, tucked out of view almost like an afterthought, he spotted a picture of him and his brother. It had been taken before their parents were killed, and the youthful innocence in their freckled faces made his chest ache. He remembered that day, all too well. They'd had a cookout and gone wading in Walker's Creek. The water had been cold, but they hadn't cared.

When they'd come back home, their parents had allowed them to cook marshmallows over the firepit. That night, Jeremy and Russell had gone to bed happy, the sound of their parents talking and laughing outside a soothing background noise.

No wonder Russell had kept this photograph. It had captured the last good evening the brothers had shared with their family still intact.

Putting the frame back on the shelf, Jeremy shook his head. The sudden ache in his throat shouldn't have been surprising, but it was after so many years.

Look toward the future. The mantra he'd often repeated while locked up still served him well.

The future. And despite what anyone might think, he knew he had a good one.

Though Holly had asked him if he had some sort of plan, for whatever reason Jeremy hadn't felt comfortable sharing it. Not yet, not while he still felt so vulnerable.

True, he had goals, both short- and long-term. Yes, he planned to settle in Blake, the town where he'd grown up.

And, once he'd worked hard to remake frayed and torn relationships, he hoped to open his own dog training business. He had zero doubts he'd succeed. He had a rare talent and unique skills. Word would get out. Hell, he'd already been contacted by some of the most prestigious dog academies on the continent. He not only had talent, but he had connections.

However, before he could do anything else, there was the matter of Russell's mysterious disappearance. While Jeremy truly didn't believe that Holly had any involvement, he also knew she'd held back information. What exactly, he didn't know. But something didn't add up.

Russell may have cut all ties with Jeremy several years ago. He had no idea that his younger brother had been wrongfully imprisoned, or that Jeremy had managed to thrive despite all the obstacles thrown at him. In fact, he'd turned his life around.

Jeremy wanted the chance to show him.

"We're going to find my brother," he announced, walking back into the kitchen. His declaration appeared to startle Holly, who stood with her back to him, cutting up something on the counter.

Thor, who'd curled up in a large dog bed in one corner, got to his feet and came over, wagging his tail in greeting. Jeremy reached down to pet him while he waited for Holly to respond.

"How exactly are we going to do that?" she asked, her tone mild. She barely glanced back at him, continuing to keep her attention on the task at hand.

"I don't know," he admitted, taking a seat at the table. Thor heaved an exaggerated sigh and returned to his bed. "Since you know him better than I do at this point, I was hoping you'd have some suggestions."

Now she did turn around, still brandishing a large knife in one hand. "I've already tried that, remember? I worked with the state police, went out on multiple searches organized by his friends in town, and we weren't able to turn up anything. Not one single clue. Russell must have really wanted to disappear, because he took great care not to leave anything behind."

"Not even a note?" he asked. "Surely he cared enough to at least let you know why he decided to take off."

He couldn't identify the raw emotion he saw flash across her expression. Pain or anger, he thought, though not sure which or why.

"He didn't leave a note," she replied, her level voice devoid of emotion. "And like I told you, I've already been over this with the police. I suggest you talk to them."

"We're on the same side here," he reminded her. "I think maybe we got off on the wrong foot. Can we start over? After all, we both want the same thing."

"Do we?" Still expressionless, still brandishing the knife, though he suspected she'd forgotten it was there, she eyed him.

"Think about how you'd feel if our situation was reversed. You waltz into my house, with no prior warning, and announce you're my ex-fiancé's brother who just got out of prison. Oh, and by the way, you're staying here." She shook her head. "You didn't bother to ask. Just decided. I'm not really comfortable with that. I don't know you. Did you ever think about that? Possibly consider you might need to find somewhere else to stay?"

"I'm sorry," he said, meaning it. "But I have nowhere else to go."

The naked truth, now spoken, and he couldn't take it back. Hell, he didn't want to unsay it. She needed to know his situation, that he hadn't decided to intrude on her life without good reason.

There was silence while she considered him, her short blond hair mussed like she'd just gotten out of bed. Sexy, he thought.

"Neither do I," she finally said. "Which I guess makes us even."

Getting up, he moved toward her and held out his hand. "Truce?"

She carefully set the knife down, and, after drying her hand on a dish towel, she slipped her fingers into his and lightly squeezed. "Truce," she agreed before tugging free.

Looking from one to the other, Thor's tail thumped on the floor as if he approved.

"But I still think we need to agree on some ground rules," she continued. "If we're going to be roommates, we'll need to split some of the chores."

Curious, he nodded. "Go on."

"Well, obviously we each do our own laundry," she said. "But I'm thinking we can switch off on the cooking duties. Maybe each of us take a week or something. And whoever isn't cooking does the dishes."

"That makes sense." He thought for a minute. "What about grocery shopping? And cleaning?"

A ghost of a smile hovered on her full lips. "We can switch off on those too. And I'll expect you to pay half the utilities too."

"I will." He paused, wary of saying the wrong thing. "What about the mortgage? I'm assuming there are payments monthly?"

"No. Russell paid the house off. Taxes have to be paid annually, but they've already been taken care of for this year."

Wow. Jeremy kept his thoughts to himself, though this secretly impressed him. While he'd known Russell had been an independent engineering consultant, he must have done really well to be able to pay off a house like this so quickly. Back when he'd been growing up, their parents had been renting it. Kudos to his brother for actually buying it.

"Anything else?" he asked, collecting his thoughts.

"No, at least not yet." Her smile bloomed across her heart-shaped face, stunning him with its beauty. "But I'm sure something will come up. When it does, we'll figure it out together."

He liked that. "Sounds good. Now, if you don't mind, I had a long trip getting here. I'm going to take a shower and then call it an early night and lie down."

"No problem." She picked up her knife again and turned back to whatever she'd been chopping. "Since your homecoming should be a special occasion, I'm making peach cobbler for dessert. It'll be ready in about an hour, if you'd like to wait up for some. I promise it's worth it."

Touched, he stared at her, finding himself at a loss for words. "You'd do that for me?"

"Yes." Her level gaze met his. "I know you were expecting something different when you came home, but this is the best I can do. I even have some vanilla ice cream to put on top."

He couldn't remember the last time he'd had peach cobbler, and even then, it hadn't been homemade. His mouth watered at the thought.

Though he'd initially planned to lie down, with this kind of bone-deep exhaustion, he knew once he drifted off he'd be out until morning.

"I'm thinking I'll postpone going to bed until I have dessert," he said, smiling. "I'm really appreciative that you've taken the time to make something like that for me."

She grinned. "Just wait until you taste it. It's my great-great-grandmother's recipe, handed down through the years."

For the first time he noticed a little twang in her accent. "Where are you from again?" he asked.

"Texas," she replied proudly. "We always say everything's bigger in Texas, but I think they've never been to Alaska."

Her humor made him laugh. "You know what? I think I like you."

She blushed. "Thanks. Let me get this cobbler into the oven. If you want to watch some TV, the remote is on the coffee table. We have satellite, so we get a lot of channels."

"Satellite?" Impressed again, he glanced at the large television. It had to be at least sixty-five inches.

"Yes. Russell had it installed long before I got here. That's another one of the monthly bills we'll be splitting." She grimaced. "To be honest, I was actually considering letting it go. It's kind of pricey."

"That's one luxury that might be worth it," he said. "You don't get very good reception up here without it."

Nodding, she returned her attention back to the cobbler, opening the oven and placing it inside.

"I think I'll go have my shower though," he told her.

"Okay. This will be ready in about an hour," she reminded him.

"Thanks." Grateful, he hurried down the hall to the bathroom. Once there, he closed the door, located clean towels in the linen closet and turned the shower on. Hot. Because hot showers had been scarce while he'd been locked up.

The anger that simmered low in his belly returned at the

thought. Though the government had compensated him, no one truly understood what it was like to spend three years of your life locked in hell for something you hadn't done. He didn't think any amount of money could make up for that.

Reminding himself that there was nothing he could do to change the past, he took his time getting clean. When he finally turned the water off, he felt much better. He'd returned home not only to make amends to his older brother, but to start his life over. In order to take care of the first, he'd need to locate Russell. He knew his brother better than most anyone, and Russell wasn't the type to run away from his problems. He'd always taken great pride in being responsible, stalwart, the one everyone else went to in order to solve their problems. No matter what the beautiful woman in the other room claimed, Jeremy figured something had to have happened. But what? He refused to believe Russell was dead. If something like that had happened, he'd have felt it deep within his heart.

Then what? If the Alaska State Police had, as Holly said, found no evidence of foul play, that would be both good and bad. Good, because it would seem more likely that Russell would be found alive. Bad, because with no evidence of foul play, the police would have abandoned their search.

Toweling off, he caught sight of himself in the mirror and shook his head. Shaggy hair and enough stubble to count as the beginning of a close-trimmed beard. He looked nothing like the eager, innocent kid who'd left Blake for Anchorage and then Seattle, intent on starting a new life.

Now he'd come back to Blake with the intention of doing the same thing. Only he'd have to find his brother first.

Once dressed, instead of going back out into the main part of the house, he went straight to his bedroom. Rummaging in the closet, he found several taped-up boxes,

neatly labeled with the words Jeremy's Things. This made
him feel slightly better. At least Russell had cared enough
not to toss everything out.

Clean, he felt refreshed. And, as the scent of peaches
and cinnamon drifted on the air, ready for some cobbler.
For the first time since arriving, he felt optimistic. Maybe
he and Holly might be able to get along after all.

Chapter 3

Holly sat down at the kitchen table and scrolled through her phone while the cobbler cooked. Baking always calmed her. Whenever she felt tense and worried, anxious or upset, the simple act of measuring ingredients and mixing them all together felt like a kind of soothing meditation.

This welcome home cobbler she'd made for Jeremy had started out exactly that. Something to calm her frazzled nerves. The idea of sharing her space with a man she didn't know upset her deeply.

She turned her need to bake into a gesture of goodwill. And the looks of incredible gratitude on his handsome face would be something she would never forget. A humbling reminder that she wasn't the only one with problems.

As if her thoughts had summoned him, Jeremy strolled into the kitchen. Hair still damp from his shower, he appeared rejuvenated. And, she thought dizzily, sexy as hell.

"We need to work together to find my brother," he announced, pulling out the chair opposite her and straddling it.

For a moment, his overwhelming masculinity made her unable to form a coherent thought. Then, as his words sunk in, her heart dropped. "If you don't mind, I think I'll let you do that on your own. I've already done everything I could to try and find him."

He cocked his head. "Are you sure?"

"I am," she replied firmly. "For the first three or four months after he left, I searched exhaustively. I talked to all of his clients, his employees and the people he hung out with the most at Mikki's. I bugged the state trooper assigned to the case until he started dodging my calls. Finally, he told me Russell's case was no longer a priority as there was no evidence of foul play."

She took a deep breath, holding his gaze as she continued. "Even then, I didn't give up. I snooped through every envelope addressed to him that came in the mail. I figured out his password for his laptop. Not only did I learn that he'd wiped his search history and email inbox clean, but he'd scrubbed his social media too. That's when I began to understand that all of this was deliberate. Russell didn't want to be found."

Judging by his skeptical expression, he didn't believe her. Fine. Let him learn the hard way, like she had.

Luckily, Jeremy didn't seem inclined to argue. At first, he opened his mouth as if he wanted to contradict her statement, but then he closed it.

The timer dinged, and she got up. Grabbing her favorite set of pot holders, she took the cobbler out of the oven and placed it on top of the stove to cool. After turning the oven off, she returned to the table. "We need to let it cool off for a few minutes."

Though he nodded, he appeared unable to drag his gaze away from the dessert. "That looks amazing," he said.

"It does," she admitted, without a trace of modesty. "People always say I should sell my desserts. I've thought about it, but if I were to open my own bakery, it would take too much time away from my art."

"Painting?" he asked.

"Among other things. I do some sculpting, but free-form. Sketching and painting are two things I enjoy the most. I just like to see where my imagination leads me. Sometimes people even offer me commissions. Depending on what they want, I usually take those. They can be quite profitable. And word gets out. Like everything else, reputation counts for a lot." She didn't mention that her local sales had dried up completely for that very reason.

"I agree." He made a show of sniffing the air. "The smell is making my mouth water."

Smiling, she took pity on him and went to get two bowls. After scooping out the still piping hot cobbler, she got the ice cream out of the freezer, put some on top and carried both bowls over to the table. Handing him a spoon, she went back for her own bowl. "Be careful," she warned. "It'll burn your mouth."

Though he nodded, he picked up his spoon and dug in, making sure to get a good bit of ice cream along with the hot cobbler.

She couldn't help but watch him as he ate. He made a sound of appreciation low in his throat, which again made her body tingle. What was it about this man, that everything he did made her want him? Maybe she'd simply gone too long without masculine attention. That had to be the reason.

After scraping his bowl clean, Jeremy sat back and sighed.

"You know, when you said people told you that you should sell this stuff, they weren't wrong," he said, pushing his empty bowl away. "That was delicious."

Though she'd heard it before, she still flushed with pleasure. "Thank you. But for me, I want to keep it a hobby. Turning it into a job will take all the fun away."

He shrugged. "I get it," he said, which surprised her. "When you get a chance, would you mind sharing with me all the information you have on Russell's disappearance?"

Just like that, her good mood vanished. While of course she, like everyone else, genuinely wanted to know what had happened to her former fiancé, since she truly believed Russell had left of his own accord, she knew he wouldn't be found as long as he didn't want to be. She'd come to accept that and even grudgingly respect it.

Naturally, she said none of this to Jeremy. "I'll give you everything I have," she said. "I have a file folder full of everything from news clippings to my copies of the police reports."

"Thank you. Did you make notes of all the people you spoke with?"

She managed to summon a smile. "Actually, I did. I'm very meticulous that way. Let me get them for you."

Moving over toward Russell's immense wooden desk, she opened the large drawer on the left side. Inside were all the hanging files, most of them containing his business records. Though she'd looked through everything hoping to find some sort of hint as to why he'd left, she'd found nothing. Still, she'd kept everything in place, afraid to toss the wrong thing.

In front of all the older records, she'd created a file of her own. Titled Russell's Disappearance, it had grown thicker the more she'd worked on locating him. She plucked it from the drawer and marched it over to Jeremy.

"Here," she said, holding it out to him. "Please don't lose anything as I haven't made backup copies. It's everything I've worked on for the past eighteen months trying to locate him."

Accepting it, he nodded. "Thank you. I promise I'll take good care of this."

"Let me know if you have any questions." Now she felt awkward. In the place that she'd gradually come to regard as her sanctuary.

When he carried the folder over to the couch and sat down to read it, she sighed. Grabbing the remote, she dropped onto the other end of the sofa. Thor hopped up between them and curled up. After petting her dog, she turned on the TV and checked what she had recorded on the DVR. When she settled on a show, she glanced at Jeremy again, but he appeared engrossed in reading one of the papers from inside the folder.

Clicking to start watching, at first she wondered if she should adjust the volume. Was it too loud or too low? But since he never looked up, she decided not to worry about it. She'd try to relax and enjoy her program.

Pushing down her resentment, she took several deep breaths, striving for calm. It wasn't lost on her that she hadn't felt this way since Russell left, which wasn't really fair to his younger brother. Though he hadn't been here long, so far Jeremy had been cordial. Except for insisting he'd be staying here, and after hearing his reasoning, she couldn't really blame him. At least he hadn't thrown her out.

Damn, she'd set the bar low. Living with an abusive narcissist tended to do that to a person.

After about fifteen minutes, she was able to lose herself in watching her favorite characters race against time to solve a case.

When the show ended, she heaved a contented sigh and realized Jeremy had looked up from his reading. As she met his gaze, something in his eyes caused her entire body to tighten. "What?" she asked, before she thought better of it.

"Nothing. Just enjoying how into the show you are."

She could feel her face heat. "Uh...thanks?"

"I've been going through all of this," he said, holding up the folder. "You've been very thorough, and I appreciate that." When he'd finished talking, he covered his mouth as he yawned.

This gave her the perfect opportunity to say what she'd been thinking. "I thought you were going to turn in early. You look exhausted."

He glanced at his smartwatch. It had been one of his first purchases once he'd been released. "I am. Maybe I'll take this with me and pick up where I left off in the morning."

Hiding her relief, she nodded. "Good night then."

Once he'd taken himself down the hall and closed the door behind him, she felt a marked decrease in tension. Oddly enough though, she also felt like all the color had gone out of the room.

Weird, she told herself. Then she clicked on the next episode of her show and settled in to watch it.

She must have fallen asleep on the couch because the next thing she knew, Thor woke her by pushing his cold nose under her chin. Gasping, she sat up. Then, realizing, she ruffled her dog's fur and said, "You need to go out, don't you? I'm sorry, boy."

After accompanying him outside and waiting while he took care of his business, she took him into the kitchen and gave him a dog treat as a reward. "Good dog, Thor," she told him. "Let's go to bed."

He followed her into her bedroom and curled up on the massive dog bed she'd bought him. He began snoring, which made her smile. After she changed into the soft T-shirt she slept in, she hurried down the hall to the bathroom to wash her face and brush her teeth. Since Jeremy's door remained closed, she felt reasonably confident she wouldn't run into him.

Finally, she shut her own bedroom door and crawled into bed.

A soft woof woke her, shortly after sunrise. She sat up in bed, rubbing the sleep from her eyes. Thor stood at the closed door, intently listening. As she watched her dog, Holly realized someone—Jeremy—was banging around in the kitchen. A quick glance at her nightstand clock showed 6:35 a.m.

Throwing back the covers, she hopped out of bed and put on a pair of shorts, a bra and tank top. Dragging her hand through her hair, she took a deep breath and went out into the hall. Thor rushed past her, tail wagging.

By the time she made it to the kitchen, her big beast of a dog stood with his front paws on Jeremy's chest, greeting him. And for his part, Jeremy appeared unfazed by this, even though Thor weighed well over a hundred pounds. In fact, he appeared to be crooning endearments to the mastiff, scratching behind the ears at the same time.

Another frozen part of Holly thawed as she watched this. It was impossible to dislike a man who treated her dog so well.

Finally, Thor jumped down and went to the back door. Shaking her head, she went to let him out.

When she returned, Jeremy had left the room. To her surprise, she realized the room felt empty without him. Which made zero sense. She'd been living here alone for eighteen months. After walking on eggshells with Russell, she preferred it that way. The sooner Jeremy moved on, the better.

Except what if he didn't?

Shaking her head at her thoughts, she told herself she'd cross that bridge when they got to it.

After a nice hot shower that he didn't really need, but wanted, Jeremy got dressed and tried to decide what he'd do first. Naturally, he wanted to get started looking for his brother, but he also needed to take care of procuring basic necessities for himself.

Clothing, toiletries and a vehicle, to start.

He wondered if Holly would be willing to take him into town. If not, it would be a bit of a walk, but the nice weather would help make the trek pleasant.

Wandering into the kitchen, he found Holly seated at the table eating a bowl of cereal. His stomach growled, but since he hadn't yet contributed to the food supplies, he felt he couldn't simply walk over to the pantry and pour himself a bowl without asking first.

"Help yourself," she said, before he even spoke. "If you want to eat, then eat."

Grateful, he did exactly that. Once he finished eating, he took his bowl to the sink, rinsed it out and then went back for hers.

"Would you mind giving me a ride into town?" he asked, turning back to face her. "I need to stop by the general store and get a few things, plus check the bulletin board to see if anyone has a decent vehicle for sale."

"Sure, I can do that," she replied. "I'm working today anyway, so you can ride in with me. But I won't be able to bring you back until after my shift. Today Kip's got me working four hours."

He'd forgotten she'd said something about working there. "What do you do again?"

"Part-time work in the stockroom. Keeps me busy, helps pay a few bills and I stay out of sight of the general public." She shrugged. "I like it. And Kip is the only one who would hire me. So there's that."

Checking her watch, she stood. "I'll be leaving in about thirty minutes. If you want to ride with me, please be ready. I'm never late."

That said, she marched on out of the room. Watching her go, he couldn't help but smile. Damned if he didn't like her.

Since he didn't have much else to do to get ready, he just hung out and waited for her to return.

A few minutes later, when she walked out of the bedroom to meet him, he did a double take. He thought he'd gotten accustomed to her beauty, but eying her now, he felt like he'd been punched in the stomach.

"I put on makeup," she quipped, noticing his reaction. "It's amazing what a little mascara and lipstick can do."

Unsure how to respond, he settled for a smile. She wore a pair of torn jeans that hugged her long legs, tan boots with a heel and a thick sweater. He suddenly felt slightly underdressed in his flannel shirt and worn work boots. But then he hadn't had time to buy many clothes since he'd gotten out. He'd take care of that soon, but he'd been more focused on getting back home.

Home. For the first time in a long time, the word brought mixed emotions. He'd carefully schooled himself to be apathetic about Blake since it was only a place. Now he wanted to belong more than he'd expected.

"Are you ready?" she asked, making him realize he'd gotten lost in his thoughts. Again.

"Yes." Instinctively, he reached in his pocket for a nonexistent set of car keys. Realizing, he grimaced. "One more thing I need to take care of. Finding a good used truck." He didn't tell her how he'd hitched a ride with a trucker going west from Anchorage, or the huge amount of walking he'd done after. He considered it a good thing he'd stayed in shape while incarcerated.

"Come on then." Sweeping past him, she opened the door to the garage.

When they reached the double bay, he stared at the expensive white Land Rover parked inside. "Russell gave it to me," she said. "He put my name on the title. Since I didn't bring a car with me, he bought me this. It's a bit larger than I like but has a smooth ride."

His brother had definitely done well for himself. "If he left this one here, what did he drive when he left?"

"A truck." She shook her head. "A big, jacked up, custom pickup that he said cost more than this Land Rover. He loved that thing."

He noticed how she used past tense but didn't comment.

They were both quiet as she drove them downtown. He, because he felt more nervous than he'd expected. He had no idea what she was thinking, though he figured she was nervous too.

She kept both hands on the steering wheel, her gaze on the road. She didn't drive too fast or too slow, barely going over the speed limit. While he could have silently admired her fresh beauty the entire way into downtown Blake, he didn't want to make her uncomfortable. Instead, he stared out the window at the passing landscape. It seemed both familiar and strange.

They pulled up in front of the general store, and she drove around the corner, entering a small lot wedged in between two buildings marked Private Parking.

"I didn't even know this was here," he mused, getting

out and hurrying around with the intent of opening her door for her.

But she'd already emerged before he even made it half-way.

"I'm even a little bit early," she said, smiling up at him.

Struck momentarily dumb by the warmth of that smile, he simply nodded.

Side by side, they walked into the general store. "I guess I'll see you later," she said. "I hope you're able to find everything you need."

"Thanks."

When she started to walk off, he called her name. "Holly, wait. How about later tonight we have dinner at Mikki's?" he asked. "My treat. It's been years since I've been there, and I'd really like your company."

She stared at him with a shocked expression, as if he'd asked her to try dancing with a grizzly.

"Are you okay?" he finally asked.

Slowly, she blinked, her gaze coming back into focus.

"I don't actually do that," she replied, her expressionless face at odds with the quiver in her voice.

"You don't do what? Eat at Mikki's?"

"Right," she answered. "I try not to go into town much at all. I work here in the stockroom for Kip and try to get all my supplies when I'm here. That's about the extent of my socializing."

Which was nothing at all, though he kept that observation to himself. "Don't you get lonely?" he asked instead, struggling to understand. "Surely you have friends in town, right?"

"Friends?" This time he could hear the bitterness in her voice. "Not really. When I came here, Russell kept me isolated. I realized later that's a tactic malignant narcissists employ."

About to protest that his older brother wasn't a narcissist, never mind malignant, Jeremy decided against it. While he hadn't ever thought of Russell that way, that didn't negate the possibility that Holly might be right. After all, he hadn't spoken to his brother in many years. Russell had never been easy to get along with. Maybe he'd grown worse.

"Anyway, by the time Russell took off, I'd gotten used to being alone." She shook her head. "And for your information, I'm never lonely. Not only do I have the best dog on the planet, but I lose myself in my art or reading or baking."

He sensed there was more to this story. Though she kept a pleasant expression on her face, he couldn't help but see the shadows in her blue eyes. "What is it that you are aren't saying?"

Though she'd started to turn away as if to indicate she was finished with this discussion, she stopped and slowly faced him. "You picked up on that, didn't you?" she asked wryly.

"I did," he agreed. "Now tell me. What's really going on?"

"Remember I told you that a few people, despite the lack of any evidence whatsoever, are convinced that I did something to Russell?"

Nodding, he waited.

"That's why I don't come into town except to work." She shrugged, overly casual. "They make it unpleasant, to say the least. It's easier just to stay away."

"Because of a few haters?" He made a face, thinking about all he'd dealt with while incarcerated. "I would have thought you were braver than that."

Though he'd framed his comment to fire her up, she

didn't react the way he'd expected. Though she lifted her chin, no spark of righteous anger lit up her blue eyes. "Since you don't know me, I have no idea why you'd expect such a thing."

"Point taken. I'm sorry. You're absolutely right."

"Damn straight. But don't pity me either. My life is good. I'm doing okay."

"Then will you think about coming to dinner with me?" he asked. "I've been gone a long time, and I'm not sure how I'll be welcomed either. I wasn't just saying I need you with me. I really could use your support."

Eyes narrowed, she studied him. "Honestly, it'd probably be better for you if you went alone."

"I doubt that." He waited a few seconds. "I don't think I can do this by myself. Please. Just think about it. Hell, maybe I could be there for you too."

Their gazes locked. He could tell the moment her decision shifted. "Fine. I'll go. But don't say I didn't warn you."

"Tonight then?" he asked. "I'm craving one of Mikki's giant hamburgers."

This made her smile. "Those are really good," she admitted. "Though it's been awhile since I've had one. What time?"

"Seven?"

"Sounds good," she replied and disappeared into the stockroom without a backward glance. He stood staring after her for far too long before turning and going to the east wall of the store.

For as long as he could remember, there'd been a huge bulletin board on that wall at Murphy's. The townspeople stuck business cards there and also posted hand-printed notes about items for sale. The only requirement was that each posting be dated. Kip went through every couple of months and removed the ones that were older.

There, Jeremy hoped to find someone with a pickup truck for sale.

"Morning." Kip sidled up next to him. "What are you looking for?"

"Something to drive," Jeremy answered. "A truck in decent shape. Doesn't have to be too new, just not a junker."

His description made Kip's smile widen. "It just so happens that one of my clerks has one for sale." He stepped closer to the bulletin board and scanned it, finally plucking one index card off and handing it to Jeremy. "His name is Neal Beezer. You can call him if you want, but he comes in to work in about ten minutes. Might as well just ask him in person."

After thanking him, Jeremy asked if he still had a clothing section.

"Come with me." Gesturing for him to follow, Kip headed up one aisle and down another. They weaved around overflowing displays, one of various seeds, plants and potting soil, and another of different types of electric tools. Kip prided himself on carrying a little bit of everything. Since Murphy's General Store was where most everyone in town shopped, he did great at anticipating their needs.

Finally, they reached the west side of the large store. "Here you go," Kip declared, waving his hand toward several circular racks of both men and women's clothing. "There are boots and shoes on that long row of shelves over there and jeans, khakis and slacks over there. Holler at me if you need help with anything."

After Kip left, Jeremy began going through the clothes. The variety and quality of the shirts surprised him. He picked out seven in his size before moving on to the jeans.

By the time the clerk clocked in and headed in Jeremy's direction, he'd assembled a decent-sized stack of clothing, including two pairs of boots.

"I'm Neal," the man greeted him. "I'd ask you if I could help you find anything, but I can see you've done a fine job all by yourself."

By the time the two men carried Jeremy's haul back to the cash register, they'd agreed on a selling price for Neal's truck.

Jeremy paid cash for the clothes, and then he and Neal walked out to the same small lot where Holly had parked earlier. "Here she is," Neal said proudly, walking up to a huge pickup truck painted a puke-inducing shade of neon green. "Barely over eighty thousand miles. You're going to love her."

"I'm sure I will," Jeremy answered. "And in time, this color might even grow on me."

This comment made Neal laugh. "Like slime," he said, grinning. "Or mold. I didn't paint her. She came that way. I'd keep her but my girlfriend refuses to ride in her, so I bought another truck. But she drives like a Cadillac, I swear."

Since that would be stretching it even for a new pickup, Jeremy just shook his head. "Do you have a clear title?"

"I do."

"Then sold." Not bothering to dicker over the price, Jeremy counted out the amount from his stash of bills. "Here you go. If you'll sign the title over to me and let me have the keys, I'll be on my way."

Though Neal accepted the payment, he sighed. "Mind if I give you a helpful hint?" Without waiting for an answer, he continued. "Walking around flashing that much money is likely to get you jumped, even in our great little town."

"In Blake?" Though Jeremy knew things changed, he still found this hard to imagine. "No one even locks their doors around here."

"I'm not sure how long you've been away, but they do now." Grimacing, Neal shook his head. "A lot of roaming workers drift through, especially this time of year when the weather's so nice. Get a checking account or something, man."

Jeremy nodded. "I intend to. I wanted to take care of basic essentials first. I plan to make a stop at the bank next."

Once Neal had signed the title over, he helped Jeremy carry out all his purchases. "Do you need anything else?"

Jeremy stuck out his hand. "Nope. Thanks for all your help."

The two men shook. "Enjoy the truck."

After Neal had gone back inside, Jeremy climbed into the cab and turned the key. The engine fired right up, sounding strong and healthy. There still was something to be said about small-town integrity, he thought. Anywhere else and he would have not only taken the truck for a test drive, but had a mechanic look it over.

Even though Neal had told him things had changed, some things remained the same.

Still, he decided to drive to the bank and open up an account. Time to start setting down roots, since from now on Blake would be his home once again. And then once he located his brother, he'd have his family too. They could all start healing from the past and look toward building a future.

Then he thought of Holly, and the fear and sorrow he'd seen in her eyes when she talked about Russell. There definitely had to be more to this story, and he'd need to work on getting some answers too.

Chapter 4

Though a truck had made a delivery yesterday and she had lots of boxes to unpack and shelve, Holly couldn't resist frequent peeks out into the main part of the store to try to catch a glimpse of Jeremy.

She still wasn't sure what to make of him. She'd never met a man like him. A study in contrasts, he looked dangerous and sexy, but acted kind and intelligent. She wasn't going to lie, she enjoyed looking at his muscular body, and in odd moments when she let her guard down, she found herself fantasizing about what it would be like to caress those huge tattooed biceps of his.

Of course, when her thoughts ran amok like that, she immediately shut them down. That kind of entanglement with the ex-con brother of the man who'd lied to her and abused her would make as much sense as walking up to a grizzly with arms wide open, hoping for a hug.

Not going to happen.

Blinking, she forced herself to stop worrying about what Jeremy might be doing and concentrate on her job. These boxes wouldn't just unload themselves.

Once she got busy working, as usual, time flew. Her stomach growled, reminding her that she'd need to take a short snack break. Working part-time shifts, she didn't usually take lunch, pausing only long enough to munch on a piece of turkey jerky or an apple. She'd eat something more substantial once she clocked out.

"Look what I got." Sauntering into the stockroom, Kip held up a white paper bag. "Norma Pachla made *kolaches* again. Mikki gave me a heads up, and I was able to get a dozen before they sold out."

In addition to a bar and restaurant, one section of Mikki's operated as a donut shop from 6:00 a.m. to 11:00 a.m. Though most of the breakfast treats were made on-site, she occasionally purchased *kolaches* from Norma Pachla, who'd learned to make them from her Czech grandmother. Everyone in town loved them, and when word got out that Mikki had some in stock, they tended to sell out within hours.

"Lucky you," Holly said, meaning it. "If I didn't have so much to do, I'd run down there and snag a dozen myself."

"Go ahead." Kip shrugged. "But judging by the line that had already started forming, I don't think there will be any left by the time you get there."

"Boo." She pouted.

"But the good news is, I grabbed some for you too." He held up a second bag. "I know how much you love them."

"Thank you." She smiled and accepted the bag. "How much do I owe you?"

"Nothing. Consider them a gift." Tilting his head, he studied her. "Are you doing all right? I know Russell's brother showing up out of the blue had to be a shock."

Unable to help herself, she glanced over her shoulder toward the door to the actual store. "I'm sure he's a nice man," she said. "It's just weird having to share the house with a complete stranger."

"I bet." Kip's expression changed, becoming serious. "I know Jeremy has had some hard times, but he's good people. He and Russell were on their own for a number of years. They relied on each other and took care of each other. Until something changed."

"What happened?" she asked, curious despite herself.

"Now, that would be the million-dollar question." He shrugged. "No one knows. You'd have to ask Jeremy."

Which she wouldn't do, since it wasn't any of her business. "Maybe Russell changed," she mused out loud. "Similar to what happened in his relationship with me."

Kip had been the only person she'd been able to talk to, the only one who'd cared enough to understand her need to tell her side of the story. Even though he'd known Russell most of his life, Kip had listened to Holly without judgment. She suspected he considered himself a sort of kindly uncle, taking her under his wing.

And she appreciated that more than she could ever say.

"Maybe so," he said, shrugging. "It was a long time ago."

"Thank you," she said again, opening the paper bag and inhaling the sweet scent of the pastries.

"No worries," Kip replied. "You just remember you can always call me if you need anything. Anything at all."

With that, he turned and went to his small office, closing the door behind him.

She finished up her shift an hour later. Grabbing the *kolaches*, she popped her head in Kip's office to let him know she was taking off. "See you tomorrow," she said.

"Definitely." Looking up from his paperwork, he studied her. "I want you to think about taking a shift working the sales floor."

Even hearing those words made her heart rate accelerate. Periodically, Kip tried to convince her to come out from the solitude of the stockroom and learn to interact with the general public. He, like Jeremy, didn't seem to understand how much almost everyone in town despised her.

"They don't, you know," Kip said, placing a gentle hand on her shoulder. "I know you think everyone dislikes you, but that's not true. It's just a few gossipy women. And they should be over it by now."

Though she begged to differ, she never argued with him. Heck, she didn't even know what she'd done to cause them to spread rumors about her. For months, she'd told herself she didn't care. Eventually, she supposed she wouldn't. Right now, it seemed better for her peace of mind if she avoided them completely.

When she didn't answer, Kip moved away. "Just think about it, okay? Not only would you have more hours, but the pay is better too. And I could definitely use the help."

As always, she felt tempted. Not just because more money would be helpful, but because she wanted to help Kip out. He'd been good to her during times when no one else would. She hated that she just couldn't summon up enough courage.

Before she'd sold or given away everything to pack up and come to Alaska, Holly would have considered herself a brave person. Or brave enough. While she hadn't gone out of her way to start drama, she'd never avoided confrontation either. If a wrong needed righting, she took care of it. Once, she would have said she was thick-skinned. While not impervious to criticism, most of the time it rolled off her like water.

Somehow, she'd let Russell steal that from her. He'd started off slowly, chipping away at her little by little, all in the name of a love that had never been real. Over time, she'd come to believe the horrible things he'd said about her.

Even worse, once he'd gone, she hadn't been able to get back to being the person she'd been.

"I'll think about it," she said out loud, but Kip had already gone back out front and didn't hear her. Which was probably for the best, since she didn't like to make promises she couldn't keep.

Which made her think of her agreeing to eat dinner out with Jeremy. At the time, she'd figured it would be the easiest way to show him how the townspeople felt about her. She still believed this, though after months of avoiding them, she couldn't squash a tiny sliver of hope that maybe, just maybe, they might have gotten over their suspicions against her and moved on.

And if they hadn't, perhaps the time had come for her to learn how to deal with it.

The rest of her shift flew by. When she finally clocked out, her muscles ached in a pleasant way. That was another one of the reasons she loved this job. She enjoyed the tangible sense of accomplishment that emptying shipping boxes and shelving supplies brought her.

In a way, it seemed the perfect counterpoint to her art.

As she headed toward the back door to her vehicle, she caught sight of Kip, now back in his small office. Lifting her hand in a wave, she stepped outside. And promptly realized that someone had egged her white Land Rover.

Luckily, it appeared to have happened fairly recently. She knew from personal experience how difficult it could be to remove once it had been there awhile, the acid from the yolk eating away at the paint. This wasn't the first time someone had done this to her, and she suspected it wouldn't be the last.

Jumping inside, she immediately drove a few blocks to

the self-serve car wash. Quickly depositing the necessary coins, she used the wand to blast the eggs from her vehicle.

"Teenagers?" a man from the bay next to her asked, shaking his head. "I don't understand how they take such pleasure in destruction of others' property."

About to inform him that no, this act of vandalism had more likely been perpetrated by adults, she decided not to get into an involved conversation with a stranger and nodded instead. Though she got right back to work spraying her vehicle, she kept an eye out for any movement.

Luckily, the guy next to her finished washing his jacked-up truck and drove away.

Once she felt satisfied she'd removed all the egg residue, she drove back toward the house. In the eighteen months since Russell had vanished, she'd come to think of it as hers, despite knowing it still belonged to him. When the annual property tax bill had arrived last December, she'd gone ahead and paid it, considering it money well spent since she didn't pay rent.

With the rest of the day hers, she went home and let Thor out. Then, she made herself a glass of iced tea and went into her painting studio. Thor padded alongside her, curling up in the giant dog bed she'd placed near the floor-to-ceiling windows. The abundance of natural light had been what had drawn her to this room. She'd known the first time she saw it that she wanted it for her studio. Lucky for her, Russell had been very accommodating then. Though he'd been using it as an office/storage space, he'd immediately taken all of his things out so she could set up the space the way she wanted.

Placing a blank canvas on her easel, she grabbed her tubes of acrylic paint and a brush and got to work. Often, when she started, she had no idea what she was painting.

The painting would gradually take shape, revealing itself brush stroke by brush stroke. She frequently surprised herself, laughing with delight when she realized what she'd portrayed.

Today, as the painting took shape, she realized she'd begun painting herself. Horrified, she paused, brush in hand, and stared. She never did self-portraits. She didn't consider herself interesting enough.

But as she eyed her work, she realized she'd revealed her thoughts and inner fears about how others viewed her. Specifically, those in town who truly believed she'd done something to harm Russell.

Art was truth, at least for her. The swirls of darkness that made up the image at first seemed startling. But she took a deep breath, settling back inside herself. Then, dipping her brush back into the paint, she ignored her misgivings and continued painting. Finally, she gave herself over to her art, losing herself in the unconscious movements of paint on brush on canvas, her fingers seemingly moving of their own accord.

As the painting took shape, the texture deepened, the subtle blending of color both beautiful and terrifying. Her art had always been the one aspect of her life where she trusted herself implicitly. Over the years, she'd grown more and more confident in her ability and talent, aware she could not always control what she painted. But in the end, the finished painting accurately reflected whatever emotions she'd been trying to express.

This one would be no different.

When she finally put down the brush and sat back to take in what she'd created, she felt like she'd been punched in the stomach. More than personal, she'd exposed her sense

of betrayal, her bitterness and her pain, on canvas for anyone to see.

Except no one would. This work would be only for her
own eyes. No one but her would ever see it. She'd make
sure of that.

Finally having his own truck felt liberating. Jeremy
pulled out from Murphy's parking lot and drove slowly up
and down Main Street, turning around in the parking lot
next to the bank. This had been the route he and his friends
had taken as teenagers, cruising Main Street.

For a brief moment, he had that sense of unlimited potential once again. As if anything could happen, all of it
good, with the future stretching wide open before him.

Then, as he made his second pass north, he came crashing back to reality. His brother had gone missing. And Jeremy not only was staying with Russell's former fiancée,
who'd admitted a lot of people believed her responsible, but
was battling a completely inappropriate attraction to her.
How much worse could the situation be?

Shaking his head at himself, he turned off the main drag
and headed toward Russell's house. His brother had bought
the place shortly after kicking Jeremy out. As kids, they'd
always loved the house and their parents had talked about
buying the place. Russell had often declared that he planned
to own the house someday. At least he had achieved one
of his dreams.

Since he'd learned long ago that melancholy and dwelling on the past only served to slow his forward progress,
Jeremy fiddled with the radio until he found the local country music station. He turned it up and sang along with Keith
Urban until he pulled into the drive.

He used his key to let himself in. Feeling like an intruder, he made his way toward the kitchen. Thor intercepted him halfway, tail wagging.

"Hey, boy." Jeremy crouched down to pet the huge dog. "I'm sure glad you like me," he said. "Come on, do you need to go outside?"

After making sure Thor took care of his business, Jeremy let him inside and gave him a dog biscuit from a jar on the kitchen counter.

Now what? At some point, he knew he wanted to contribute groceries and household supplies. But that was something he needed to coordinate with Holly. And while he'd gone over everything in the folder she'd given him, he wasn't any closer to figuring out what had happened to his brother.

He knew Holly had tried to locate Russell. She'd documented every single step she'd taken. She'd even listed phone numbers and names of various Alaska state troopers who'd worked on the case. He might as well start there. Grabbing the folder, he sat down at the kitchen table and began making calls.

Thirty minutes later, he wanted to throw his phone across the room. Not a single person on the list of seven names had been available to take his call. Though he'd left voicemails, he somehow doubted anyone would return his call. Hopefully, he was wrong.

Getting up, he began prowling the house, looking for some sort of clue as to what might have driven Russell to do whatever he'd done. Sadly, he knew very little about his brother, especially since it had been years since they last spoke. A lot of water had flowed under the bridge since then.

Wandering from room to room, he saw more of Holly's personality that Russell's. She'd added little feminine touches here and there. Artwork, decorative items, even rugs and pillows. While he had no clue what the place might have looked like before she'd arrived, he suspected her additions had added warmth to a more sterile, masculine space.

But then, he'd never know for sure.

Reaching the bookshelf, he paused. Here, he spotted authors he knew had always been his brother's favorites. John Grisham, Stephen King and Dean Koontz, to name a few. Most in hardback, though a few well-worn paperbacks occupied places of honor on the shelf.

He plucked one out at random and thumbed through the pages. As he did, a slip of paper fell to the floor. Curious, he picked it up, but it was only a business card for a yard service. Russell must have used it as a bookmark at some point.

Moving on to the kitchen with Thor right behind him, he began opening cabinets. It didn't help that he felt like an intruder in Holly's house. But if he wanted hints, any kind of hints, about what had made Russell tick, he had to start somewhere.

Naturally, nothing in the kitchen revealed anything of his brother's personality. Or Holly's for that matter. There was only so much meaning pots, pans and storage containers could impart.

Grimacing at his own foolishness, he moved on to the main bedroom. He paused at the doorway, loathe to enter. Since Holly had made it her own for the last year and a half, he doubted any trace of his brother remained. He couldn't help but wonder if Russell and Holly had shared the huge king-size bed. Since they'd been engaged, it seemed likely. The fact that this bothered him, even a little bit, was deeply concerning.

Yet eyeing the pale pink and yellow bedspread and the feminine wall art, he understood why he couldn't rummage around in that room. It hadn't been his brother's in a very long time.

Since he had a few hours until Holly came home, he stopped trying to discover something that clearly wasn't there and went out back. Having lived in Alaska his entire life, he knew firewood for the colder weather would always be needed. He found the axe in the shed and began splitting logs. The sheer physicality of the work not only released tension, but as the woodpile grew, his satisfaction at the tangible evidence of his labor had him grinning.

"Wow!" Holly said, startling him. He turned to see her standing on the back porch. "That's a lot of firewood."

"Yes, it is." He set the axe down. "I figured I might as well get a head start since I know how much is needed for winter."

Her level gaze gave nothing away. "True. Even though we've got a few months, it never hurts to be prepared."

Sweating, he nodded. "You didn't have much wood," he pointed out, wondering how she'd made it through last winter. "Did you split this yourself?"

"I did. But I'm not very good at it, so I definitely appreciate the help. Thank you."

"You're welcome."

She cleared her throat, her gaze traveling the length of him. "I saw Neal's old truck in the driveway. Did you buy it?"

He grinned. "I did. He said his girlfriend refuses to ride in it because of the color."

"I can't say I blame her," she replied, though her slight smile hinted she might be teasing. "Are you still wanting to go into town to eat tonight?"

"As long as you don't mind if we take my truck."

This made her laugh. The sound made warmth coil inside him. "I don't mind. Secretly, I kind of like the color."

"Then, yes." Feeling like a giddy fool, he didn't even need to check his watch. "I still have plenty of time to shower."

"Yes, you do." As she turned to go, he half expected her to turn back and say she'd changed her mind, but she didn't.

Two hours later, after unpacking his new clothes, he showered. Clean, he realized he felt better than he had in months. Immediately after this thought, he felt a stab of guilt. Not only was Russell still missing, but Jeremy knew damn good and well that his brother wouldn't appreciate an uninvited houseguest.

Shrugging off the disconcerting thought, he got dressed in a new pair of jeans, new shirt and—heck, new everything. Surveying his image in the dresser mirror, he looked nothing like the man who'd hurried through the prison gates with only the clothes on his back. He looked, he thought, normal.

He went out into the living room to find Holly and Thor sitting on the couch watching TV. The giant mastiff stood upon seeing him and wagged his tail.

"Hey boy," Jeremy greeted the dog. He felt immediately gratified when the black beast got down and lumbered over to him.

As he scratched behind Thor's ears, Holly looked up and smiled. He felt the beauty of that smile low in his chest.

"You got new clothes!" she exclaimed. "You look nice."

Nice. A tepid word at best. But coming from her, with that smile, he'd take it.

"Thanks. Are you ready to go?"

"Let me take Thor out first," she said. Hearing his name, Thor followed Holly to the back door.

When she returned a moment later, the smile had left her face. "I'm still not sure about this. But since I said I would go, I won't go back on my word."

"Do you want to ride in my new truck?" he asked, feeling like a kid eager to show off his ride.

"That green monstrosity?" she asked, laughing a little. "I've watched Neal try to sell that truck for years. I think I'll wait until you get it painted."

Though she had a point, he couldn't resist teasing her a little. "I might not paint it," he replied. "That color grows on you."

"In that case, let's take my vehicle."

Since the house wasn't too far from downtown, they didn't have a long drive. In just a few minutes, they pulled up to Mikki's. She found a spot right in front of the entrance and parked.

Turning to him, she left the key in the ignition and the engine running. "Are you sure you want to do this?" she asked.

Not sure whether to be amused or worried, he said yes.

"Okay." She killed the engine and pocketed the key. "Don't say I didn't warn you."

With that enigmatic statement, she got out of the car.

He joined her, and they walked into Mikki's together. Since it was prime dinnertime, the place was packed, even the bar area. There were quite a few people who looked vaguely familiar, both at tables and seated at the bar.

Though No Smoking signs were posted everywhere, the scent of stale cigarette smoke still lingered.

"I used to love playing pool here," he mused. "Do you like to play?"

For the first time since they'd left the house, she smiled. "I do. Russell taught me. I'm pretty good at it, I think."

He made a mental note to make her prove it.

As they made their way to an empty table, several people turned and watched them go past. Head held high, shoulders back, Holly ignored them. Following her example, Jeremy did the same.

Once they'd taken a seat, a waitress dropped off menus but didn't stop to chat. Since the tables around them all had their food, Jeremy found this mystifying, though Holly didn't act as if she found this unusual.

"Is it okay with you if I have a glass of wine?" Holly asked. "I don't want to drink around you if that's an issue."

"It's fine," he replied. "Have whatever you want."

She dipped her chin. "Thanks."

When the waitress arrived, Holly ordered Pinot Grigio. Jeremy got a diet cola. They went ahead and ordered burgers too, since they knew what they wanted.

"I'll get that order in," their waitress said, smiling. She took off and a minute later returned with their drinks. "Here you go."

Two older couples sat at the table next to them. Though the men appeared oblivious, the two women kept sneaking looks at Holly and whispering to each other.

Meanwhile, Holly sipped her wine and ignored them.

Their burgers arrived, both with a heaping side of seasoned fries. Just the aroma made his mouth water. He and Holly shared a smile before she picked up one half of hers and took a huge bite.

"Shameless," one woman hissed, just loud enough for them to hear. Her husband immediately tried to shush her, which Jeremy suspected wouldn't go well.

Jeremy followed Holly's lead and sampled his burger. The meaty taste exploded in his mouth. Rolling his eyes, he made a low sound of pleasure.

"As good as you remembered?" Holly asked, smiling.

"Maybe even better," he responded. "This is amazing."

As they both took their second bites, the same woman at the adjoining table narrowed her eyes. Glaring at them, she said something to her friend, who nodded. When her husband put his hand on her arm in a futile attempt to quiet her, she shook him off and lurched to her feet.

"I've seen enough," the woman declared, her shrill voice carrying to every corner of the room. She marched over to Jeremy and Holly's table. "How dare you parade in here with your latest man. You can't even be bothered to honor Russell's memory, can you?"

Though Holly's mouth tightened, she didn't look up from her plate.

"Actually, I'm Russell's brother," Jeremy drawled, pushing to his feet. "Do you have a problem with me, or are you just harassing Holly for no good reason?"

As the woman sputtered something unintelligible, her husband rushed over, taking her arm and hustling her back to their table. "My apologies," he said, looking at Jeremy.

"Don't apologize for me," the woman screeched, though she allowed herself to be steered back to her chair. "You know my opinion of that woman!"

Apparently noticing the commotion, Mikki herself came over. "Brenda, you know how I feel about bar fights. If you're itching to start one, then I'm going to have to ask you to leave."

Jeremy waited. Across from him, Holly appeared to have withdrawn into herself. She still didn't look up, and she'd stopped eating, as if the altercation had caused her to lose her appetite. This made his chest tighten.

Chapter 5

When Holly realized Jeremy was staring, she looked up and met his gaze. The fierce look on his handsome face had her breath catching in her throat.

"You deserve an apology," he muttered, pushing to his feet. He ignored her quiet protest. A few steps took him to the other table. Holly wished the floor would open up and swallow her.

Mikki, who'd started to walk away, stopped and did a double-take. "Jeremy Elliot? Is it really you?"

"Evening, Mikki," he responded with a curt nod. "It is me. And this rude woman here said some awful things to my brother's fiancée. I believe she owes Holly an apology."

When Brenda heard that, she opened her mouth, clearly intending to protest. Her husband elbowed her, hard. "She was just about to do that," he said. "Weren't you, Brenda?"

All the diners at the tables near them had gone silent, watching the little drama play out. Once again, Holly silently reminded herself never to come to town again. Something like this always seemed to happen. It just wasn't worth the aggravation.

Still, she had to admit having someone stand up for her felt pretty darn amazing. The fierce outrage on Jeremy's handsome face made her go all warm inside. She took another sip of wine and watched, curious to see how this would all play out.

Mikki, who had a reputation for fairness and had always been pleasant to Holly, crossed her arms and shot Brenda a hard glare. "Well?" she prompted. "If you have something to say, spit it out."

"I..." Brenda glanced around the room, apparently checking to see if she had any support. When instead she was met with hard stares and disapproving frowns, she swallowed. "I'm sorry," she mumbled. "I didn't realize you were visiting with Russell's brother."

Suppressing a spurt of anger, Holly set her wine glass down and looked at the other woman. Normally, she tended to take the path of least resistance since she hated confrontations.

But today, with so many clearly on her side, she decided to stand up for herself. "It shouldn't even matter," she said, her clear tone carrying. "You don't even know me. How dare you make judgments about a woman you've never even met."

Jeremy looked like he wanted to applaud. Holly sincerely hoped he wouldn't. Instead, he followed Holly's lead, sitting quietly and waiting to see how Brenda would react.

While Holly didn't know Brenda personally, she knew a lot of people like her. Quick to judge, their assumptions were apparently based on Holly's appearance. She'd been told she looked citified, too Southern, and she'd even been called fake, despite the fact that she wore little to no makeup. Other women automatically assumed Holly would make a play for their man. Brenda was no exception. If Holly thought she'd reiterate her apology, or even try to explain her actions, she was wrong.

A look of utter disgust crossed Brenda's face as she stood

and snatched her purse up from her chair. "Come on, Joe. We're going home." She marched off without waiting for her husband.

Though he stared after her, poor Joe made no move to go after his wife. Instead, he looked around the bar at everyone still watching and shrugged. "I guess she can wait in the truck," he said. "I'm going to finish my meal and my beer."

Most people laughed. A few shook their heads.

At that, everyone in the room went back to what they been doing prior to Brenda's outburst. Mikki clapped her hand on Joe's shoulder, before striding back off toward the kitchen.

"Are you okay?" Jeremy asked Holly in a low voice.

Slowly, she nodded. "Yes, I am. Thanks for standing up for me. I really appreciate it." Glancing around, she lowered her voice even more. "But now you see why I try not to come to town. That woman is not the only one who feels that way about me."

"I'm sorry," he said. "I don't understand what the reasoning could possibly be behind such accusations. I'm guessing there must be something you haven't told me."

She would have laughed, except she still felt raw. "You mean like some detail big or small that would persuade people to consider me a bad person?"

Slowly, he nodded.

"Well, I don't have one." She shrugged. "Apparently, around here it doesn't take much. I have no idea. Maybe just the way I look rubs women like Brenda the wrong way."

Jeremy nodded and picked up the rest of his burger. Holly eyed hers before pushing away her plate. "I'll take the rest of this home." She watched Jeremy eat and finished her wine, a calmness finally seeping into her, quieting her nerves.

The light over their table put shadows over Jeremy's rugged face. His longer hair and the intricate tattoo on his bicep gave him a bit of a dangerous look. Which she had to admit she found sexy as hell.

He was nothing like Russell. Nothing at all.

Russell favored a neat appearance, bordering on fussy. Until things had started changing, he'd always worn a button-down shirt, pressed khakis and soft leather shoes. With his T-shirts and jeans, Jeremy dressed more like Holly.

That wasn't the only thing. The two brothers' dining styles couldn't be more different. Russell had been particular with his meals. It had taken him forever to get everything on his plate arranged the way he wanted before he could start eating. He'd cut up his burger into neat fourths, pour ketchup over the fries and use salt and pepper, all before he took his first bite.

Whereas Jeremy attacked his food, eating with a single-minded intensity, as if he hadn't eaten a burger in months. Considering where he'd been, she suspected that might very well be possible. She had to admit, he seemed more vibrant, more alive, though that might just be her loneliness rearing its head.

Because no matter what she might have told Jeremy, she sometimes struggled with her self-imposed isolation.

"Are you okay?"

Blinking, she realized that Jeremy had finished his burger. He studied her, his gaze curious. To her surprise, she felt her face heat. She hadn't blushed so much since she'd been a teenager.

"I'm fine," she said. "I just got a little bit lost in my thoughts."

From the corner of her eye, Holly noticed her antagonist sailing across the room toward them. Great. She braced herself for yet another outburst. Instead, Brenda marched over to her own table. Hands on ample hips, she glared at her husband, her face bright red with anger. The other couple at the table focused on their food, studiously ignoring her.

"Joe. What are you doing? I've been waiting in the car. What's taking you so long?"

Her husband barely glanced up. "I'm finishing my dinner," he said, his tone mild. "I suggest you sit down and try to do the same."

Brenda inhaled sharply, but then, apparently cognizant of the way everyone in the area had looked up and gone silent, closed her mouth.

"Sit," Joe ordered, still quiet. "And let me enjoy my meal in peace."

"I can't," Brenda whined. "The stink from that other table makes me gag."

A few people gasped. Immediately, everyone looked to Holly to see her reaction. Instead of looking at Brenda, she was busy watching Jeremy.

The fury she read in Jeremy's handsome face both alarmed and gratified her. "Don't," she ordered quietly. "There's no need to say or do anything. Believe me, it will only make it worse."

Jaw tight, he met and held her gaze. She could tell he hated not being able to defend her, but she also realized she could defend herself. Or, she could simply ignore Brenda and let everyone around them see her make an ass of herself.

Craving peace and quiet, she decided to do the latter. "Are you ready to go?" she asked Jeremy quietly.

"Only if you are."

When she nodded, he looked around for their waitress so he could ask for the check.

Mikki stood close by, apparently having been alerted that Brenda had returned to cause more trouble. She hurried over to Jeremy and Holly. "This one's on me," she told them. "I'm sorry you had to endure that awful woman. She won't be welcomed back, though you two certainly are."

Picking up on this, Brenda began screeching. "You can't ban me. I've been coming to this place for over twenty years. I'm a loyal and paying customer."

Instead of looking at her, Mikki jerked her chin at Brenda's husband. "Joe, I'm sorry. You definitely can eat here. Just don't bring her with you."

Then, while Brenda sputtered, Mikki sailed back toward the kitchen.

Everyone nearby applauded. To her surprise, Holly couldn't stop smiling. When Jeremy took her arm and they walked to the door, she felt like royalty. It had been far too long since anyone had treated her like she had value. Despite her smile, tears pricked her eyes.

Once they were outside, Jeremy pulled her close for a quick hug. "Sorry, but I think you needed that," he said, releasing her. "That woman is awful."

On the verge of informing him that there were numerous others just like Brenda, she didn't. The last thing she needed was having Russell's brother feeling sorry for her.

"I'm good," she told him, maybe a bit too brightly. "And it was really kind of Mikki to comp our meal."

As they climbed into the Land Rover, she wished their evening could have ended on a better note. But then again, she'd tried to explain why she avoided going into town. Now that he knew, he'd understand.

"It's wrong, you know," Jeremy said, his intent gaze making her glance his way. "You shouldn't have to adjust your life because of people like that."

"True," she agreed, keeping her attention on the road. "But when stuff like that happens over and over again, it's exhausting. It sucks all the joy out of the day."

They stopped at one of the two traffic lights between downtown and home.

"Holly," Jeremy said.

The instant she turned toward him, he slanted his mouth over hers.

Shocked, stunned and incredibly turned on, she found herself kissing him back. It wasn't until someone honked their horn behind them that she realized the light had changed from red to green.

Feeling as if every nerve ending had caught fire, she gulped in air, pressed down on the accelerator and moved the SUV forward.

Neither of them spoke again, not even once she pulled into the driveway and opened the garage using the automatic opener. Though she knew she should say something, she had no words. Stunned, bemused and surprisingly angry, she killed the ignition, jumped out of the Land Rover and strode into the house. She didn't look back to see if Jeremy followed.

Hurrying to her bedroom, she closed and locked the door behind her. Later, she knew she'd have to talk to him, let him know that such a thing couldn't happen again, not ever. But right now, she needed to sit with herself and sort through all the emotions coursing through her.

Chief among them, desire. Completely inappropriate desire. While aware she'd gone far too long without an embrace, a caress, the raw sensuality of Jeremy's kiss had drawn her in, making her crave more, like a wounded moth to a life-affirming flame.

Foolish. And so, so wrong.

This was Russell's brother, for Pete's sake. She already had most of Blake believing whatever nonsense Russell had been spreading around about her before he'd left. Once Jeremy heard—and she had no doubt he would eventually—he'd regret that kiss.

She'd need to be clear it could absolutely never happen again.

Slowly getting out of the car, Jeremy noted Holly's rigid back as she marched into the house. He waited a bit before following, mentally berating himself. What had he been thinking? He hadn't been, clearly. Just something about her bravery, her generosity of spirit, and the way she didn't seem aware of her own beauty, got to him.

The kiss had been impulsive. And to be honest, pretty damn awesome. His entire body had gone full DEFCON arousal.

Not a good thing, not a good thing at all. Tasting her had only made him want her more. Now he'd need to learn to manage the craving. No more stolen kisses.

No matter what, he had to make sure it didn't happen again.

When his arousal finally settled down enough so he could walk, he made his way into the house. He saw no sign of Holly, and when he noticed her closed bedroom door, he understood.

He'd need to apologize, big-time. No matter that she'd kissed him back, he'd been the one to initiate it and he shouldn't have.

At a loss as to what to do to occupy his time until they could talk, he decided to go back into Blake by himself tomorrow and do some poking around to see what he could find out.

Though he'd read over Holly's incredibly detailed notes several times, Jeremy also knew that most of the locals would have reservations talking to a stranger about one of their own. Even if she was the fiancée of the man who had gone missing. So Jeremy would head into town and make a point of questioning as many people as he could.

After all, everyone knew Russell. He had been outgoing and popular with a lot of friends. Jeremy didn't figure his brother would have changed much in the last several years. Someone had to have an idea where he'd gone. Maybe they hadn't wanted to tell Holly, but surely they'd open up to Jeremy.

Holly didn't come back out. He turned on the TV, tried to focus long enough to watch a show or two, but found himself pacing. Torn between giving her time and knocking on her door to see if she'd be willing to talk, he finally decided it would be best to let things settle down. He'd crossed a line, massively. And while he intended to apologize and promise such a thing would never happen again, he still needed to puzzle out what foolish impulse had driven him to kiss her in the first place.

Finally, around ten thirty, he gave up, turned off the TV and went to bed. The second he closed his bedroom door, he heard her and Thor moving down the hallway. A moment later, she let her dog out.

In the morning, he slept a little late. Surprised to realize it was already seven thirty, he got up, made himself a cup of coffee and headed to the shower. When he emerged to a quiet and empty house, he realized Holly had already gone.

If anything, this made him feel worse. He'd hoped to smooth things over between them, and now that would have to wait until she got off work.

Deciding to grab something for breakfast in town, he

jumped in his truck. It started right up, which made him happy.

Mikki's sold donuts in the morning, so he drove there. After parking, he went inside and ordered two plus a coffee, sitting at the counter to eat them. Most of the other customers were there to grab donuts to go, and no one paid him any attention.

After finishing, he took his coffee and went back out to his truck. He drove two blocks north and parked in the middle of all the shops along Main Street. Jingling his keys, he walked to the corner, stopping in front of the old building there. For as long as he could remember, this building had housed an odd combination of businesses just as the sign outside proclaimed. Outfitter/Fishing Guide/Tourism and finally Real Estate Office.

Taking a deep breath, he pushed the door open. The instant he stepped inside, nostalgia hit him. He'd spent a good portion of his summers working part-time here, helping the few tourists who'd managed to make it this far into the Alaskan wilderness.

The young girl behind the counter looked up from her phone. "Can I help you?" she asked, managing to sound both friendly and bored all at the same time. She had a faded baseball cap pulled low over her face and wore her long brown hair in a ponytail. She appeared to be around the same age as Jeremy had been when he'd worked here, back in the day.

"I'm looking for Walker," he said. "Is he around?"

"I'm not sure." She returned her attention to her phone. "I haven't seen him in a while."

Since Jeremy knew Walker lived in an apartment upstairs from the business, he had to be close by. "Would you mind calling him and letting him know I'm here?" he asked. "My name is Jeremy Elliot."

Bored expression unchanging, she shrugged. "I'll text him and let him know."

A few minutes later, taciturn Walker Quinten, a tall man built like a linebacker, strode into the office. For as long as Jeremy could remember, Walker had owned and managed the multiple businesses housed here. Though he was at least ten years older than Russell, the two men had become good friends. Jeremy had often tagged along with them and had learned a lot about hunting and fishing from Walker.

"Jeremy Elliot!" Voice booming, Walker held out his hand. Once Jeremy took it, the older man all but crushed his hand. "I haven't seen you in forever. I heard you ran into a spot of trouble in Seattle, but since you're here, I'm guessing you're done with that. What brings you back to town?"

"I decided to move back home," Jeremy replied. "And when I got here, I was surprised to hear that my brother had up and disappeared. I'm hoping you could give me a little more information about that."

"You can't be serious." Bushy brows raised, Walker eyed him in disbelief. "Russell and I haven't talked in forever."

Perplexed, Jeremy scratched his head. "But you and he were good friends. I remember all those fishing and hunting expeditions the two of you went on."

If anything, Walker's expression hardened. "Your brother changed, man. He treated all of us like dirt, the same as he did you right before you left." He took a deep breath. "Russell always was self-involved, but he never went out of his way to hurt anyone before. The last couple of months before he left, he turned it into kind of a sport. Hurting people, making them feel like crap. Especially that poor girlfriend of his, Holly."

Stunned, Jeremy stared. "I didn't know," he said, wondering how he could get Walker to elaborate.

"Yeah, I figured." The big man crossed his massive arms. "You were gone for, what, at least ten years? I didn't think you'd be back, after he kicked you out."

"I deserved it," Jeremy said.

"No. You didn't. You were only sixteen. Who the hell tosses out a teenager with nothing more than the clothes on his back? Especially in the middle of winter? Come on, now."

Not wanting to go into what he considered personal family business, Jeremy nodded. "You say Russell changed. In what way?"

Walker snorted. "I'm guessing your plan is to go around and talk to people who once were his friends. I'll bet all of them will tell you the same thing. Russell did what would benefit him and only him. Just like always."

Something must have shown on Jeremy's face, because Walker chuckled. "Not what you were expecting to hear, is it? Well, let me give you one more bit of information. If Russell took off, he had his reasons. It's likely he doesn't want to be found. Best keep that in mind."

Then, before Jeremy could even react to this, never mind comment, Walker turned and went to the door. He held it open. "I'm sorry, but I don't want to talk about Russell anymore," he said, jerking his head toward the sidewalk. "Despite everything, it still hurts. But it was nice seeing you again."

"Same," Jeremy replied, though he didn't mean it. Three seconds after he stepped outside, Walker closed the door and locked it with a decisive click.

Weird. Russell had lost his best friend. This made Jeremy wonder what or who else he'd lost.

Deciding to leave his truck parked, Jeremy walked over to Murphy's. Kip had told him to stop by anytime he needed to talk, so hopefully he'd be more receptive than Walker had been.

He spotted the store owner by the hardware aisle and hurried over.

"Back so soon?" Smiling, Kip clapped Jeremy on the back. "What'd you forget to buy the other day?"

Jeremy smiled back. "Nothing yet, though I'm sure I'll find stuff if I walk around. I wanted to see if you had a minute to talk."

"Sure. Let's go back to my office. Follow me." Kip led the way into the back.

As they walked through the stockroom to Kip's small office, Jeremy spotted Holly. She had her back to them as she unloaded a large box.

Once inside the tiny room, Kip closed the door. "Sit." He gestured to a folding metal chair before taking a seat behind his desk. "What's on your mind?"

"I wanted to talk to you about Russell," Jeremy began. Immediately, Kip's friendly expression became guarded.

"What's wrong?" Jeremy asked. "You can level with me."

Kip heaved a sigh. "Okay, I will. I'm going to guess you're talking to all the people you remember as being in Russell's circle of friends."

"I am."

"Well, the thing is you've been away for a while."

"Which is what Walker said. But he wouldn't elaborate, other than saying my brother seemed to enjoy going around hurting people. Including those who once were his friends." Jeremy leaned forward. "I trust you. Tell me the truth. What was going on with my brother?"

"I'm not sure how to say this." Clearly uncomfortable, Kip shifted in his chair. "I'll start at the beginning. Even before Russ brought Holly out here, he changed. As you know, he's always been a bit self-involved, but he reached new levels of bad behavior. He slept with his buddies' wives, lied to just about everyone and, in short, acted like a total ass. I suspect he might have been on something."

For a heartbeat, Jeremy thought he'd heard wrong. "I don't understand."

"Drugs." Kip grimaced. "There, I've said it. A couple of us even confronted him, tried to stage an intervention of sorts. But he blew us off."

None of this made sense. Earlier, Holly had said something similar, that Russell was on drugs. He hadn't believed it then, nor did he now. His brother had been the most virulent anti-drug crusader Jeremy had ever known. "But that's why he kicked me out of the house," he protested. "He caught me using."

"When you were sixteen." Kip's mouth twisted with disgust. "He should have gotten you help instead of throwing you out into the street. Several of us tried to talk to him about that, you know. Hell, me and Walker even went looking for you to offer you a place to stay. But we couldn't find you."

Because he'd hitched a ride with a trucker all the way to Anchorage. He'd done the same when he'd moved to Seattle. "I appreciate the attempt, but that's all in the past. I've turned my life around and come back to make things right with my brother. Instead, I find he's been missing for over a year with a former fiancée living in his home. No one seems overly concerned about what might have happened to him. Including Holly."

"Don't." Gaze hard, Kip stood. "You have no idea what Russell put that poor woman through. Not only did he make sure that just about every other woman in town despises her, but he came damn close to making her hate herself. Holly doesn't deserve any of that."

Taken aback, Jeremy nodded. "I wasn't talking bad about Holly. I barely know her. I'm just trying to find my brother."

"Why?" Kip asked bluntly. "You and he didn't part on good terms. What makes you think he'd welcome you with open arms if he were still here?"

Jeremy held the other man's gaze. "I never thought that he would, to be honest. But we're family, the only blood relatives each other has. Since I decided to come home, I figured the time had come to patch things up between us." He swallowed hard. "Time has a way of smoothing over old wounds. I figured I could convince him to give me a chance. I still do, if I can find him."

Though some of the hardness in Kip's face softened, he shook his head. "I hate to break it to you, but until Russell wants to be found, he's going to stay missing. I'm not sure what he did, but whatever it was, it must have had some awfully bad consequences to make him decide to go into hiding."

"Once again, Walker said something similar."

"They used to be best friends," Kip pointed out. "If anyone knows Russell, Walker does. Or did," he amended. "And I'm sorry, but no matter how many people you talk to, they're all going to say the same thing. The Russell you knew from before hasn't been around in years."

Jeremy struggled to wrap his mind around this. "When I left here, Russell was one of the most popular guys in town." He left the rest unsaid. Even at sixteen, he'd ached to be part of his brother's inner circle. To be drawn into the warmth and laughter instead of being forced to watch from a distance, an outsider standing in the cold.

Though Russell had made sure Jeremy had a roof over his head and food in his belly, he'd seemed to draw the line at offering any kind of emotional connection. He'd been pleasant enough, on the surface. Just…distant. And then he'd kicked him out.

Shaking off the old memories, he sighed. "Maybe I'm delusional. But I know I have to at least try."

Kip nodded. "I respect that. If I can think of anything that could help you, I promise to give you a call."

"Thank you."

Leaving the general store, he decided to go speak with Greg Norman, the mayor. Greg, who bore a striking re-semblance to Santa Claus had, along with his wife, Jane, always been kind to Jeremy when he was a kid. Jeremy had fond memories of hot cocoa and access to a seemingly end-less library of children's picture books that the couple had bought for their grandchildren.

Since the mayor's office was also the couple's home, Jeremy rang the doorbell. Waiting on the front porch, he almost felt like a kid again.

"Well, hello, there!" Jane opened the door, smiling broadly. "I heard you were back in town, young man. Now, come here and give me a hug."

Happy to comply, Jeremy wrapped his arms carefully around the older woman. While Jane had always been trim, she seemed more fragile than he remembered.

"Let me find Greg," she said once they broke apart. "He'll be thrilled to see you."

Before she'd even finished speaking, Greg strode into the kitchen. But instead of greeting Jeremy with a smile, he stopped short and frowned. "What the hell are you doing here?" he demanded. "Get out. Now. People like you aren't welcome in my house."

Chapter 6

Holly hadn't been able to stop dwelling on *the kiss*. Possibly because it had been ages since anyone had kissed her like she was a desirable woman, but more likely because she hadn't been able to throttle her wild attraction to her ex-fiancé's younger brother.

Worse, she didn't feel ashamed. Not in the slightest. Instead, she'd had to physically avoid Jeremy to prevent herself from doing something stupid, like throw herself into his arms.

Though it felt cowardly to hide out in her bedroom, that's what she did. When she finally heard the TV go off, she knew he'd likely taken himself off to bed.

Immediately, she took Thor out and rushed down the hall to the bathroom to brush her teeth and wash her face.

And in the morning, she managed to avoid him entirely. After a quick shower at 6:00 a.m., she got dressed and ready for work in record time. Since today she'd be working in the stockroom from eight until ten, and then she'd agreed to try working the sales floor from ten to twelve, she felt extra nervous. Kip had promised to stick around and help her if she ran into trouble, and she planned to hold him to it.

So when Jeremy had walked into the back room of Murphy's with her boss shortly after eight, she'd immediately tensed up. She'd successfully avoided glancing at him. Surely he knew better than to bring their personal issues into her place of work.

Instead, Kip had taken Jeremy into his office and closed the door.

She'd kept herself busy, so she hadn't noticed when Jeremy left. Which likely was a good thing, considering she had other things on her mind, like dealing with a potentially hostile public. All jangled nerves, she hoped her jitters wouldn't show. Either way, the closer it got to ten, the more she kept checking her watch.

"Are you ready?" Kip appeared, all smiles. "I'm going to have you shadow Neal today. That'll help you see how everything works."

"Sounds good." She liked Neal. He'd always been kind to her, even helping her unpack stock when the store itself was slow.

Though Blake was a small town, the remote location meant that Murphy's acted as a kind of catchall store. They sold nonperishable groceries, with the exception of produce and meat brought in by locals. People actually bartered when they had items they knew would be of value. Those with chickens brought in their surplus eggs, and in the summer and early fall, over-producing gardens meant Murphy's carried lots of fresh fruits and vegetables.

In addition to the food, they had a clothing section, plus a section where locals sold their crafted items on consignment. Holly had several of her own paintings and other artwork on display here. There was a hardware section, carrying various tools and things like grass seed and birdseed. She'd often wondered how Kip managed to balance such a varied inventory, but he'd been doing it for years and had the skill down to a fine art.

The first time Russell had taken her into Murphy's, she'd been amazed at how one general store served the entire town's needs. Over time, she'd come to appreciate the place even more.

"Are you ready?" Neal asked, walking over to her with a smile.

Summoning up her own smile, she nodded. "Lead the way."

The rest of her shift went quickly. She watched closely, standing by while Neal helped numerous customers. Friendly and helpful, he seemed to know not only where everything was located, but what else each customer might need to buy to go with his or her purchase.

"You're really good," she told him, meaning it.

"Thanks." Neal smiled. "You'll be just as good once you've done this a few times, I promise."

Though she privately doubted that, she simply shrugged. "We'll see."

"I think someone is here to see you," Neal said, gesturing toward the door. "Either that, or he's here to complain about the truck I sold him."

She looked over to see Jeremy making his way toward them. Her heart skipped in her chest. Though at first glance he appeared casual, something about the way he held himself told her something had happened.

"Afternoon, Neal," Jeremy said, dipping his chin at the other man before turning his attention on Holly. "I came by to ask you what time you get off work. I really need to talk to you."

Immediately, she thought of the mind-blowing kiss they'd shared. To her absolute horror, she felt her face heat. Blushing bright red was one of the major downsides to having a pale complexion.

Neal, bless his heart, appeared oblivious to any undercurrents. "I think she's off in ten minutes," he said to Jeremy, before looking at Holly. "But since it's quiet right now, if you want to go, I'm cool with it."

"Or I can wait," Jeremy said, even though she could feel the tension practically radiating from him.

"No need. Let me go clock out and I'll be right back." She hurried into the back, grabbed her time card and inserted it into the old-fashioned machine on the wall. Once stamped, she put the card back into its slot, grabbed her backpack and hurried out front.

Since Neal had gone to help a new customer, Jeremy waited alone. Hands jammed in his jean pockets, he stared off into the distance, clearly lost in thought. As she approached him, she took a moment to study his rugged profile, anticipating the familiar tug of attraction. When he finally registered her approach, he swung his head around and met her gaze.

"Are you all right?" she asked quietly, lightly touching his arm.

He stared at her a moment before answering. "No. I'm not. Would you mind walking with me?"

Though walking down Main Street was generally something she avoided, she nodded. "Sure."

Outside, the bright sunshine and perfect temperature made her inhale in appreciation. Summer might be short in Alaska, but that only made it more precious. She wished she had the right to link her arm through Jeremy's, though the second that thought crossed her mind she regretted it. Russell had been particular about public displays of affection, refusing to even allow her to stand too close.

They walked a block in silence before she stopped and

turned to him. "Are you going to tell me what happened?" she asked.

Before answering, he swallowed. The pain in his brown eyes made her catch her breath.

"I went around town and tried to talk to all the people I remembered as being my brother's friends," he began.

Instantly, she understood. "And you learned a lot had changed since the last time you were in town." She too had been surprised to learn how unpopular her new fiancé actually was. Russell had painted himself as popular and well-liked by everyone in the small town.

"Right. All the people who used to be close friends with Russell now despise him." Disappointment and shock echoed in his voice.

"I'm sorry," she said, meaning it. "From what I've been told, your brother changed a lot. I know he did even after I arrived. He didn't seem to care how many enemies he made." Or how he treated the woman he professed to love.

Grim-faced, he eyed her. "But in Mikki's last night, that woman was hateful to you. Almost like she was defending him."

Holly shrugged. "It seems Russell was quite the ladies' man." She didn't try to keep the bitterness from her voice. "Most of the townsfolk who believe I had something to do with his disappearance are female. I'm not entirely sure why, though more than a few people have hinted that Russell had more than one side chick."

At first, he didn't comment. Instead, he turned and jammed his hands into his pockets before resuming walking. She kept pace, deciding to let him talk when he felt ready.

"That's not the worst part of it," he finally said, still moving and keeping his gaze straight ahead. "I stopped by the mayor's. Greg and Jane have always been like family to me. Not this time. Jane welcomed me in, but the instant Greg saw me, he ordered me to leave."

Shocked, her steps faltered. "Why? The Normans are some of the kindest, most welcoming people I know."

"I know, right? That's why it hurt so badly. He said people like me aren't welcome in his house."

She took a minute to consider his words. Though she wasn't sure how or what he'd done, she suspected Russell had something to do with all this. For now, since she had no proof and she figured Jeremy wouldn't want to hear it, she kept her suspicions to herself.

"Maybe I should ask Jane," she said. "She's always been friendly toward me."

He stopped and turned to face her. "I appreciate the offer, but please don't. I'll figure this out on my own, when I can. Right now, I want to focus on finding my brother."

"I'll help you any way I can," she promised, even though she believed Russell wouldn't allow himself to be found until he was good and ready. Which might mean never.

Several people had come looking for him in the weeks immediately after he'd disappeared. Since they'd all been relatively courteous, she truthfully hadn't thought anything of it. But when she mentioned this to Jeremy, he appeared startled.

"What did they want?" he asked, stopping again and facing her.

"I'm not sure. Each one asked for Russell. When I told them he wasn't there and that I wasn't sure when he'd return, they accepted it and went away. The first month, at least once a week someone would stop by. Sometimes more."

"Did you get any of their names?"

"Yes, I wrote them all down. They're in the folder I gave you." She swallowed. "Though to be honest, I'm pretty sure the names they gave weren't real."

"Why do you think that?" he asked.

"Because when I tried to find them later, they didn't exist. Not on social media or in the town directory of residents. I'm not sure why they felt they had to hide their identities though. They never came out and said what they wanted Russell for."

"Come on." He turned and began walking back the way they'd come. "Thank you for listening."

This touched her far more than it should have. "You're welcome. I just wish I could be of more help. I've gone over all this too many times to count. Not only with the police, but with myself, trying to make sense of it."

They'd reached her Land Rover. Jeremy waited while she unlocked the vehicle and got inside. Though she felt like she should say something more or do something else, she went ahead and closed the door and started the engine.

As she drove away, she glanced back once. Jeremy remained where she'd left him, watching her go.

After walking Holly to her vehicle, Jeremy stood and tracked her SUV as she drove away. Before going back to his own truck, he decided to head on down to Mikki's and see if she had anything to add to the mounting list of complaints against Russell. He might as well get it all at once. No sense in ruining another day when this one had already tanked.

When she saw him coming, Mikki sauntered over with a welcoming smile. "Back so soon? I could swear you were in here earlier for a couple of donuts and a coffee."

"I was." He smiled back. "I wondered if you had a few minutes to talk to me about Russell."

Just like that, her smile vanished. Noticing this, he groaned. "Not you too," he said.

"I have no idea what you mean," she replied, her voice lofty. But he knew that she did.

"Come on, Mikki," he pleaded. "I know I've been away for a lot of years, but I'm just trying to locate my brother. I tried to talk to several people today who were once Russell's friends, but no one will even tell me the truth."

She crossed her arms. "What did they say then?"

"Just that he'd changed. And not for the good." He took a deep breath. "They all said that he hadn't been the same person he was when I left. Honestly, I didn't expect him to be. All in all, it's been over ten years. People change. I get that. But Russell was a good person at the core. I don't understand the hostility."

Still watching him closely, finally Mikki sighed. "Follow me. We'll go talk in my office where we can have some privacy."

Finally. Walking through a door to the left of the bar, they passed the kitchen, a small break room and then a larger stockroom. Mikki led him to a portioned area on the other side of that.

"Come on in. Take a seat." She closed the door behind him before moving to the other side of a rickety metal desk. Lowering herself into an ancient chair that squeaked, she sighed. "I know you're having a tough time, Jeremy. But you've been gone the better part of a decade, and I'm guessing people don't feel they really know you."

Stunned, he could only stare at her. "I don't understand," he said. "What difference does that make?"

"A lot. No one wants to tell someone horrible things

about their older brother if they can help it. Especially since they don't know how you'll take it."

"Horrible things." He focused on that. "Please explain what you mean."

"I don't even know where to begin," she admitted, leaning back in her chair. "I know everyone has been telling you this, but Russell changed. More than you could ever imagine. I vaguely remember how awful he was to you when you were a teenager and how you acted out, just trying to get his attention."

Again, Jeremy had to hide his surprise. He'd never thought of his relationship with his older brother like that. Yes, he'd definitely wanted more than Russell had been able to give, but still…

"Anyway," Mikki continued. "Russell was always self-involved, but after you left and he had no one, he took that to new levels."

His expression must have shown he didn't understand, because Mikki sighed. "Booze, drugs and women," she finally said. "I don't know how much more succinct I can be than that."

"That doesn't sound like my brother," Jeremy said. But then, realizing he'd protested, exactly what Mikki had said he would do, he amended. "Or the brother I remember from a long time ago. Please, tell me what you know. You can be honest with me."

"Are you sure about that?" Expression skeptical, Mikki gave him a long look.

"Yes." He kept his voice firm. "Maybe then I can figure out his disappearance."

"There's really nothing to figure out," Mikki replied. "Russell took himself off for a reason that only he knows. And he's not going to show back up unless he wants to."

Since he'd heard that over and over today, he nodded. "Tell me about the other things. The booze and women and...drugs." This last was the most difficult to swallow.

Mikki took a minute to answer. "Jeremy started hanging out here at my bar," she said, clearly choosing her words carefully. "He always drank a lot, but it seemed like he could handle his liquor. We only had to cut him off a few times, and made sure he had a ride home."

"Loneliness?" Jeremy guessed, still trying to figure out what had made his brother tick.

Mikki snorted. "Not hardly. That boy wasn't lonely. He had just about every woman in town hanging all over him. Older and younger both. And he didn't discriminate between single and married either." She leaned forward and lowered her voice. "I hate gossiping, but you asked. When he slept with Josie Quinten, that pushed Walker over the edge."

"He slept with his best friend's wife?" Jeremy could hardly believe it. His brother had always held them both to high standards, coming down hard on Jeremy when he didn't meet them. "No wonder Walker could barely bring himself to say my brother's name."

"Yes." She shrugged. "For a while there, it seemed like Russell couldn't help himself. Wives, sisters, girlfriends, he didn't care. And he wasn't after any sort of relationship situation either. He made that clear."

No wonder his former friends despised him. Jeremy couldn't blame them. "Wow," he commented. "That's a lot to take in."

"I know." Pointing to a minifridge on the table behind her desk, she asked him if he wanted a soft drink or bottled water.

Suddenly parched, he asked for a water. Once she'd

handed it to him, he drank several long draughts. "Where does Holly figure into all this?" he asked. "How did he go from serial womanizer to getting engaged?"

"That's what just about everyone in town wanted to know," Mikki said. "But I will say this. There are only so many bridges you can burn in one town. In addition to that, as whatever drug he was using claimed more and more hold on him, his physical appearance and hygiene deteriorated. The women stopped coming around. Since Holly came from the lower forty-eight, I'm guessing he met her on a dating app."

Since Jeremy didn't plan to discuss Holly at all, he simply waited.

"Except for Tanya," Mikki mused. "That woman pursued him like a bear after salmon. She didn't care what he did, or who he hurt."

"Tanya?" This was the first time he'd heard the name. "Who is she?"

"One of his lady friends. But while most of them went away as Russell started getting really bad, she dug in. In fact, rumor had it that she helped him with some of his more outrageous schemes."

Schemes. Her choice of words didn't escape him.

"I want to ask about those, but I'm not sure I want to know. I'm having a difficult enough time digesting all this. I'm not sure I can handle anything else."

"Another time," Mikki agreed. "But when you want to know why people like Brenda hate Holly so much, it's because of Tanya. She went around to all of Russell's old flings and got most of them to believe that Holly had something to do with his disappearance."

This made him frown. "Something how? Like she talked him into leaving?"

"While that would make the most sense, no. It's not what I heard. It seems Tanya has convinced herself that Holly killed off your brother and hid his body so she can stay in the house and continue to drive that fancy white Land Rover."

Dumbfounded, he scratched his head. "First up, she owns half the house. And Russell gifted her that SUV. Her name is on the deed and the vehicle title."

"So she claims, according to Tanya. She thinks Holly has everyone believing that, but that it's a load of nonsense."

"Have any of these people actually *met* Holly?" he asked, incredulous. "Lying about that doesn't seem like something she would do."

"And you've known her how long?" Mikki asked gently. "A couple of days at best, right?"

It took a moment for her words to register. "Are you saying you think she might have actually done something like that?"

"No, not at all. I'm just letting you know what rumors are out there."

"I see." Though he wanted to push to his feet, he forced himself to wait. "Is there anything else you can tell me? Like maybe what kind of drugs Russell was using and where he got them."

"I'm sorry, I mustn't have made myself clear. Everything I've told you, I got secondhand. It could be true, it might be all lies. I don't know much more than what I've already told you. Except one final thing. Russell wasn't just using, he was selling."

Now this, of all the bizarre accusations, was too much. "No." He shook his head. "Russell wouldn't do that. I know him."

"You *knew* him," she gently pointed out. "And those in

the know say he had quite an inventory. Mostly opioids, I've heard. But some stimulants too. Now, bear in mind, I don't have proof of this, so don't take any of this as fact. These are all bits of gossips I've heard floated around the bar. People say a lot of things they shouldn't when they've had a few drinks."

Jeremy nodded. "I appreciate you being honest with me. I admit, I'm struggling to believe any of this."

"I imagine you are. But you should know, your brother was never a nice person, even when you knew him. Before he left, he'd become downright awful. As hard as it might be to say to you, most people don't really mind that he's missing. A few probably downright celebrated."

Though he'd wanted the truth, the knowledge sat heavy on his shoulders. He couldn't help but wonder how much of this Holly knew. If she'd come here to marry a man most people couldn't trust or like, what did that say about her?

"Thank you," he said. "At least I have more information than I had when I started. Where can I find this Tanya? I think she's who I need to speak with next."

"That, I don't know," Mikki replied. "She used to come into the bar nightly when she knew Russell would be here, but she's only been off and on in the past year. I only know she's still around because some of my other customers mention her from time to time."

"Which means if I want to locate her, I need to come to the bar and talk to people."

She made a face. "You can certainly try. At least you don't look too much like him."

"What do you mean?" Puzzled, he met her gaze. "For as long as I can remember, people always said they could tell we were related."

"Maybe the eyes." Mikki shrugged, looking him up and

down dispassionately. "And maybe you share the same chin. I'd have to say you both are good-looking men, though in a different way."

"Thanks." He dipped his head. "Back to this Tanya woman. Blake is a pretty small town. Surely there's got to be some way I can find her."

She laughed. "You know how people talk. I'm sure word has already gotten out that you're back in town. Start coming around the bar a few nights a week. I bet she'll show up just to check you out."

Oddly enough, his first thought in that scenario was that he didn't want to leave Holly alone. This shocked him, given that he barely knew her and she'd been living by herself ever since his brother had disappeared.

"I'd rather be more proactive," he said instead. "Are you sure you don't know anything about her, like where she works?"

"I don't, but I'm guessing some of the regulars might. Come in tonight around eight. Most of them will be here by then."

"I'll do that." Pushing to his feet, he turned to go. "Thanks for being so up-front with me. I really appreciate it."

Standing also, she came around from behind her desk. "I hate to be the bearer of bad news, but somebody had to tell you."

"True." Something else occurred to him. "One more question before I go. Does Holly know about Tanya?"

Mikki shrugged. "I have no idea. That'd be something you'd have to ask her yourself."

Chapter 7

Driving home, for the first time in far too long Holly felt happy. Truly happy. As in, she couldn't stop smiling. She almost didn't recognize this feeling, it had been so long. While she'd made her peace with her solitude and greeted each morning with a kind of quiet contentment, she couldn't remember the last time she felt so alive. For so long she'd been existing merely in the moment. While she'd been refusing to dwell on the past, she'd also been afraid to dare to think about the future.

She might have no clear picture of what she wanted to do with her life, but she knew what she didn't want. Russell and his mind games, turning what she'd believed to be love into something twisted and rotten. And though she'd come to appreciate Alaska with its stark, rugged beauty, sometimes she felt life in a small town like Blake wasn't right for her.

Then there were days like today. Where everything meshed just right and she knew her place in the universe. No matter what else she lost, she had her art and her online store. Her part-time job at Murphy's with friends like Kip and Neal to have her back.

Today, with Kip coaxing her to work out front instead of hiding away in the stockroom, she realized she just might be done with staying out of sight. People like Brenda didn't deserve the right to take away her sunshine and relegate her to the shadows. She'd done nothing wrong. Perhaps the time had come to refuse to allow anyone to treat her as if she had.

And then there was Jeremy. Her unwanted attraction to him made absolutely zero sense. She knew better than to allow herself to act on that. After all, look what had happened with his brother.

In hindsight, she'd been a fool, falling for Russell on the basis of a four-month, long-distance relationship. Sure, he'd traveled to see her a few times. And she'd truly believed they'd had a connection, that he loved her. Her heart had leaped for joy when he'd asked her to be his wife and promised to take care of her the rest of her life if she'd do the same for him.

She'd given up everything—her possessions, her apartment, her friends—and traveled to Alaska to be with him.

Rose-colored glasses firmly in place, the first months after she'd arrived in Blake, Alaska, had been among the happiest of her life. She and Russell had done everything together, and if there'd been warning signs, she'd willfully chosen to ignore them.

Until she couldn't any longer.

The first time Russell had gone on a rampage, he'd been drunk. He'd hurled accusations at her like knives, the words sharp enough to cut deeply. She'd been too stunned to fight back, too incredulous to even understand what she'd done to set him off. Instead, she'd retreated to the bathroom where she'd locked the door and sat and cried.

Russell hadn't spoken to her again that night. In fact, when she'd finally gathered the courage to emerge, she'd found him passed out on the couch.

The next morning, he'd apologized profusely. He'd sworn

he hadn't meant any of it and it would never happen again. "Let me make it up to you," he'd begged. "Please don't leave me. I can't live without you."

Fool that she'd been, she'd believed him. And for numerous times after that, as her fiancé had gotten worse and worse and she'd begun to suspect it wasn't just alcohol fueling his rages.

And then she'd learned about the other women. Not just one, or even two, and apparently Russell hadn't worried about any sexually transmitted diseases he might have brought home to her. She'd moved to the other bedroom, the one Jeremy used now, and learned how to tell if the Russell arriving back at the end of the work day would be civil or a screaming, raging monster.

Each vicious cycle had chipped away at her until little by little, her love for him had died. Though she had nowhere to go, she'd tried to give him back his ring when she informed him their engagement was over. He'd refused to take it, which is why she still had it. She'd also let him know that she planned to remain in the house until either he bought her out or they sold it. To her surprise, Russell had shrugged and told her that was fine.

And two days later, Russell had disappeared.

She'd learned his company, the one he'd built from the ground up, had been sold several months ago. What Russell might have done with the profit from that sale, she didn't know. Likely she never would.

Tired of dwelling on the past, she shook off the bit of melancholy and took Thor out for a walk. Despite his size and massive strength, he'd always been a pleasure to walk. He never pulled, not even when he caught sight of a squirrel or rabbit.

After circling the block, they returned home. Thor happily curled up on his cushiony dog bed while she debated going into her art room to work on some new creations. She'd recently been making small sculptures, all modeled after Thor, and begun painting them in swirls of vivid color. They sold well, and she'd gotten a few emails asking her to do another breed of dog. She wanted to try her hand at this too.

Settling down to work on her third attempt to make a dachshund, she'd been lost in the clay for only thirty minutes when Jeremy's green truck pulled into the drive. Thor alerted her by going to the front window and letting out a single loud woof as if welcoming Jeremy home. Her dog stood, fluffy tail wagging, facing the front door, waiting for Jeremy to come inside.

Holly got up and stretched her legs, walking into the main part of the house where she could see her dog.

"You really like him, don't you, boy?" Holly asked. Thor actually glanced back at her before refocusing on the door. She could have sworn her dog was smiling.

When Jeremy let himself in a few moments later, Thor greeted him with the same level of enthusiasm he usually reserved only for Holly. Watching, she had to admit she liked the way Jeremy made a fuss over the large canine, tangling his hands in Thor's thick fur and talking to him as if he were human, the same way she did.

When Jeremy finally straightened, Thor trotted back to Holly's side. Settling at her feet, he heaved a contented sigh. She decided not to return to her art room, not just yet. She spotted tension in the way Jeremy carried himself. While she knew it wasn't any of her business, she also suspected he could use a friendly ear.

"How'd the rest of your day go?" she asked, keeping her voice casual.

Slowly, he shook his head. "Enlightening, I guess. Though not in the way I expected. After you left, I went to talk to Mikki." Jeremy walked into the kitchen, leaving her and Thor to follow. Jeremy dropped into one of the chairs and leaned back. "Unlike everyone else I talked to, she opened up and told me everything she knew about Russell. Which was a lot."

Holly nodded, searching his face for some kind of hint as to how that might have affected him. "Are you okay?" she finally asked.

"I'm not sure."

His blunt honesty surprised her. "I'm sorry," she said. "Let me know if there's anything I can do to help."

"Actually, there is. I need to ask you something." He barely paused for her to nod before continuing. "Did you know about Tanya?"

Just hearing the name again made her feel sick. "What about her?" she asked. "I assumed Mikki told you about her stalking me."

"What?"

Judging by his surprised expression, she'd guessed wrong. "Tanya is a woman who became obsessed with Russell," she said. "He told me about her long before he disappeared. He met her at Mikki's, and she wouldn't leave him alone."

"Did he sleep with her?" he asked. Something told her he already knew the answer.

"I'm sure he did." She shrugged, as if the knowledge had never hurt. "One time when Russell was under the influence, he bragged about how many women he'd been with, and not just in the past before me. He didn't seem to realize that I might take offense."

"Ouch." Jeremy winced. "I don't know what to say. I'm sorry."

"It's not your fault," she replied. "Russell's actions have nothing to do with you. But why are you asking about Tanya?"

"Mikki mentioned her. I thought maybe if I could find her and talk to her, she might have some idea where Russell went."

Holly snorted. "I doubt that. She's convinced that I killed him and hid his body. She has several of her women friends believing that as well."

"Like Brenda when we were trying to eat dinner?"

"Exactly," she replied. "She used to call all the time and say awful things to me, until I changed the landline number and made it unlisted. Then she'd drive by and tape notes to my front door, or leave bags of horse manure in my mailbox."

"Is she dangerous?" he asked.

"I don't think so. She's a bit deluded, but she hasn't bothered me in at least a month. I'm sure she continues to try and spread rumors about me around town, but by now I think most people have moved on." She sighed. "I'm afraid if you reach out to her, she'll start back up again. And I really don't want to go through that all over again."

He acknowledged her statement with a nod. "If I try to find her, she won't know that you have anything to do with me."

"Maybe not. But you bring up Russell, and she thinks of me. She never could stand that he brought me here, asked me to marry him and gave me a ring."

"Still, I don't think it would hurt to see what she has to say," he said.

"You're not going to let this go, are you?" Part of her

couldn't blame him. He wanted to explore any potential avenue that might lead to his brother. And he had no way of knowing how volatile Tanya could be.

"I'm not," he acknowledged. "But if I find her and she brings you up, I'll make sure she understands that I'm on your side. Will that work?"

"Since I don't have a choice, I suppose it will have to."

"Do you have any idea where she works or anything?" he asked.

"No." She folded her arms. "I don't. I've made it a point to know as little about her as possible."

Though he raised a brow, he didn't comment.

Since changing the subject seemed the right thing to do, she got them both a bottled water before taking the seat across from him.

"Off topic, but I'm genuinely curious. Since it seems like you're going to be here awhile, what are you planning to do for work?" she asked, her voice guarded. "I know we discussed you paying your share of the utilities and groceries, but I'm thinking you're eventually going to want to find a job, right?"

Judging from the way he stared at her, she might have gone too far. "You're the first person who's asked me that. I'm thinking of starting my own business."

Now it was her turn to be surprised. "Like Russell did? I was surprised to find out he'd sold it a few months before he left."

"What did he do, exactly?" he asked.

"Remote IT work. Companies would contract him to handle their IT needs. He was very good at it, or so he said." She crossed over to the kitchen junk drawer, opened it and rummaged around. Finally, she found what she'd been looking for—one of Russell's old business cards. "Here," she said, handing it to Jeremy. "This was his."

He studied it, turning the card over in his hand. "Do you mind if I keep this?"

"Not at all." She sat back down. "But you still haven't answered my question. What kind of business are you planning to open?"

Now he glanced at Thor. The instant he did, her dog left her side and went over to Jeremy, curling up to lie at his feet. When Thor did this, Jeremy broke out into a huge smile. "I train dogs," he said. "I was part of a dog training program in prison, and it turned out I'm really good at it. I studied up on the market, and it turns out there's a real need for skilled people to train dogs. That's what I'm planning to do."

Fascinated despite herself, she nodded. "What kind of dog training? Are you talking about regular obedience training? Or something different, like service dogs?"

"I thought I'd start out with search and rescue dogs," he said, as if that wasn't a huge undertaking in itself. "I wanted to apprentice under some of the more well-known training centers, but no one wants an ex-convict working for them. Even if he's been cleared of any wrongdoing."

He said that so matter-of-factly that at first the words didn't register. When they did, she shook her head. "Even once you explained?" she asked.

"They didn't want to hear it. No matter. I've watched a lot of videos and I've read a lot of books. Plus, I got a lot of practical experience while I was incarcerated. My plan is to train one dog and then reach out to various organizations that might be interested." He shrugged. "It's a solid plan. And I'm good. You'll see."

"Judging by the way Thor has taken to you, I'm thinking that your plan just might work."

Again he smiled, though it didn't reach his eyes. "Now it's my turn to ask you something. Do you actually want my brother to be found?"

"I want to clear my name," she replied, aware it wasn't really an answer. "And since the only way to do that is for him to show up, alive and unharmed, I do."

"Except you don't sound entirely certain," he pointed out.

She thought about that for a moment. "Since today is your day to hear hard truths, I might as well be brutally honest with you. Russell made my life a living hell. In the end, he destroyed everything that we'd begun to build together. Since he left, my life has been quiet. Peaceful even. If Russell came back to this house, I'm not sure I could stay. I've been saving up money to get my own place, so I'd figure something out."

"He probably wouldn't let me stay either," Jeremy said quietly. "But I still want to find him. Maybe I can help him turn his life around."

Though she thought Russell was too far gone for that, what did she know? Maybe Jeremy was right. If all Russell needed was a brother's caring guidance, then she was all for it.

"Let me ask you one more thing," Jeremy continued. "I know everyone, including you, believes my brother just took off on his own. But is there even the slightest chance that someone might have harmed him? Like this Tanya person?"

"Anything is possible. I brought that up to the police," she said. "They said they'd look into it, but I never heard anything back. Maybe if you call them, since you're next of kin, they might fill you in."

"I plan to do that." He got up and began prowling around the kitchen, his movements surprisingly graceful for a man of his size.

Fascinated, she watched silently, wondering how two brothers could be so different. And how she could find herself battling attraction to one of them so soon after the other had nearly destroyed her.

There were a lot of undercurrents swirling in the words that Holly didn't say. Jeremy watched her as she struggled to find the right phrases. He could tell she walked a fine line, torn between wanting to be honest and not completely crushing his feelings. While he appreciated that, he also valued Mikki's earlier brutal honesty.

He'd begun to understand that he carried around an idealized, fictional image of his brother. The man he believed Russell to be rather than who he actually had become. Yet until he saw for himself, he found it impossible to comprehend that his older brother could be that bad. After all, for most of his life, Jeremy had wanted to be more like him. The entire time he'd been incarcerated and fighting for his freedom, he'd often wished he'd had Russell on his side. Only envisioning the look of disappointment he'd known he'd see on his brother's face had prevented him from making the attempt.

Now he wondered if not contacting Russell might have been a good thing.

"I don't have anything to go on," he said out loud. "I can see you've investigated every angle. I put in a call to the state police, but I haven't heard back yet. So this Tanya woman is all I've got."

Holly made a face but didn't comment.

"Would you be interested in coming with me to try and find her?" he asked, pretty sure he already knew what Holly's answer would be.

"What?" Her huge blue eyes widened. "That'd definitely be poking the bear. She seems to have backed off from me for now. Why would I want to risk starting her harassment all over again?"

"You don't think maybe she's over it by now?"

"Was Brenda over it the other night when we were trying to have dinner?" she countered. "As long as Tanya's friends continue to treat me like a stain on the earth, I'm not taking a chance. While I hope you find her, if only to get a few more answers, I also wish you luck. You have no idea of her level of instability." She took a deep breath and then exhaled. "The only advice I have for you is to just be careful."

"Thank you," he answered solemnly, though again he battled the urge to kiss her. Instead, he forced himself to stay on track. "I'm thinking the best place to try and connect with Tanya would be Mikki's. Maybe I should go for a nonalcoholic drink a few nights a week. I'll talk to people, let everyone know I'm Russell's younger brother, and I'm thinking word will get out to her. Eventually, she'll show up, if only to check me out."

Holly agreed that seemed like a good start. "Unless it's hard for you to be around alcohol and not drink."

"I think I'll be fine," he said, though he actually had no idea since he'd never tried. "Alcohol wasn't ever really one of my issues. The main reason I prefer not to touch it is because it lowers my inhibitions. I can't afford to take a chance of losing control of my willpower."

She studied him for a long moment and then nodded.

"Sounds like you have a solid plan. Again, I'm definitely not going to go with you," she said. "There's no way Tanya will go anywhere near you if she spots me."

He agreed. "You have a point. Can you tell me a little about what she looks like? Without you there, I'll have no idea who I'm talking to."

Her smile captivated him. "How to describe Tanya. Let me just say that you won't be able to miss her. She's had a lot of work done in order to make herself into her version of every man's perfect woman."

He tried to figure out what that might be, but all he could see was Holly. Shocked, he realized that if he were asked to describe his ideal woman, Holly immediately came to mind.

Damn, he was in trouble.

"Thanks," he managed. "But can you be a bit more specific? Is she tall or short? Thin or curvy? What color is her hair?"

She waved his questions away. "Blond, but that's all I'll say. I promise, if she comes into Mikki's, you'll know it's her right away."

Though he wasn't sure he believed her, he thanked her anyway. "I'm going to go tonight for an hour or so."

"Suit yourself." Spine stiff, she turned away. For the first time he wondered if his plan to meet up with Tanya upset her.

But then why would it? There'd be no way for Tanya to link him to Holly. Suddenly, he realized he had to know.

"Holly, wait."

She froze, turning slowly. "What?"

"Are you okay with me searching for Tanya?" he asked, watching her face closely.

"What do you want to know? You've already decided." Stone-faced, she took a couple steps toward him. "Since you've been here you've done whatever the hell you wanted, so I don't see why you'd all of a sudden care what I think."

He met her furious gaze. "Holly, I'm just trying to find my brother. I won't let Tanya get to you, I promise."

"You won't let." Now she sounded as if she'd clenched her teeth. "I think that's a huge part of the problem. You show up here, disrupt my life and act like you're in charge. Well, I had enough of that with Russell. I refuse to allow anyone to treat me like that ever again."

With that, she spun around to stalk off.

"Wait." He reached out and grabbed her arm, intent only on stopping her. Instead, she lashed out at him, fighting as if defending herself against a physical attack.

"Don't touch me!" Her voice rose. "I'm not putting up with that anymore."

Immediately, he dropped his hand and backed away. In that instant, sickened, he realized Russell must have physically abused her.

"I'm sorry." He held his hands up, a gesture of surrender. "I never should have grabbed you. I didn't realize…" Unable to actually say the words aloud, he let them trail away.

Breathing hard, she watched him, the fear and confusion in her expression breaking his heart.

"I'd never hurt you," he continued. "Please believe me."

Still eyeing him, she slowly nodded. "You're not him," she said. "I know that. But still, when you grabbed me…"

"I didn't know. It won't happen, not ever again."

"Clearly I'm not over it. I guess I must have a kind of PTSD. I thought after all this time I'd healed. Obviously not." She cleared her throat. "I'm sorry."

And then, before he could tell her not to apologize, she crumpled, wrapping her arms around her midsection as if hugging herself. He longed to pull her into his arms but didn't dare. Instead, he stood empty-handed, aching to offer comfort, but keeping his distance instead because he didn't want to frighten her again.

Finally, breathing harshly, she raised her head. Her eyes shone bright with tears. "I never told anyone," she said, her steady voice at odds with her shattered expression. "Not even Kip. I didn't mean for you to find out just yet. You've heard enough bad things about your brother."

Even traumatized, she worried about his feelings. Right now, if he were to turn around and see Russell, he'd be hard-pressed not to punch him in the face.

"I'm sorry," he said, not knowing what else to say. He took a slow step toward her, but reconsidered. "Would it be all right if I hug you?" he asked quietly. "Or would you rather I keep my distance?"

Wiping at her streaming eyes, she swallowed. "I think I could really use a hug," she finally said.

Carefully, he took her into his arms. At first, she held herself stiffly, but gradually she began to relax. Holding her, he wanted to rip apart the man who had done this to her, even though it was Russell. No, *especially* because it was Russell.

In that moment, breathing the clean, floral scent of Holly's hair, her body so slender and fragile pressed up against him, he realized he'd do anything to protect her. No matter what it took.

"I'll never let anyone hurt you ever again," he swore, the promise in his quiet voice more of a solemn vow.

She shifted in his arms and raised her face to his. Even with her eyes swollen with tears and her nose pink, she was the most beautiful woman he'd ever seen.

"I want you to kiss me," she said, her voice low. "And make love to me. I need to feel…like a woman again."

His entire body tightened. "Are you sure?" he rasped, his sudden arousal fierce and instant.

"Yes. And I don't want you to be gentle or slow. I want to feel alive." Her voice quivered with the confession.

She stood up on tiptoe and pressed her mouth to his.

Just like that, any shred of self-control he'd managed to hang on to evaporated. The instant their lips met, he claimed her, putting all of his pent-up desire into the kiss.

She met him with a passion of her own, taking as well as she gave. Somehow, they managed to shed their clothes, still kissing, until their bodies were pressed skin to naked skin.

Hot. So. Damn. Hot.

Standing with her back against the wall, his massive arousal pressing into her soft belly, she arched herself over him and guided him inside of her. Almost wild with lust, he took her then, with them both unsteady on their feet. Fierce and wild, completely out of control. He was unable to speak or think of anything but the tight, wet warmth of her body surrounding him.

With each thrust, she moaned, rotating her hips just enough to drive him over the brink. When she let out a little half cry and her body shuddered around his, his release built. Right before he climaxed, he realized he'd failed to use protection.

Chapter 8

"No regrets," Holly told him, meaning it. She then stepped back to untangle herself. "I've got to go to the bathroom," she said, hurrying down the hall.

Once she'd closed the door, she used a washcloth and warm water to clean herself up. Eyeing herself in the mirror, she mentally congratulated herself on making yet another bad decision. Nothing good could come of this. Having sex with Jeremy would only complicate things.

But what's done was done. While she hadn't been able to afford actual therapy, she'd done a lot of reading and learned she couldn't focus on the past.

Plus, she had to admit the sex had been amazing. Exactly what she'd needed and wanted at the moment. She not only felt more alive than she had in forever, but sensual and sexy too.

For all the good that did her.

The way she mentally countered every good thought made her shake her head and smile at her mirror image wryly.

Humming under her breath, she opened the door and went to rejoin Jeremy. As she walked into the room, his stricken expression made her falter. "Talk about having regrets," she said, keeping her tone light. "Are you okay?"

"We didn't use protection," he said, meeting her gaze. "I'm sorry, it all happened so suddenly."

She froze. "That never even occurred to me. And I'm not on any form of birth control, since after Russell left I had no reason to be." Taking a deep breath, she shook her head. "Hopefully, we'll be okay."

"I'll make sure to buy some condoms in case there's a next time," he said.

At first, she almost told him that there wouldn't be. But then again, she didn't want to make promises she couldn't guarantee she'd be able to keep. Better to be prepared than sorry.

"Are you still going to go out tonight?" she asked, changing the subject.

"I don't think so. I just thought I'd hang out around here, with you. If that's all right," he added.

Determined to keep things casual, she smiled as she got dressed. "Fine by me. But I'm planning to hole up in my art studio and get back to work. You're on your own."

Even though that was her feeble attempt at letting him know she really didn't mind if he went looking for Tanya, Jeremy didn't appear to care. But then again, he didn't need her permission to do anything.

She made herself a tall glass of iced tea and retreated to her art room. From his spot on the couch, Thor raised his head but made no move to jump down and accompany her. Instead, he looked from her to Jeremy, as if weighing his options. Comfort definitely won out, as her dog lowered his muzzle back to the pillow and closed his eyes.

Noticing, Jeremy grinned. "Do you mind if I take him for a walk while you work?"

For a moment she froze, not sure how she felt about that.

"I'm not sure he'll go with you," she said. "No one has ever really walked him except me."

"I'd like to try. It's been a while since I've been able to work with a dog, especially one as smart as him. Maybe I'll even teach him a few new tricks."

Though she highly doubted that, she didn't want to burst his bubble. She knew her dog better than anyone, and Thor had a stubborn streak a mile wide.

"Knock yourself out," she finally said. "His leash is hanging from a hook in the laundry room. And there's a jar full of his favorite dog treats on the kitchen counter."

"Thanks."

"You're welcome." Glancing at her still sleeping furry beast, she sighed. "He does enjoy the exercise."

With that, she went into her little studio and closed the door. Silly as it might be, she didn't want to watch Thor do Jeremy's bidding with the same amount of eagerness that he usually reserved for her.

Despite trying not to, she couldn't help but overhear Jeremy calling Thor's name. A moment later, the front door opened and closed. She rushed to the window just in time to see Jeremy holding a leash, with Thor walking smartly at his side.

The magnitude of the moment didn't escape her. If she were to be cast out into the world with nothing, as long as she had her dog, she knew she'd be okay. Trusting Thor with someone else made her insides twist, but only for a moment. Thor had made it clear that he liked and trusted Jeremy. So she would too.

Putting any other worries from her mind, she gathered her supplies, closed her eyes and took some deep breaths, and then got to work.

The endorphins from great sex definitely fueled her creative juices. More inspired than she'd been in ages, she lost herself in her art, moving from the little sculptures on to her favorite medium, painting. Acrylics on canvas were her most successful pieces, and she'd always found the sensation of creating with brush strokes and paint cathartic.

Making art was her own form of therapy. When she created something, all her worries melted away.

When she finally emerged from her creative haze, she checked her phone and was startled to realize several hours had passed. Standing, she stretched, still pleasantly achy, but feeling much more Zen than she had earlier. She considered the ability to lose herself so thoroughly in her art one of the greatest gifts the universe could bestow.

Opening the door, she walked out to discover Thor and Jeremy, both dozing on the couch. Thor had his head on Jeremy's leg, eyes closed. The TV, while on, had the volume turned down low, she guessed so it wouldn't disturb her.

She couldn't help but get out her phone and snap a quick picture. The sound made Jeremy open his eyes.

"Hey," he said, his sleepy smile making her insides melt. "Did you have a good session?"

"I did." She found herself smiling back. Thor blinked but didn't move, the traitor. "How was your walk?"

"Excellent. You've done a great job training this big boy." He ruffled Thor's thick fur. She could have sworn her dog smiled.

"Thanks. I watched videos online. Plus, Thor is smart."

"Yes, he is." Now Thor was definitely smiling. "I made sandwiches for dinner. Yours is in the fridge."

Surprised, she thanked him and went and got it plus a glass of water. She took a seat on the opposite end of the couch, balancing her plate on her lap while she ate. What could have been awkward wasn't. She grabbed the remote, turned up the volume and began searching for something they could all watch together.

They settled on an irreverent game show and passed the next hour trading guesses and cheering when a contestant got a correct answer. When that ended, they watched another, and then the local news. She couldn't remember the last time she'd enjoyed an evening of television so much.

When she finally got up to take Thor out before bedtime, she glanced over at the handsome man relaxing on the couch. She'd never had this kind of chill, quiet evening with Russell, not even in the beginning. He'd had a kind of angry, manic energy that required running on the treadmill or physical labor to vanquish. When she wanted to watch a movie with him, he always had to be doing something else. Playing games on his phone, scrolling social media or online shopping. He'd rarely given her 100 percent of his attention. She'd managed to forget what it was like to have someone actually be present in the moment.

"Thanks for a fun evening," she said as she passed by on her way to her room.

Sitting up, he dragged his hand through his already disheveled hair, which only made him look unbearably sexy. "What do you mean?" he asked. "We just watched TV."

This made her laugh. "I guess I have a very low bar when it comes to what I consider an enjoyable night. I'm just trying to say this could have been awkward after what happened earlier. It wasn't. I appreciate that."

Then, without giving him a chance to respond, she turned around and sailed off, her dog right behind her. After taking Thor out for a walk around the block, which helped her get back to feeling like normal, they returned. She made a quick stop in the bathroom to brush her teeth and wash her face before heading to her bed.

Thor grunted and heaved a sigh before curling up in his orthopedic dog bed. She ruffled his fur, changed into the soft, oversize T-shirt she slept in and slipped beneath her sheets.

If she'd thought she'd have difficulty falling asleep, she was wrong. With her head on her pillow, she allowed herself a moment to think about what it would be like if Jeremy were to join her and then she drifted off.

When she next opened her eyes, it was shortly after 9:00 a.m. Thor whined, letting her know he needed to go out.

Since she didn't have to work at Murphy's today, she'd slept in. She'd always loved the luxurious feeling of waking without an alarm.

Stretching, she realized she felt pleasantly sore. Another benefit from such an enthusiastic bout of lovemaking. She found herself contemplating doing it again, properly this time, like in an actual bed.

Thor whined again, louder this time, bringing her back to reality. She took him out, watching from the patio while he took care of his business.

Then she went to make herself a cup of coffee and find Jeremy.

Except a quick search of the house revealed he wasn't even there. Just to confirm, she checked outside and saw that his green truck wasn't parked in the driveway.

Shrugging, she went for coffee instead.

She'd just finished breakfast when her doorbell chimed. Thor shot to his feet, instantly alert, though he didn't bark. Mystified, Holly went to look out the peephole. Around here, no one really pressed the doorbell. They either knocked or texted ahead that they were on their way.

She didn't recognize the man standing on her front

porch. Despite the warmth of the day, he wore a leather motorcycle jacket covered in patches.

Barely cracking the door open, she peered out. "Can I help you?" Beside her, Thor nudged her leg, reminding her of his support.

"I'm looking for Russell Elliot," the man said. "I've been told this is his residence."

Unsure how to answer, she opened the door a bit wider but didn't step out onto the front porch. "He's not here right now. Is there a message you'd like me to give him if I— *when* I—see him again?"

"Not really. It's personal. Do you have any idea when you might expect him back?"

She almost laughed out loud. But since this stranger clearly had no clue, she didn't. "No, I'm afraid I don't."

That said, she started to close the door. Instead, the man moved fast, placing his foot just enough inside to prevent her. "Not so fast," he said. "I'm not done."

Anger mixed with a healthy dose of fear coursed through her. "I advise you to remove your boot," she said. Thor, hearing her emotion, growled his own warning.

"What are you going to do if I don't?" the stranger asked.

Now she moved aside, allowing him to see her giant beast of a dog. "I wouldn't advise that."

Eyes widening, the man cursed. "Fine. But you tell Russell he'd better pay up what he owes me. His payment came due three weeks ago, and he's not returning my calls. I drove all the way here from Anchorage to collect. He knows what's going to happen if he doesn't settle his debt."

"What debt?" she asked, her curiosity getting the better of her. "Surely you're aware Russell has been missing for over eighteen months now."

"Missing?" he snorted. "Hiding out is more likely. He

owes me a large sum of money or a significant amount of inventory. And no one dodges the organization I work for. No one."

Once again she tried to get specifics. "Money for what? And what kind of inventory? I learned Russell sold his business a few months before he disappeared."

Instead of answering, he glowered at her. "If you know what's good for you, pass the message along. I'd hate for a pretty little thing like you to get hurt for something you had no part of."

Then, threat delivered, he marched off, climbing into a black Mercedes-Benz with dark windows and no license plates. A moment later, he drove off.

Holly's first instinct was to call Jeremy. But then she realized she didn't actually have his number. Nor did he have hers. Something else she'd need to rectify.

Oddly enough, she wasn't frightened. There was something off about the whole thing. Why would Russell have taken out a loan when he had enough free and clear assets that he could sell to raise money? Even his half of the house would have fetched a tidy sum, never mind his monster truck.

How much had he needed to go into hiding?

Since she had no idea and no one to bounce ideas off of, she did what she usually did on her days off. House cleaning, laundry and grocery shopping. She always tried to throw in a long hike with Thor and, if she had enough time left in the day, something for herself, like a home facial.

As she got started cleaning, she realized Jeremy must have done his own tidying up while she'd been at work. The kitchen and bathroom just needed a few tweaks to make them sparkling. While the washer ran, she vacuumed, Thor watching with a long-suffering expression, and mopped the kitchen floor. Then she grabbed Thor's leash, called him to her and left to take him for a long walk. Walking always helped clear her head. Though she and Russell hadn't shared funds, she needed to figure out a way to access his bank accounts, if only to get a handle on things. If what her visitor had said was real, a direct look at deposits and withdrawals could confirm that. Unless of course, Russell had moved the money somewhere else.

She decided to hold off from discussing this with Jeremy until she had more concrete information. If she found something, it might be time to go to the police.

Waking up early, Jeremy had made himself a cup of coffee and decided to take it to go. He'd glanced at Holly's closed bedroom door and briefly considered seeing if she'd allow him to join her in bed, but decided against it. For one thing, he still hadn't purchased the necessary condoms, and for another, sleeping with his brother's ex-fiancée didn't seem like the right thing to do.

Even though he wanted to. More than he could ever explain.

Rummaging around in the cupboard, he found a stainless steel insulated tumbler with a lid. That would keep his coffee hot. As he headed out to his truck, he found himself wishing he had a dog to go with him. Maybe someday. For now, occasionally spending time with Thor would have to do.

Though he hadn't said anything to Holly, he spent part of their walk yesterday working with Thor on some basic commands. The big dog already knew the commands "sit" and "down," and he caught on to recall quickly enough that Jeremy suspected he'd been taught that too. To his surprise, when Jeremy had told Thor to heel, the huge animal had immediately fallen into step on Jeremy's left side. He'd trotted along, plumed tail high above his back, happy and confident.

When Jeremy stopped, Thor sat. Jeremy rewarded the very good boy with a treat. Clearly Holly, or someone, had spent some time working with this beast of a dog.

Instead of just strolling around the block, Jeremy went a bit farther. Walking in the fresh air had cleared his head, and he'd wanted to give Holly uninterrupted time to focus on her work.

By the time he and Thor had returned to the house, he felt the start of a deeper bond had been forged. He would have given a lot to have been able to take the big dog with him now.

Instead, he went alone. Driving toward the Neacola River, he parked in the small lot near the trailhead of what had once been one of his favorite hikes. During his time living in the lower forty-eight, he'd missed the wild Alaskan land the most. The time had come to try and reconnect with it.

He'd made this hike often as a teenager. Hiking had been his form of meditation, a way to free his mind. More than anything, all of the information about his brother had confused and saddened him. He'd returned home hoping for a simple reconciliation. Instead, he'd gotten a lot more than he'd expected. Not only the mystery of his brother's disappearance and complete change in character, but his attraction to the beautiful woman staying in Russell's house.

While he liked Holly a lot, and had certainly enjoyed their lovemaking, something about her story just didn't add up. Why would Russell, who from all accounts had become a selfish bastard, allow the woman who'd spurned him to drive an expensive vehicle he'd bought her? He'd let her keep the ring too. Jeremy would have thought Russell would have demanded Holly buy out his half stake in the house instead of simply walking away.

Not only that, but a large segment of Blake appeared to believe Holly had done something to Russell. Whether she'd driven him away or physically harmed him, Jeremy wasn't sure. This was why he really wanted to find Tanya and talk to her.

How had Russell changed so much in ten years? And was his brother actually hiding out somewhere, as most people seemed to think, or had he met a violent end?

This last thought made him shudder.

Against his will, he thought of Holly. Though she and Russell were no longer engaged, she'd remained living in the house they shared and using his luxury SUV. Plus from what he could tell, his brother had treated her badly. She seemed to have more reason than most to do away with Russell.

And if she had, did that mean he might be in danger as well? Something to definitely think about. He didn't know Holly well at all. The chemistry between them might have blinded him. He'd need to be more careful, learn what made her tick and determine if there was even the slightest possibility she might have taken her problems with Russell into her own hands. While he couldn't envision it, that didn't mean he should discount the idea outright.

Finishing the hike, he walked back to his truck, glad he'd gone. While he hadn't solved any problems, he felt as if he'd cleared his head and gotten some perspective. Tonight, he planned to stop by Mikki's and hang out for a bit in the bar. Hopefully, word would get out and Tanya would come searching for him.

Holly and Thor were gone when he returned to the

house. He got cleaned up and settled down at the kitchen table with the folder she'd given him. He made another phone call to the state police, left a second voicemail and began rereading Holly's notes.

If she were trying to cover something up, she didn't act like it. Her meticulous research appeared to be that of someone desperately trying to find a missing person.

When she and Thor returned, the large dog greeted him enthusiastically. Holly said hello, grabbed a bottled water from the fridge and retreated to her art studio.

Which suited him just fine. More time to try to figure things out.

That night, after making them both hamburgers on the grill, he went to get cleaned up before driving downtown. The entire situation felt weird to him. Years ago, before he'd left, he couldn't wait to be old enough to legally have a beer at Mikki's. Now, ten odd years later, not only did he not drink, but he'd rather sit out on the back patio with Holly.

Damn. Again. He couldn't understand how she managed to affect him so strongly. Sharing the same space with her, he found himself walking around in a constant state of arousal. He woke up every single morning aching for her. Worse, as far as he could tell, he didn't have the same impact on her. With the tension building inside him, if he didn't find a release soon, he felt like he might explode.

Maybe meeting other single women in a bar might not be a bad idea after all. He didn't expect Tanya to make an appearance until he'd gone there a few times. Since he no longer drank alcohol, club soda would have to do. Even if he found himself really wanting a beer, he felt confident he could resist.

As he headed toward the door to leave, Holly called to him, holding her phone. "Do you mind giving me your number?" she asked. "Text me so I'll have it, and that way we can contact each other if we need something."

"Good idea." He couldn't believe they hadn't exchanged numbers. She read out hers and he put it into his contacts and sent her a text.

Sure you don't want to come with me?

Laughing, she shook her head. "Have fun," she said.

He got into his truck and drove the short distance to downtown, all the while wishing Holly were at his side.

When he walked inside Mikki's, he took a seat at the bar. Since it was a weeknight, the place only seemed half-full. When Mikki herself came over to take his order, she smiled when he asked for a club soda with a lime. She brought it quickly, told him it was on the house and went to take care of another customer. Leaving Jeremy to sip his drink and survey the bar.

While there were a few families out for a meal, by and large most of the customers seemed to be singles. A group of five guys, coworkers from the looks of them, occupied one of the tables, but other than that, there were mostly people who might have stopped by to have a drink after a long day at work. He could picture his brother doing the same.

"You're new around here," a slender brunette said, sliding onto the bar stool next to him. "Except for some reason, you look familiar."

She did too. He studied her, searching his memory. "I grew up here," he finally admitted. "My name's Jeremy Elliot."

"Seriously?" She beamed. "We went to school together. We were in the same class from kindergarten all the way to twelfth grade. Sheila Pearson." Then she hugged him.

When she pulled away, the strong scent of her perfume lingered.

"Where have you been all this time?" she asked. The bartender brought her a glass of white wine without her even ordering.

"I moved to Seattle," he said, deciding to omit any details. "After I left Blake, I wanted to get as far away as I could."

"Wow." Sipping her wine, she appeared impressed. "Most people move to Anchorage or Fairbanks to get out of here. But now you're back. I guess you couldn't stay away after all."

Again, he decided to let that one go.

"Have you heard what happened to your brother?" she asked, her half smile telling him she knew he had. "Rumor has it that woman he brought up from Texas had something to do with his disappearance."

"Yeah, when I found her living in his house, I admit it came as a shock," he replied, sticking with the truth. "But most people I've talked to seem to think Russell just took off on his own."

She shrugged. "I suppose that's possible too. But if anyone would know, it would be Tanya. She and Russell were together for years. I think he just brought that Holly woman in because he and Tanya had a fight."

Now they were getting somewhere. Careful not to reveal his excitement, he took a sip of his club soda. "Does Tanya ever come in here to have a drink? I'm thinking I might need to talk to her."

His comment made Sheila frown. "Not too often, thank goodness. I can say this. Most men, once they get a look at Tanya, they swear off everyone else." She fluttered her eyelashes at him. "I really would hate for that to happen with you. Blake has a limited supply of eligible bachelors."

For a second he could only stare at her. As a child, he'd played in the sandbox with this woman. They'd studied for history tests together and not once had there ever been a single spark of romantic interest between them.

Not sure how to respond without offending her, he looked down at his drink. When he met her gaze again, he kept his expression serious. "I'm not interested in starting a romantic relationship with Tanya, or with anyone else for that matter. I know she and my brother were close, and I want to see if she has any idea where he might have gone."

"Gone?" She gave him a pitying look. "You've been talking to that Holly woman, haven't you? Don't let her fool you. She'd like everyone to believe that Russell just up and walked away from everything he owned. There's just no way."

"Did you know my brother well?" he asked.

"Not really," she admitted. "But the one thing you could say about Russell is how highly he valued his possessions. When Holly broke off their engagement, he went ballistic. Do you really think he'd have no problem with her staying in his house and driving that Land Rover after she broke his heart?"

"When you put it like that, you have a point," he said, careful to keep his tone neutral. "Except she actually owns half of the house and the SUV. She has just as much right to be there as he does."

"You really buy into that load of nonsense, don't you?"

"I do," he responded, then decided to get back on track. "But then what do you think happened to Russell? If he didn't just take off, where is he?"

Clearly uncomfortable, she shifted on her stool and

slugged back the rest of her wine. After signaling to the bartender that she wanted another, she heaved a dramatic sigh. "I don't know, but there are quite a few people around Blake who believe Holly did something to him."

"Something like what?" he pressed, even though it seemed obvious where she was going with that.

"I really can't say," she finally admitted, chickening out. "But you need to talk to some other people around town and get their input. Russell's sudden disappearance was one of the most highly discussed topics when it happened. Lots of folks have strong opinions about the circumstances around it."

"Thank you. If you happen to run into Tanya, will you please let her know Russell's brother is looking for her? I'd really appreciate it." After drinking the last of his club soda, he got to his feet. "It was nice seeing you. Take care."

That said, he headed toward the door.

Mikki intercepted him before he made it halfway. "Be careful around that one," she said, taking his arms. "She's part of a group of what we call Mean Girls. They've had it in for Holly ever since she arrived."

He nodded. "Thanks. I kind of suspected as much. She's another one who blames Holly for Russell being gone. She even insinuated that she thinks Holly might have harmed him."

"Oh, I know." Mikki rolled her eyes. "The town has been divided on that ever since Russell vanished. Some think he took off under his own free will. Others seem to believe Holly killed him and hid his body."

"I suppose either one is plausible," he said. "Though Holly is a tiny little thing. Unless she used poison, I don't see her being able to take my brother down."

His words caused Mikki to stop in her tracks, yanking

on his arm. "I don't believe Holly has anything to do with Russell's disappearance. He treated her like dirt and I suspect even hit her. So she had plenty of reasons."

Fascinated, he waited to hear the rest.

"But if you get to know Holly, you'll see she's not like that. Most of the women, Tanya included, are jealous of her." She sighed. "And most of the men are in her corner. I'm sure you can understand why."

Chapter 9

After Jeremy left for Mikki's, for a half second Holly regretted not going with him. She got over that quickly though. While she might be regaining confidence, she knew several of Russell's previous lady friends tended to hang out there. Seeing her would likely blow their minds, and she wasn't up for another vicious confrontation. She shouldn't have to constantly defend herself against baseless accusations.

Yet the thought of Jeremy in Tanya's clutches made her feel queasy. From what she'd seen, no man could resist Tanya's oversexed, siren's lure. Even Kip had admitted to spending time with her. He'd at least had the grace to be embarrassed.

Holly just knew Jeremy would be putty in Tanya's skillful hands. And she had to admit, she felt jealous.

Without reason. She barely knew the man, for one thing. And sleeping with him seemed like something Tanya would do. Holly wasn't like that. Until now, she never had been one for casual sex. Even she and Russell hadn't shared a bed until they'd been dating three months.

But something about Jeremy just got to her. Maybe she'd been alone too long, but every time she looked at him, a shiver of longing ran up her spine and her insides turned to mush. She didn't regret what they'd shared. Even worse, she longed to do it again.

What did that make her?

Trying to put all thoughts of Jeremy from her head, she decided to bake something. A comfort cake. While she wasn't as skilled at baking as she was at painting, she enjoyed the process. And the finished product usually turned out delicious.

Grabbing one of her cookbooks, she paged through the dessert section until she found what she wanted. Lemon cake. She just happened to have all the ingredients, since she'd been craving one for a good while. Once she had that going, she planned to look through Russell's computer. He'd left both his laptop and an older desktop that she wasn't sure even worked. She'd figured out Russell's passwords to get into the computers a few weeks after he'd left. Hopefully, she'd be able to find a way to access some of the bank records.

She'd just put the cake in the oven when her phone chimed, indicating she'd received a text message. Assuming it to be Jeremy, she grinned and checked.

Instead, she didn't recognize the number showing on the screen. When she opened the message, a chill made her shudder.

I'm still going to make you pay. Wait and see. And I will make sure you suffer.

Holly didn't know whether to laugh or to cry. After a few months of silence, it appeared Tanya was back to her old tricks. Had Jeremy talked to her? It seemed unlikely, since he'd only gone to Mikki's tonight. No, it seemed much more possible that one of Tanya's many friends had mentioned seeing Holly out and about the other night with Jeremy. The mere notion that she'd dared to poke her face outside of the house would be enough to trigger Tanya.

Oddly enough, Russell's side chick had made it her mission to ruin Holly's life. She'd thrown around baseless accusations to anyone who would listen, stoked conspiracy theories without a shred of factual evidence and had drummed up calls for Holly's arrest despite Holly having committed no crime.

For several months after Russell's disappearance, Tanya had turned Holly's life into a virtual hell. The few friends she'd made since moving to Blake ghosted her. Total strangers glared at her and whispered behind her back. But no one, not one single person other than the police and the mayor, asked Holly directly about Russell's disappearance.

In the months following his leaving, Holly had thrown herself into trying to find him, if only to clear her name. Since no proof of foul play turned up and the police pointed out Russell was an adult and could come and go as he pleased, Holly had eventually conceded the point and abandoned her search.

Tanya however, still appeared determined to persecute Russell's ex-fiancée. Drunken drive-bys, text messages from random phone numbers, bags of excrement left on her doorstep and in her mailbox and hate mail had continued for months. She'd had to change the number for the landline even. Only recently had Tanya slowed her efforts. Just long enough for Holly to start to have hope she could take back her life.

Shaking her head, she blocked the number from texting her again, though she took a screenshot of the text first. She always kept them, just in case Tanya actually took things further than a threat and carried out an actual attack.

As the scent of the baking filled the house, she logged in to the laptop and then typed in the web address of their small-town bank. Russell had kept some money there for convenience sake, but he'd often bragged about the two large national banks he used out of Anchorage.

Since he'd had the computer save his password, getting into the account was easy. And when the words Account Closed came up, she wasn't surprised. While she supposed she should have tried to do this right after he left, she'd also been focused on living independently. She and Russell hadn't ever shared bank accounts, so she'd felt it wasn't any of her business. Until now.

The other two banks did not have the passwords stored. And because she knew if she made too many attempts to guess, she'd be locked out, she didn't even try again. If Russell kept funds in any of those accounts, he didn't want her to have access to them. That also made sense. She couldn't really blame him.

When headlights swept the front window, she tensed up and closed the laptop. "Thor," she said quietly. "Come here."

Immediately, her protector got up from where he'd been dozing on one of his numerous dog beds and trotted over. She not only felt safer with him by her side, but she also wanted to protect him if necessary.

Though his shoulder touched her knee, Thor kept his attention focused on the entryway. He didn't bark or even seem alarmed, which meant it must be Jeremy rather than an intruder.

The front door opened, and Jeremy came inside. Thor jumped to his feet and trotted over to greet him, tail swishing. As usual, Jeremy crouched down to pet him, tangling his fingers in Thor's thick fur. Her dog grunted, eyes closed, tongue lolling from his mouth. She couldn't help but grin.

"Dog massage," Jeremy said, meeting her gaze. "It's a real thing. Helps soothe them, but can be particularly helpful in dogs with arthritis or similar issues. I took some classes. That's another thing I've been considering making part of my business, if I can see a need."

Impressed despite herself, she nodded. "Well, it appears Thor would give you a recommendation for sure."

Jeremy got to his feet and gave Thor one final ear scratch. "What have you been up to?" he asked, noticing her laptop.

She decided to go ahead and tell him about her earlier visitor.

"He said Russell took out a loan?" He frowned. "I've been told he sold his business, which must have netted him some cash. Did the guy say what he used for collateral? Hopefully, it wasn't this house."

"I didn't even consider asking that," she admitted. "But I'm guessing that man would have said something if that were the case. I will say that I was thinking about all of the other assets that he could have liquidated for funds. His half of this house and that fancy pickup truck would have brought in significant cash."

Jeremy went quiet. "Did that guy actually use the word *loan*?"

She thought for a moment. "Now that you mention it, no he did not. He also used the word inventory. And said the people he worked for didn't mess around. It reminded me of a mobster movie or something."

"Drugs," he said, his jaw tense. "I wonder if that's the inventory he meant. If Russell took a bunch of drugs intending to sell them, then took off without making payment, no wonder he's taken deep cover. If that's the case and they find him, his life will be worth nothing."

Unsure how to respond to that, she simply didn't.

"But my brother is super smart," Jeremy continued. "He wouldn't let himself get tied up in a mess like that. There's got to be another explanation. Did you happen to get that guy's contact information?"

"No. I was too shocked and he got angry and stomped off. He drove a black Mercedes-Benz sedan with dark tinted windows."

This description made him shake his head. "Like a movie or something. I'm guessing he'll be back when he doesn't get paid."

"You never know," she said. "Maybe Russell ordered some inventory for his business before he knew he'd be selling it and simply forgot to pay the supplier back. I think if it had been drugs, this man wouldn't have been so upfront talking about inventory."

"It's possible," Jeremy replied, though his tone would seem to indicate he didn't believe that. "Promise me that you won't speak with him alone again. If he comes by and I'm not here, don't answer the door."

This startled her. "Why? Do you think he's dangerous? Because I didn't get that impression from him at all."

"Maybe, maybe not." He grimaced. "You never know. Better to play it safe."

"True," she agreed. "But I think it's more likely one of Russell's lady friends attacks me than this man."

He reached across the table and touched the back of her hand. The simple gesture made her go all warm and fuzzy inside.

"How'd it go at Mikki's?" she asked, deciding to change the subject. "I'm guessing you didn't run into Tanya."

"No, but I didn't expect to this early on in the game. Word has to get out among her friends that Russell's younger brother is hanging around asking questions about him. I'm betting she won't be able to resist coming by to check me out once she hears."

"Probably not," she agreed, taking a deep breath. "Then I guess you're not the reason she threatened me by text today. It's been a while, so I figured something must have set her off."

"What?" Instantly alert, he met her gaze. "She sends you threatening text messages from her phone? Then all you have to do is show those to the police."

"I have no way to prove it's her. She either uses one of the apps that sends texts from a random number, or she buys disposable phones that can't be traced."

"Do you mind if I see it?" he asked.

Instead of responding, she did face recognition, pulled up the screenshot and held out her phone. "I've already blocked the number."

He read the text. "How do you know it's from her?" he asked. "It's pretty generic."

"True." Taking her phone back, she shrugged. "But who else would it be? Tanya has been threatening me since the week after Russell vanished. She'd let up a bit recently, so I have no idea what might have inspired her to start in again."

"Maybe I'll ask her that too, when and if I finally get to meet her," he said. "I figure I'll have to go back a few more times before that will happen."

"Probably so," she agreed. Part of her hoped he'd never meet Tanya. She'd hate for him to fall under the other woman's spell.

The instant the thought occurred to her, she jumped to her feet, her heart racing. She didn't need to be thinking about Jeremy like that. She had no claim on him, nor did she want one. "I think I'm going to turn in," she said, more flustered than she should have been. She headed toward the back door, calling Thor, finding anywhere else to look other than at Jeremy.

Once Holly had gone and holed up in her bedroom, Jeremy had to throttle a strong impulse to follow her. Instead, he went outside to sit on the back patio under the stars. He needed to get his arousal under control. These days, just being around Holly had him hard.

One thing going to Mikki's had proved. His reaction to Holly wasn't due to how long it had been since he'd made love with a woman. Sitting next to Sheila Pearson, he hadn't felt even the slightest interest in kissing her.

He wanted Holly. Only Holly.

Which meant he'd gone beyond asking for trouble. He was now buried up to his neck in it.

Sitting outside, the night breeze cooling his skin, he wondered if he should go about the business of beginning his new life. Keeping everything in limbo while he searched for his brother seemed counterproductive, at the very least.

He'd continue trying to find Russell, of course. But since he couldn't spend every hour of every day looking, he needed to get started on scouting a location for his business. Once he'd secured a lease, then he'd need to find a police department willing to negotiate. They'd provide a dog, and he'd train it for a heavily reduced price if they'd promise to spread the word. He'd done so well with the weapon and drug detection dogs he'd trained while in prison, that several organizations had complimented him and promised to give him a letter of recommendation. He planned to take them up on that.

Making the decision to once again move his life forward did wonders for Jeremy's frame of mind. Feeling better than he had in a good while, he finally got up and took himself off to bed.

The next morning, he woke to the homey sounds of Holly puttering around in the kitchen. Since the clock showed 7:00 a.m., he knew she must be getting ready to go to work.

That didn't stop his body from wishing she were in his bed.

Since this had become a normal occurrence, he got up, pulled on a pair of boxers and made his way to the bathroom. Oblivious to his dilemma, Holly continued whistling in the kitchen and he reached his destination without interruption. Now he could either have a cold shower, or a warm one and take matters into his own hands.

He already knew which one he'd choose.

Later, dry and clean, he went back to his room to get dressed. After, when he headed to the kitchen for his first cup of coffee, he was surprised to find Holly seated at the table with a book.

"Good morning," she said, looking up and smiling. "Did you sleep well?"

If she meant had he tossed and turned all night, aching for her, then he supposed he had. Otherwise, no. "I did," he replied, smiling back. "Are you going in to work today?"

"Nope. I'm extremely part-time, so Kip only has me come in when he needs me. The next delivery isn't until Tuesday, and Neal is scheduled to work the front, so I'm off for a bit."

She stretched, drawing his attention to her body.

"What are your plans for the day?" she asked, clearly oblivious to how she affected him.

"I'm thinking about going downtown and looking for a place to rent to start my dog training business," he said, aware that once he spoke the words out loud, there'd be no going back.

"That's awesome," she said, grinning at him. "I'm guessing you'll need a space large enough for you to work the dogs, right?"

"Exactly. I don't need something the size of a warehouse, but a small office/reception area and a large back room would be perfect. I know Blake probably has a few vacant buildings, so I'm hoping I can find and rent one that will suit my needs."

As he poured himself a cup of coffee, his phone rang. He didn't recognize the number, but decided to answer anyway. Not too many people had his contact information, so the call might be important.

"I know where to find Russell," a man's voice said.

Jeremy froze. "Who is this?" he asked. "I don't recognize your number."

"Man, I'm sorry. It's Gary Acosta. Your brother and I went to school together. Back then, we didn't do a hell of a lot of partying." Gary chuckled. "Things change."

"That they do. How did you get my number?"

"You can get anything off the internet," Gary replied. "For a small fee."

"Okay." Trying to puzzle out the reason why his brother's old high school buddy would call with such a strange claim, he tried to get the conversation back on track. "And you say you know where Russell is?"

Hearing that, Holly sat up straight, her gaze intense.

"I do. Any chance you could meet me at the turnoff by the Neacola in an hour?"

Now alarms were definitely sounding. "Why don't you just tell me now? I don't see what the point is in meeting up."

"Wow. I'm hurt." Gary sounded angry. "You sound like you don't trust me. Any friend of Russell's should be a friend of yours. Yet you don't even want to take fifteen minutes to say hello in person."

"That's not it," Jeremy protested. "You said you know where to find my brother. He's been missing a good while. So if you're telling me the truth, just let me know where I can find him. You and I can meet face-to-face another time."

"Look, show up or don't. I couldn't care less. I'll be at the turnoff in one hour. I'll wait ten minutes. If you don't come, that's fine with me." Then, before Jeremy could comment, Gary ended the call.

Some of his unease must have shown on his face. He carried his mug over to the table and took a seat across from her.

"What was that all about?" Holly asked. "Obviously, I heard part of it."

"Some guy Russell went to school with is claiming he knows how to find him. But he won't just tell me. Instead, he wants to meet at that tourist turnoff by the bridge over the Neacola."

"That's weird." Putting her book down, she locked her gaze on his face. "I take it you don't trust him."

"I don't know him," he said. "But I'm getting really bad vibes. He's got some ulterior motive. If he really knows where to find Russell, just pass along the info. Once that's settled, there'd be a time and a place to get to know each other."

"True."

If he got up, a few steps would put him close enough to reach out and cup her face in his hands and then kiss her.

He almost followed through with his thoughts. Instead,

he took a deep breath and looked away. "I have a bad feeling about this. If what Gary says is true, why hasn't he come forward before now? What's with the cloak-and-dagger nonsense?"

Blushing, she shrugged. "I think we should go," she said. "We've got nothing to lose. And if he has somehow spotted Russell, that would be amazing."

One lesson that had been hammered home to him during his time in prison had been to understand if something seemed too good to be true, it usually was. And if this went sideways, he didn't want to take a chance and risk Holly.

"If I go to meet him, I'm doing this alone," he told her.

"No, you're not. I'll be your backup." Arms crossed, the look she gave him dared him to contradict her. "And if it turns out to be a bust, which you clearly think it's going to be, maybe we can do a little fishing after."

Her words were so unexpected that he had to laugh. "Deal. But I don't have anything to fish with at the moment."

"That's okay, I do. Or Russell does." She made a face. "When I first moved here, Russell took me fishing all the time. He was really patient with teaching me, and the kinder he treated me, the more I realized that coming here hadn't been a mistake after all."

Fascinated, he waited for her to finish.

"But then one time when I didn't put enough weight on the line, Russell got furious. He started yelling and throwing things. I realized if I didn't get away from him right that instant, he was going to hit me or do something worse. When he started talking about holding my head underwater, I took off."

"Where'd you go?" he asked. There wasn't much of anything out by that trailhead.

"Home," she replied, once again startling him. "I hiked just above the road, taking care that I stayed hidden in case he came looking for me. Luckily, I had Thor with me. I knew he'd keep me safe if I encountered any wildlife."

Both amazed at her grit and disturbed that his brother had made her feel so unsafe, he capitulated. "Fine, we'll go together. And if turns out to be one big bad of nothing, then I intend to hold you to that promise to go fishing."

Her grin lit up her blue eyes. "Awesome. Should we take Thor with us? Not only will he enjoy the outing, but I always feel safer when he's by my side."

"As well you should." Again he battled a strong urge to kiss her. This time, he gave in, pushing to his feet and closing the distance between them.

When his lips met hers, she gave a little squeak. She wrapped her arms around his neck, getting as close as she could. His body instantly responded.

She broke away, her eyes wide. "We'd better stop now. If we keep going this way, we'll end up naked in bed and miss the meeting."

About to tell her that's what he'd rather do, he gathered up his tattered self-control and nodded. "You're right," he said. "I'm going to go get cleaned up. We'll head out in a little bit."

He went into the bathroom, where he splashed some cold water on his face. It seemed strange that Gary wanted to meet at the exact same place Jeremy had used as a starting point for his hike. He had a sneaking suspicion that Gary wanted something and wasn't above using a lie to get it. This wouldn't be good.

Forty-five minutes later, he, Holly and Thor were all inside his truck, heading toward the river. He parked in the same small lot he had before, noting there were only two other vehicles there.

Opening the doors, he smiled as Thor bounded out, tail wagging, panting happily. He saw no signs on anyone else, which meant that the drivers of the other cars were likely hiking the trails. "I should have asked Gary what he'll be driving."

"I'm sure he'll be here any moment," she said, touching his arm. "I can't wait to hear where he thinks Russell is hiding."

"Me too."

A black Mercedes-Benz pulled in, parking a short distance from them. "Oh, no," Holly muttered.

A short, stout man in a button-down dress shirt and slacks got out and made his way toward them.

"That's the guy who rang my doorbell," Holly said, grabbing Jeremy's arm.

Hearing the edge of panic in her voice, Thor placed himself between her and the other man.

Approaching them, he took one look at the giant dog and his steps faltered. "Jeremy, it's me. Gary Acosta. We spoke on the phone."

Now Jeremy remembered this guy, even though he'd only seen him from a distance. Despite being Russell's friend, Gary had been the guy everyone in Russell's class went to for alcohol or drugs. Jeremy had always wondered why he and Russell had hung out. He'd figured his brother had made it his mission to help Gary back onto the straight and narrow.

"You don't know where to find Russell, do you?" If looks could kill, Jeremy felt confident Gary would crumple to the ground.

"Not yet." Gary's cold smile included Holly. "But like

I told her, Russell owes the people I work for a significant amount of money."

Jeremy shoved his hands down into his pockets so he wouldn't accidentally use his fists to do something he might regret. "What kind of drugs, Gary?" he asked. "Oxy, or something else? Are they laced with fentanyl?"

Eyes narrowed, Gary took a step closer. Thor growled a warning, stopping the man in his tracks. "I'm not here to talk about anything but the money I'm owed."

"Then I suggest you go to the police," Jeremy said. "Or get yourself a lawyer and file a lawsuit. Because not only do we not know where to find Russell, we don't have any of his money."

"I strongly suggest you figure out a way to find it."

Chapter 10

So tense she quivered, Holly kept her gaze locked on Gary. What a nice, normal name for such a vile person. She couldn't believe she'd thought him to be a loan officer instead of a drug dealer.

The thought also made her realize they might be in danger. A quick glance at Jeremy told her he too understood the risk.

She didn't own a gun. Heck, she knew how to shoot one, thanks to Russell. He'd been determined to teach her how to handle a weapon, due to the constant threat of wildlife. Plus, occasionally drifters wandered through town, and all single women understood it wasn't safe to be alone when they were nearby.

The untamed frontier referred to more than the landscape.

For the first time, she found herself wondering if Jeremy might be armed. His alert body language told her he also understood the risk they were taking.

Thor growled again, the sound louder and more menacing. Though grateful for the protection her pet provided, Holly would do anything, including sacrifice herself, to make sure nothing happened to her dog.

"I repeat. If you don't have money to pay me, you'd better find it," Gary continued, barely moving his gaze away from Thor's menacing stance.

"Or what?" Jeremy drawled. "You'll go to the police? Since I know for a fact that you won't do that, how do you propose to get something we don't have? I just got out of prison, and Holly here works part-time at the general store. Neither one of us is sitting on piles of cash. And anything to do with drugs is not something I want to be involved in."

Gary shrugged. "My bosses will want me to do whatever it takes to make Russell show up and make good on his debt. If it means we have to hurt his girlfriend or his brother, so be it."

"Don't even think about touching one single hair on her head," Jeremy said, taking a step toward the other man. Thor moved with him, low to the ground, ears pinned back. Watching, Holly could easily believe if Jeremy gave the command, her beast of a dog would attack.

Swallowing nervously, Gary clearly thought that too. He took a step back, but then pulled out a pistol and pointed it at Thor.

Holly's heart stopped. "No," she shouted. "Thor, come."

Thor, though clearly reluctant, immediately turned away and went to Holly's side. Never had she been so glad she'd taught him recall.

"Lower your weapon," Jeremy ordered.

Though Gary narrowed his eyes, he brought his pistol down to hold at his side. "I mean it," he said. "I'll do whatever it takes to make sure we get paid."

"*We?*" Jeremy zeroed in on that word. "Since when did you get mixed up with the bad guys, Gary? From what I remember, back in the day, you were mostly small-time."

"I've worked hard to get where I am," Gary replied, the pride in his hard voice making Holly feel sick. "From what

I hear, you could have done the same thing if you'd made different choices."

"Done the same thing?" Jeremy shook his head. "I went to prison because someone framed me for a murder that I didn't commit." He took a deep breath. "And I wouldn't be surprised to learn that someone was part of the same organization you work for."

"I wouldn't know. That's not my area." Yet Gary's flippant tone suggested he might very well have an idea about what had happened to Jeremy. "I heard about it though. It was a couple years ago, right? You were down in Seattle?"

When Jeremy didn't reply, Gary chuckled, a nasty sound. "I think maybe you might have been in the wrong place at the wrong time."

The sudden tension in Jeremy's large body had Holly paralyzed in fear. "Jeremy, don't," she cautioned. "He's not worth it."

"Jeremy, don't," Gary mocked, bringing his pistol back up. "You of all people should know you can't play in the big leagues and expect to walk away."

"Walk away. That's what we're going to do right now." Though she felt like she was babbling, Holly grabbed Jeremy's arm. "Come on. Let's go."

For a second she thought he might resist, but he finally turned and stalked away. Thor stayed right with them.

Gary let them get half the distance to his truck before calling after them. "Don't forget. Find Russell. He needs to pay up. Or someone is going to get hurt."

Neither Holly nor Jeremy acknowledged his words.

Once in the truck, with Thor panting happily in the back seat, Holly heaved a huge sigh of relief. "That was awful," she said.

Jaw tense, Jeremy started the engine and shifted into

Drive. He didn't speak until they were out of the parking area and on the road heading back toward Blake.

"He knew," he said. "Three years of my life were wasted, rotting away in prison for a crime I didn't commit. I was set up and railroaded, despite a lack of evidence. My attorney and I both suspected the prosecutor took a large bribe to make sure I was convicted."

He pounded the steering wheel, gaze straight ahead. "And Gary knew, despite being up in Anchorage. I'm not sure how or why, but I think he might have been part of the entire thing."

Though she wasn't sure of the timing, she decided to ask. "I know you said you were exonerated. And when they let you out, they made restitution. I'm going to go out on a limb and guess that was a fair amount of money, since you were locked up for three years."

"Maybe," he acknowledged. "But not enough to give me back all that time. What's your point?"

She took a deep breath. "What are the chances that someone else knows about your settlement? Someone in the gang or cartel or whoever it is that Gary works for. They could definitely believe you would use that to pay them back."

"Not a chance in hell." He cursed again. "That's my seed money to get my business started. Not only that, but I figured Russell wouldn't want me living with him forever, so I planned to eventually purchase a place of my own."

"That's wise," she said. "I've been saving up to try to do the same thing. But for me, I'd be renting."

"Whatever Russell got mixed up in, there's got to be another way out."

"I hope so," she replied. "But obviously, he didn't think so. Why else would he run?"

"Maybe because he's still using. Drugs can mess with your head and make small things seem impossible." He swallowed. "Though this doesn't sound small. It's pretty damn huge. Which means we've got to find Russell. He's the only one who can put an end to this."

"Except he doesn't appear to want to be found, and I'm beginning to see why."

"Me too." Glum expression matching his voice, he swallowed hard. "I came here to show my brother that I'd finally gotten my life together. And now it seems like I'm mixed back in the exact same type of situation that I want to be far away from."

For the first time she understood that Jeremy could be at risk. Once before he'd been implicated for something he hadn't done. Though she couldn't imagine how, she could understand why he'd want to make sure it didn't happen again.

"Maybe you should distance yourself from this," she said. "At least as much as possible. Though I don't know how."

He looked at her like she'd started speaking gibberish. "I have to find my brother. That's the only way to make this go away. Russell needs to pay those people what he owes them and then put himself into an addiction treatment facility."

"Is that what you did?" she asked softly. "To get healed?"

"No. I quit on my own and attended Narcotics Anonymous meetings."

"How long were you clean before you were sent to prison?" Though she couldn't let Jeremy know, the answer was very important. She'd experienced firsthand how Russell's behavior had changed as he'd sunk deeper into his addiction. She never wanted to experience that again.

"Three years," he told her. "I had a steady job and was

saving my money. I kept going to meetings. At first, in order to help myself. Later, I wanted to help others. That's why when one of my friends from NA relapsed and decided to go score, I knew I had to try and stop him."

"And that's when you got arrested."

"Right." He sighed. "It was pretty damn awful."

"Did he get arrested too?"

"Yes, he did." Voice tinged with sadness, he looked down. "After he did his time, once he got out, he began using again. Last I heard, he died of an overdose on the street in Seattle."

She reached out and touched his arm. "I'm sorry. That's sad."

"It is," he agreed. "I want nothing to do with drugs or people who use them. That's what makes this entire situation with Russell even worse. I'm right back in the thick of that, which is the last place I want to be."

Slowly, she nodded. "Once you saved yourself, you tried to help others. That's amazing."

"Maybe so, but it cost me two entire years of my life. I'm not so eager to let that happen again." He took a deep breath. "But I've got to help my brother. And hopefully we all will emerge unscathed."

She thought of how quiet her life had been once Russell disappeared. She'd discovered a new kind of peace and she'd flourished. Solitude had allowed her to create, unfettered. To others she knew she appeared mousy and boring, but one look at her art, and she might be viewed as a wild woman. At least she thought so.

This thought made her think of how she'd felt making love with Jeremy. Untamed, fully in the moment.

Worse, she wanted to do it again.

As soon as possible.

* * *

Though careful not to reveal how he felt to Holly, the incident with Gary had rattled the hell out of Jeremy. All of this, the drugs, the money, the threats, brought back horrible old memories from a life he'd left far behind. The knowledge that his older brother was now living that kind of life made him want to punch something.

He had to find Russell. But how?

"Are you going back to Mikki's again tonight?" Holly asked. "I think maybe talking to Tanya is going to be your best bet. She's involved in all of this drug stuff, you know. I'm pretty sure she's the one who got Russell using."

Again he felt that flash of fury. Not at Holly, never her. Despite what some of the women believed, he found it increasingly difficult to believe she had anything to do with Russell's disappearance. Or his drug habits. Tanya however, was another story. He'd reserve judgment for now, but in his experience, if she'd been close to Russell, the two had likely partied together.

"I think I need to," he replied. "Hopefully after a couple of nights, word will eventually get out to her and she'll come by to take a look at me herself."

She nodded. "A couple of nights. From what I've heard, she's like a piranha when it comes to new blood. She might be by sooner than you think."

Before he could stop himself, he leaned over and kissed her on the mouth. Just a quick peck, though the instant their lips touched he had to battle the temptation to deepen the kiss.

When they broke apart, they were both breathing heavily.

"What was that for?" she asked, sounding bemused.

"No reason." He forced himself to move away, trying like hell to sound casual. He looked over to find Thor watching him, tongue lolling. If Jeremy hadn't known better, he would have said the dog was laughing.

"I'm going to make a few phone calls," he said. "And if you don't mind, could I use your computer? I need to do some research on the internet."

"No problem," she said, her expression still dazed. "That's Russell's laptop. As you know, he scrubbed it clean. But I wrote the password on a sticky note, so use it however long you need to. I don't get on it much. My phone pretty much does anything I might need to do."

Thanking her, he sat down and opened the computer. Once it powered on, he typed in the password and got to work. Holly got up and disappeared into her studio, leaving Thor with him.

He spent several hours searching for police reports of large drug busts. He started in Anchorage and branched out to Fairbanks, Juneau and then smaller towns like Homer. He wasn't surprised to find quite a few in Anchorage, and he combed through those, looking for any similarities, like names. From experience, he knew unless the DEA had an undercover operation and performed a sting like the one that had sent him to prison, all the people arrested in these were small players. They posted bond, got out and went right back to doing what they'd been doing.

Immersing himself in the data online, the sound of Holly calling Thor made him look up.

"Hey, there," she said, smiling. "Not trying to be annoying, but if you're planning on going to Mikki's tonight, you might want to start getting ready." That said she opened the back door and went out with her dog.

A quick glance at his smartwatch revealed several hours had passed. Logging out, he closed the laptop and got up to stretch. Then he went to get cleaned up for his second night out on the town.

Holly waved him off with a smile, wishing him luck. Though he would much rather have spent the evening with her, he smiled back. Then he got in his truck and made the short drive over to Mikki's.

This time, when he walked up and took a seat at the bar, Mikki brought him a club soda with a twist of lime without asking. "Back so soon?" she asked, brows arching.

"I have a plan," he said, thanking her for the drink. "I'm hoping Russell's friend Tanya drops by. I need to talk to her."

"Since I saw you talking to her friend Sheila last time, I'm sure Tanya knows you were here. She's only been in a few times since Russell went missing, but I bet you she shows up tonight."

"I hope so." He leaned forward. "Please tell me what she looks like. All anyone will say is that I'll know her when I see her."

This made Mikki laugh. "They're not wrong, you know. Think Jessica Rabbit in the flesh." With that, she walked off to help another customer.

Swiveling in his seat to survey the half-empty bar, he noticed most of the clientele seemed to be the same from his previous visit. Same guys, in small groups. The occasional single guy, intent on drowning his sorrows. A few tables of two or three women, enjoying their glasses of wine and each other's company.

He could easily understand why people would come here. Even hanging out by yourself here would be a hundred times better than sitting at home all alone.

The front door opened and a woman strutted in. Almost everyone in the bar stopped what they were doing to stare.

Instantly, just like everyone had told him, he understood that this was the mysterious and elusive Tanya. Jessica Rabbit in the flesh, indeed.

She sashayed over to the bar and made a show of climbing onto the barstool next to Jeremy. As she did, she deliberately gave him a show of leg and more. He actually looked away, hiding his stunned reaction. Had to give her points for brazenness.

"Well, hello, there," she drawled, looking him up and down, her false eyelashes fluttering. The way she let her gaze drift hungrily over him made him feel as if she were undressing him with her eyes.

Settling back, he forced himself to do the same with her. Everything about this woman seemed overdone. From her huge, likely enhanced bosom, the artfully applied makeup and bright red lips, to her clearly expensive dress and sky-high heels.

"I'm Jeremy," he said, holding out his hand for her to shake.

Ignoring that, she waved to Mikki and ordered a glass of wine. "I know who you are," she finally said, once Mikki brought it. "You're my Russell's baby brother, though I'd have to say you're definitely all grown-up." And she licked her lips suggestively.

For the life of him, he couldn't understand what his brother had seen in this woman. But right now, because his best chance of getting information would be to pretend he was into her too, he grinned. "I am that. And you are?"

"Oh, honey, surely you've heard of me. I'm Tanya. Everyone in Blake knows who I am."

Though tempted to comment, he decided to let that one go. "I'm kind of new to town," he said instead. "What's your last name, Tanya?"

For whatever reason, this question made her laugh. A practiced, tinkling sound, reminiscent of someone sounding scales to warm up before singing. He found everything about this woman annoying. Seriously, he struggled to understand how Russell could have chosen her over Holly. They were as opposite as night and day.

"I don't use a last name," she finally said. "Just Tanya. Like Cher, or Pink, or Madonna."

He pretended to find this fascinating. "I get it. Did you happen to know my brother very well?"

Again, she found his question amusing. Either because she understood he already knew about her relationship with Russell, or because she thought that he didn't. Either way, all he cared about was getting some answers. He figured he'd have to be careful not to scare her away.

"Russell was my lover for years, sweetheart," she drawled, once again looking him up and down. "Long before he brought that other girl up from the lower forty-eight, and long after. But if you're about to ask me what I think happened to him, you'd be questioning the wrong person."

He pretended not to understand what she meant.

"His pretend fiancée," she replied, not bothering to hide her impatience. "That woman stays in his house, uses his Land Rover and makes no pretense about being glad he's gone. I'm not the only one who feels she had something to do with his disappearance."

Now he'd need to tread carefully. "I gathered that," he said, deciding not to point out Holly's ownership rights to both the house and the vehicle. Not yet. "But I've also talked to several of his friends who think he took off on his own."

She made a dismissive sound. "That's nonsense. He has a perfectly good life here. No debt, and he'd just sold his business and said he was taking an early retirement. The only thorn in his side was Holly. She refused to leave, even after he dumped her. She's greedy and thought she could get him back."

Since none of this even came close to matching the Holly he'd come to know, Jeremy said nothing. He just kept his gaze on Tanya's face, pretending to be fascinated.

All the attention made her preen. "You're staying there with her, aren't you?" she asked. "Since you're Russell's next of kin, you have the authority to kick her out."

"Do I?" Trying to find the right words and failing miserably, he decided to go with his heart. "Right now, I'm just trying to find Russell. If I do, then he can tell me who he does or doesn't want staying in his house. Since you and he were close, is there anything he said to you that might tell me where to look for him?"

She started to open her mouth, no doubt to shoot off another cutting remark. Instead, she closed it. "I miss him," she finally said, her voice quiet and reflective. "Your brother was a good man at heart. But to answer your question, no. He never talked to me about leaving. Not even once."

Because he sensed she had more to say, he waited.

"I love him, you know," she continued. "And it really hurt when he brought some other woman into his home and told me he'd asked her to marry him. That broke my heart."

"But none of that is Holly's fault," he felt compelled to point out. "Russell didn't tell her anything about you or any of the others."

Her bright red lips tightened. "I tried to cut him off after he brought Holly back. That's why he started sleeping around. Even though I took him back, he kept it up."

He decided not to point out that it should have been Russell doing the cutting off. Why bother to get engaged, to ask someone to spend the rest of their life with you, if you had no intention of honoring your vows?

"What about when he and Holly broke it off?" he finally asked, keeping his tone neutral. "Did you and Russell get back together?"

Her heavily made-up eyes flashed. "As if I would ever allow him—or any man—to make me their second choice."

"I take it that's a no, then?"

Tossing back the rest of her wine in one gulp, she signaled to Mikki that she wanted another. "Let's just say I tried and leave it at that."

"But he never said anything to you about leaving or where he might have gone?"

Slowly, she shook her head. "No, he didn't. And that hurt almost as much as him bringing in Holly." Her wine arrived. She thanked Mikki and took another large swallow. "Look, I don't know you. Russell might have mentioned once or twice that he had a younger brother, but that was the extent of it. But if you are actually sharing Russell's house with Holly, you need to watch your back."

"Why?" he asked, genuinely curious.

"Because she had something to do with Russell vanishing." Gaze steady, Tanya sighed. "I'm aware a lot of people here in town don't believe me. But I know it in my heart. Russell wouldn't simply turn his back on the people and place he loves. He worked too hard to get where he is. He'd never just abandon everything and walk away."

Since she claimed to know his brother well, Jeremy decided to bring up the elephant in the room. "Do you think maybe the drugs might have had something to do with it?"

Glass halfway to her mouth, she paused. "You know about that?"

"Yes. I assume you do also."

After taking another sip from her glass, she slowly nodded.

He decided he might as well just come out and ask her. Even though he already knew the answer, he couldn't help but be curious as to what she would say. "Was Russell dealing drugs?"

"I don't know," she replied. "While I do enjoy my wine and the occasional gin and tonic, I'm not into that scene. As far as I'm aware, Russell indulged in recreational drug use from time to time." She sighed. "I have to admit, I used to be. Russell and I used a few times together. He hurt his back and really liked how the opioids made him feel. When he needed more, I helped him get it. But he didn't stop there. I quit. He didn't. Right before he went missing, I believe it got away from him. If anyone would know more details about that, it would be Holly. You should be asking her."

Since he had no intention of discussing Holly with Tanya, he nodded. To his surprise, he kind of liked her. She appeared to genuinely care about his brother, despite her misplaced animosity toward Holly.

"I'll do that," he said. "But Holly isn't the bad guy in all of this. Russell hurt her too."

"Sure, she's really suffered." Tone full of mockery, Tanya glared. "She got rid of the abusive boyfriend and ended up with the house and the Land Rover. You can't tell me you don't think she came out ahead."

"Abusive," he said, focusing on that one word. "So you knew about that too."

"Russell was abusive to a lot of people," she said, her frosty tone matching her expression. "And in my opinion, his abuse gave Holly even more reason to harm him."

"Was he abusive to you?" Jeremy pressed. "Did he hit you?"

She looked down, suddenly finding one of her rings fascinating. "If he did, I forgave him."

"I wouldn't have. Growing up, Russell always told me a man should never lay hands on a woman."

"Yet you said he threw you out when you were far too young to take care of yourself," she pointed out. "And here you are, all these years later, wanting to reconcile. You have no room to judge me."

"That's the last thing I'd ever do," he replied. "Despite what you might think, when my brother kicked me out, I deserved it. I was stealing, skipping school and using drugs. He only did what he thought was right."

"By tossing a sixteen-year-old kid into the street? The better thing to do would have been to get you help. Did he even offer to do that?"

This Tanya had a way of cutting to the chase, he'd give her that. "Maybe so, but all of that happened over a decade ago. It's in the past. Maybe it needs to stay there."

"Suit yourself." She shrugged, still sipping her wine. "But if you leave deep issues unresolved, they tend to fester inside. Believe me. I speak from personal experience."

Suddenly weary, he thanked her for her candor. Scribbling his number on a napkin, he handed it to her. "I'd honestly hoped you might have more information about where Russell might have gone. I appreciate you sharing with me what you did know. If anything comes up, call me."

"You're welcome. And I will." Now smiling, she blew him a kiss. "I'll say this one last time. Holly comes off as the girl next door, all innocent and sweet. Look deeper if you really want to find out what happened with your brother. And whatever you do, don't sleep with her. All of Russell's troubles began when he met her. Watch your back."

Jeremy walked away, hoping his expression hadn't revealed it was already too late for that.

Driving home, he forced himself to consider Tanya's words. Despite her appearance, she seemed genuine, though a little misguided. But some of the things she'd said made good points. Holly and Russell had been living together. If anyone would know what was going on with his brother, she'd be the one.

His gut twisted. He didn't like doubting Holly. She'd been nothing but kind. Though to be fair, he had to wonder if the overwhelming attraction he felt toward her might have affected his judgment.

Tanya had cautioned him not to sleep with Holly. Not only had he already done so, but he hadn't been able to stop thinking about the one time they'd made love. At the time, he'd believed everything had happened naturally. Neither of them had been able to resist the passion that had blazed between them so unexpectedly. They'd allowed it to propel them into a place of intimacy where they likely shouldn't have gone.

Yet he found himself wanting her again and again. And while he had no idea whether or not she felt the same way, he had to take into consideration that all of that lust might have blinded him from seeing the truth.

Except he had no idea what the truth might be.

Chapter 11

After Jeremy left for Mikki's, Holly took advantage of the longer daylight to go outside into the large backyard. Thor trotted happily at her side.

As soon as they reached the backyard, Thor found himself a sunny patch of grass and plopped down, happy as could be. Watching him made her smile.

She continued on to the back corner of the yard, a patch of earth she'd cultivated just to see if she could. Her little garden turned out to be something she really enjoyed. She'd planted it in the spring, using seeds she'd grown in little pots over the winter, keeping them inside until they were large enough and the weather mild enough for them to be moved.

Chicken wire protected the area from rabbits and deer, and she'd already gotten a head of lettuce, some zucchini and a bunch of peppers. The tomatoes were coming along nicely too, and she anticipated a nice crop of them in a month or less, well before the first frost. Two rows of corn would be ready in the fall as well.

She found tending to her garden soothing and peaceful. Another activity she'd never even suspected she might like and which now she knew she couldn't live without.

A shadow, something moved, just on the edge of her

vision. It was right behind the fence line, where the chain link made a corner. Beyond that was a grove of trees that deer often frequented. Holly froze, her first thought going to Tanya. The woman had stalked her before, though that had been months ago.

Holly looked at Thor, well aware that his superior hearing and sense of smell would notice an intruder long before she would. But instead of being on alert, her beast rolled around on the grass, tongue lolling. Everything about his relaxed posture told her no danger existed.

Maybe it had been a deer. Thor allowed them to pass unbothered, watching them graze with a kind of patient benevolence.

Still, as she pulled weeds from her small garden, she kept a watchful eye out just in case. Between Tanya and Gary, she felt she now had to watch her back. This didn't sit well with her, not at all. But until Russell reappeared and made things right, she had no way to make it all stop.

If and when Russell did return, she'd immediately need to find a new place to live. Which meant she not only needed to sell more art, but see if Kip would give her additional hours at the store. The more she could make, the more she could save.

At least Jeremy was no longer hovering over her.

In truth, as soon as he'd driven off, she'd found herself wishing she'd gone with him. Since such neediness wasn't part of her nature and she didn't like it, she'd made herself get busy.

Working in the soil, fingers in the dirt, she'd felt her worries melt away. Until that darn shadow, or whatever it had been, had brought her crashing back to reality.

She found herself thinking about Jeremy, wondering if Tanya had paid a visit to Mikki's yet. While Holly wasn't fond of the woman, the level of hatred Tanya felt for her rivaled the heat of a hundred suns. The few times Holly had come face-to-face with the woman, she'd been able to feel the animosity from across the room.

Both intimidating and frightening, the first time it had happened, Holly remembered asking Russell if she'd done something to offend Tanya. He'd laughed and said something about how he and Tanya had once dated and Holly shouldn't worry about it. Since they were in the beginning of their engagement, Holly had believed him without reservation. She hadn't known then what she knew now. Russell lied. About almost everything.

Since they were brothers, she'd found herself wondering if Jeremy shared some of the traits of his sibling. At one point, she'd considered doing an online search to learn if the story he'd told her was true or, in fact, fiction.

In fact, once she finished working in her garden, tonight would be the perfect time to do that.

Though she kept glancing toward the area where she'd thought she'd seen something, nothing else moved or appeared out of the ordinary. And Thor continued to doze contentedly, so she finally relaxed and focused on her gardening.

Finally, with all the weeds pulled, she watered her plants and called Thor. The two of them headed inside.

Right before they reached the back door, Thor spun around, suddenly on full alert. He appeared to be staring at the same spot where she thought she'd seen something earlier.

She called his name, keeping her voice low but her tone urgent. "In the house. Now."

For one heart-stopping moment, she thought her dog intended to ignore her. Instead, he snapped out of his intense fixation and followed her inside.

Once there, she locked the back door and then went from room to room, checking each window just in case. An overabundance of caution would be better than having someone let themselves in through an unsecured window.

The minute she'd satisfied herself that she was as safe as she could be at the moment, she went into the living room and dropped down onto the couch. She almost reached for the remote, with the intention of turning the TV on, but then realized she was afraid to have anything hamper her hearing. If someone tried to break into the house, she wanted to be ready.

She hadn't been this anxious since the first few months after Russell left. Tanya had made her life a living hell, showing up at all hours of the day and night, calling, demanding Holly tell her where Russell was. She'd refused to believe Holly when she said she didn't know.

If Tanya was starting up again, that meant something had to have happened to set her off. But what? Maybe Jeremy might know.

When his headlights swept the front window, she almost cried with relief. She didn't like feeling so vulnerable.

Thor lifted his head at the sound of the truck pulling into the drive, but didn't get up.

The instant Jeremy strode into the house, Holly launched herself into his arms. He caught her, let her hold on tight and wrapped his arms around her. "What happened?" he asked. "You're shaking."

Breathing in the outdoorsy scent of him, she continued to hold as she explained. "I think Tanya has started stalking me again."

"It couldn't have been Tanya," he said, pulling back so

he could look at her. "Because she was at Mikki's, talking to me."

The sudden flash of jealousy that hit her low in the gut took her by surprise. "If not her, then who?" she wondered out loud. "Because someone was out there, watching me." She thought for a minute. "I was so sure it had to be her, I didn't even consider anyone else. Maybe it was Gary."

"That's possible, but not likely. He made a big show of warning us already. So far, he hasn't been shy about letting us know he's out there. Why would he start skulking around now?"

"Maybe he thought if he stays hidden, we might lead him to Russell," she said. "I don't know who, but I think someone was out there. Thor sensed it too."

"Did he go chase them down?" Jeremy asked.

"No. But even if he had, they were on the other side of the fence." She thought for a moment. "But what seemed odd was that he didn't even bark. He just froze and stared at the spot where I thought I saw movement."

"Thought you saw?" He picked up on her choice of words. "Does that mean you didn't actually see someone? Or did you?"

"No," she reluctantly admitted. "Just a flash of movement. I'd just about convinced myself that it must have been a deer or moose until Thor went on full alert. But he didn't bark or chase after anything, so I have no idea if I'm just being paranoid."

He thought for a moment. "Since it's dark out there now, I don't see any point in going to check for prints. I'll take a look in the morning."

"Or I will," she countered, slightly annoyed for no reason. Actually, she knew why. She stepped back. "How'd your talk with Tanya go?"

Instead of answering, he went and got himself a glass of ice water. Then, gesturing at the table, he pulled out a chair and dropped into it.

"She's not what I expected," he said, his tone pensive.

Again the gut punch of jealousy. Ignoring it, she forced herself to keep her expression neutral. She took her time pulling out a chair and sitting. "How so?"

"Well, her appearance is deceiving. Underneath all that, she seems to really care about my brother."

"That's about the only thing she cares about," she said, not bothering to hide her bitterness. "She's convinced herself that I'm some kind of Mata Hari. Early on, when she'd come to me with all kinds of wild accusations, I tried to talk to her. To defend myself and give her my side of the story. She wasn't interested in hearing it."

"Yeah." His wry smile made her breath catch. "She warned me all about you. She claimed Russell's life was just fine until you came to town."

To her dismay, her eyes filled with tears. "I don't know why she thinks she can blame me for everything. The only thing I did wrong was fall for Russell's lies."

"Honestly, I think it's because he spurned her for you," he said slowly. "She's managed to convince herself that you did something to him. Because she can't stand the thought of him going away without letting her know where he went."

"Maybe so," she admitted, wiping at her eyes with the back of her hand. "I just wish she'd listen to reason."

He leaned across the table and touched her arm lightly. "She's still in too much pain. From what I'd heard about her, I thought she'd try to come on to me, but she didn't. She flirted a little at first, but when I didn't reciprocate, she calmed right down and was willing to talk about Russell."

"I see. And I assume she had quite a bit to say about me as well."

"She did." His slow smile made her feel warm all over. "The sad thing is, she actually believes what she's saying. Or appears to." Continuing to stroke her arm, he sighed. "The end result of it all is that she apparently has no idea where my brother might be. In fact, she tends to think you killed him and hid his body."

This made her groan out loud. "I can't tell you how many times I've defended myself against that claim. She tried to get the police involved. I allowed them to search the house and yard, and I even took a lie detector test. They told her they found no reason to believe what she said was true."

Finally, he moved his magic fingers away. Which was a good thing, as she'd found herself unable to catch her breath. "That should have been the end of it then."

"Right? Except it wasn't. She convinced herself I'd somehow gotten the Alaska State Police on my side. Or under my spell, I believe she said. I honestly used to just wish Russell would contact her so she'd know I hadn't killed him. But he never did."

Jeremy tipped back his glass and downed half of it in one swallow. Somehow, she even found this sexy. Her entire body ached for him. She didn't even recognize herself around this man.

When he met her gaze again, heat blazed in his brown eyes. "I couldn't understand how my brother could be with her when he had you," he said, his low voice raw.

That did it. Pushing out of her chair, she went to him. She slid herself on top of him, straddling him, and covered his mouth with hers.

As it always did, heat and fire flared. Devouring each

other, neither of them could get enough. His instant arousal only fueled her desire.

She'd given up trying to figure out what it was about this man that got to her. Since she appeared to be powerless to resist it, she simply gave herself over to all-consuming desire. If there were consequences, she'd deal with them later. Right now, she'd simply enjoy.

After making love, Jeremy had held Holly close until her trembling subsided. Though he'd been sure to be prepared this time, he'd barely managed to break away long enough to grab a condom. And the seductive touch of her fingers as she helped him put it on had nearly undone him.

This had matched the intensity of their first time. He'd never experienced anything even close to the way Holly made him feel. Judging by her actions, she felt the same way.

When she finally fell asleep, he carefully eased himself out of the bed and went to the bathroom to clean up.

Returning to the bedroom, he stood and gazed at her. Somehow, despite everything that should have separated them, he couldn't imagine living a life without her in it.

Shaking his head at his impracticable thoughts, he carefully climbed into bed and pulled her close. Breathing in her honeysuckle scent, he closed his eyes.

In the morning, he woke aroused but alone in her bed.

Contemplating finding her, instead he hurried to the bathroom and took a quick cold shower. Once clean, he followed the smell of coffee. Thor met him halfway, tail wagging. Jeremy scratched the dog around the neck before continuing on to the kitchen.

The instant he walked in, she smiled. Clearly, she'd already showered and gotten dressed for the day. "Good morning. I was hoping to see you before I disappeared into my studio. I'm planning on spending most of the day painting."

He poured himself a cup and sat down. "About last night," he began, not entirely sure what he wanted to say.

"Shhh." Shaking her head, she waved his words away. "Please, we don't need to make a big deal out of whatever this is. I say we just see what happens and enjoy it while we can."

Then, while he racked his brain trying to figure out how to respond to that, she got up, poured herself another cup of coffee and headed to her studio.

Even though Thor watched her go, at first he didn't follow. But as she started to close the door, the big dog shook himself, heaved a sigh and trotted after her. When he looked back, Jeremy could have sworn he smiled right before Holly shut them in.

For one split second, Jeremy found himself envying Thor.

After eating a bowl of cereal, he had just poured himself a second cup of coffee when his phone rang. Though he didn't recognize the number showing on his phone, he went ahead and answered it anyway.

"Well, hello, there and good morning," a sultry voice drawled.

He recognized her instantly. "Tanya. What's up?"

"Someone said they saw Russell." For a second she dropped the pretense, sounding breathless and a little hopeful. "I'm not sure what to think. This is the first time anything like this has happened since he disappeared."

"Who saw him?" he asked. "Are they credible?"

"Greg Norman," she replied. "I'd say the mayor is about as credible as they come."

Jeremy cursed. "He is, but he won't talk to me. I have no idea why, but when I went to see him right after I arrived back in town, he threw me out."

"Oh, I know why. He thinks you were behind all of Russell's drug problems."

This so shocked him that he nearly dropped the phone. "What? But I was incarcerated for three years. And clean a long time before then. From what I understand, Russell's issues started in the time I was gone."

"I know. But you have to understand, people only can go with what Russell told them. And I'm guessing that's what he told the mayor." She sighed. "He always had a way to excuse anything."

Hurt, though he shouldn't have been, he had to ask. "Is that what he told you? That it was my fault he started using?"

"Not at all." The quickness of her response should have been reassuring. "In fact, he barely mentioned you at all. I know for a fact that the mayor confronted Russell about him bringing drugs to Blake. Russell told me. Though he didn't go into detail about what was said, it's easy to imagine."

Sadly, he agreed. "Whatever happened, I can't talk to Greg about his supposed sighting. I'm assuming he told you himself. Were you able to get any details?"

"Oh, I haven't talked to him. You know how quickly gossip spreads around this town."

Any flicker of hope he might have had instantly vanished. "Which means you haven't actually verified if this is even true, right?"

"Most gossip is," she replied. "Especially something like this. No one ever talks about the mayor. And Russell has been gone for so long, the idea that anyone would even say this has to mean it's true."

While he wasn't sure he agreed with her analysis, he sure as hell didn't plan to argue. "Would you mind speaking with Greg personally and see what he has to say? If he did see my brother, details would be helpful."

"I don't know." She sighed. "I'm not exactly popular with the mayor either. He's always been civil, but not overly friendly."

"Do you want to find Russell or not?" he asked, his tone sharper than he intended, but that couldn't be helped. Why would Tanya pass on a rumor like this without validating its truthfulness?

"I do. I'll try to talk to Greg. I'll keep you posted."

Thanking her, he ended the call. Then went to find Holly.

Though she'd closed the door to her art studio partway, he was able to nudge it open silently. Holly stood with her back to him, painting on a large canvas she'd propped on an easel. Thor, who'd curled up in a large dog bed in one corner, raised his head when he spotted Jeremy but didn't bark.

Jeremy stood in the doorway, watching Holly. He couldn't get a clear view of her painting, but she appeared to be so engrossed in her work that she didn't even register his presence.

Finally, she paused and put her brush down. Getting up from her stool, she stretched and turned just enough to notice Jeremy standing in the doorway.

"Oh, hi," she said, grabbing a paint smeared towel to wipe off her hands. "Did you need something?"

He told her about Tanya's call, noting the way she stiffened when he said the other woman's name. "Obviously, after what happened, I can't go talk to Greg."

"And you were hoping I would do it."

"Yes. Though to be fair, I also asked Tanya if she would."

Holly stiffened, but she didn't comment.

"I figure if Greg won't talk to her, he might to you."

"Right. Tanya first," she said, her tone grudging. "I get it. Thank you for being honest with me."

"Does that mean you'll do it?" he asked, hoping she wouldn't let the knowledge that her archenemy had agreed to help color her judgment.

"Yes. I can try. I haven't exactly formed any kind of relationship with the mayor and his wife, though the few times we spoke, they were kind."

"Thank you." He took a few more steps into the room. When he saw her painting, he caught his breath. She'd painted an eagle with a large fish in its talons. The detail was incredible, but more importantly, she'd somehow managed to convey the wild beauty of the bird's freedom.

Awestruck by the raw emotion the painting brought, he couldn't stop staring. "That's beautiful," he finally said.

"Thanks," she replied. "I confess I haven't gone out of the way to try and make friends with the mayor or his wife."

Though he found this astonishing, he kept his mouth shut. "Well, maybe now would be a good time to start. If this rumor is true and Greg thinks he saw Russell, we need to know where and when and how certain he is."

Gaze locked on his face, she nodded. "Let me get cleaned up and I'll go talk to him this afternoon."

"Thank you." Again, he found himself looking at her painting. "Is that something you'll be selling once you've finished it?"

"Yes," she replied. "I do really well with my Alaskan wildlife series."

"I want to buy it," he said, his voice husky. "Name your price, but please sell it to me."

For a moment, looking from him to her artwork, she

didn't speak. Finally, she nodded. "Of course. I'll let you know when it's done."

"Thank you."

Some of the rawness of his unexpected emotion must have shown in his face.

"Are you all right?" she asked, studying him. "Has this news about a spotting of Russell got you reeling?"

Facing her, the most beautiful, genuine woman he'd ever met, he came awfully close to spilling his guts. But he knew if he told her that he couldn't stop thinking about her, and wanted to be closer to her every time they were in the same room, he'd scare her off.

Instead, he reached for her at the same time she reached for him. They came together, her softness melting into him. Fingers tangled in her hair, they kissed.

Tangled up in each other, only Thor's frantic barking brought them out of their embrace.

The instant they broke apart, Jeremy smelled it. Smoke.

"Did you leave something on the stove?" he asked her.

"No." Expression alarmed, she took off for the kitchen with him right behind her. As soon as they hit the living room, he realized the smoke was coming from the opposite direction.

"My bedroom," he said, pivoting to head that way.

"I've got a fire extinguisher I keep in the garage." Running, she went to get it. Thor went with her.

The smoke appeared to be coming from outside. He'd left his window open to get fresh air. Instead, smoke poured in. He slammed it shut and locked it just as Holly came running in with the extinguisher.

"It's out here." He sprinted toward the kitchen and the back door, Holly right behind him.

As soon as they rounded the corner, they saw the fire.

Several of the bushes near the house were burning, and luckily the flames had not yet spread to the structure itself.

"It smells like gasoline," she said, lifting her extinguisher and pulling the pin and spraying. She put the fire out fairly quickly before it could damage the house.

"Good thing you had that," Jeremy said.

"Yeah. Most folks around here do. We have propane, plus I work with paint thinner sometimes." Her voice wavered, making him realize she was on the verge of tears.

"Holly," he began. "It's okay. The house wasn't burned."

"This time," she replied. "This didn't just come out of nowhere. Someone deliberately set this fire. Probably whoever I saw lurking around the outskirts of the fence."

"But why?" he mused. "Even if the house is insured, they usually exclude arson."

"True. And also, a homeowner's policy pays out to the owner of the house. Which is also Russell, though we'd each have to sign off on the check. So why would someone do something like this?"

And do it poorly, he thought, though he didn't say the words out loud. If someone had truly wanted to set the house ablaze, they'd have splashed the accelerant on the wood instead of the bushes. "Maybe this was meant to be some kind of warning."

"Like from Gary and his associates?"

"Maybe. But again, that also isn't logical. If we're injured in a fire, or even just displaced, how does that help them get their money?"

Making a sound of frustration, she eyed the charred remains of the evergreen bushes. "Then I have no choice but to assume someone did it out of spite. Just to hurt me. That's the only explanation that makes sense."

Chapter 12

Despite Jeremy's attempts to come up with an explanation, Holly squashed down her rage. She'd had enough. Whether the fire had been set by Tanya or by Gary, this needed to stop. With Jeremy right behind her, she marched inside and grabbed her phone. Since she needed to talk to the mayor, now seemed as good a time as any. The few times she'd met him, he'd been friendly and seemed efficient. She could tell he really cared about the town. She'd report the fire and, after that, ask him if the rumors about Russell being spotted were true. If they were, someone needed to fill Tanya in.

"Greg Norman," he answered. Then, before she could identify herself, he continued. "Holly. I'm really glad to hear from you. How have you been?"

Since she'd never called him before in her life, she wondered how his caller ID had identified her number and asked.

"I have everyone's number," he answered, an undercurrent of humor in his voice. "It's part of my job as mayor to be able to reach any citizen at any given time. As for yours, Russell gave it to me right after you moved in. I saved it in my phone contacts."

He took a deep breath. "I'm guessing you're calling because of the gossip going around."

"Well, that too," she said. "I have another reason for contacting you, but since you brought it up, did you really see Russell?"

He paused for a few seconds. "I thought I did. To be honest, at first I was positive. But the more I think about it, the more I wonder if it was really him."

Holly met Jeremy's intense gaze and gave a slow nod. His jaw tightened, but he didn't speak.

"Where were you when you saw him?" she asked. "And what was he doing? Please, tell me everything. I really need to know."

"I see." Greg cleared his throat. "I was hiking up those trails that start at the observation area of the Neacola River. Usually when I head up that way, I'm alone. But this time, I could tell someone was up ahead of me. Far enough that I didn't feel like I was encroaching on his privacy, or he on mine. I'd just catch glimpses here and there when rounding turns or when the trail climbed."

She waited while he went quiet again, apparently gathering his thoughts.

"Anyway," he finally continued. "He got to the top ahead of me and turned to make his way back down. That's when he realized he wasn't alone. I got a clear glimpse of his face, and he looked like Russell."

"What did he do once he realized you were there?" she asked.

"He took off through the woods. Running. That's when I realized it had to be Russell. Why else would someone act that way?"

He had a point. "Which would mean Russell is hiding out somewhere close to home," she said. "Thank you, Greg."

"You're welcome. Now, what was your other reason for calling me? You said you had one."

She told him about the fire, taking care to use Jeremy's name a couple of times just to hear his reaction.

"You really think someone set it deliberately?" he asked, his voice incredulous.

"Yes," she replied. "Not only could I smell gasoline, but only the bushes caught on fire. Since there were no lightning strikes or downed power lines, that is the only way a fire like that could have started."

"I think you should file a police report," Greg advised. "Even though you'd have to call the state police in Anchorage, at least you'll have it on record."

"I'll do that."

"Good, good." He paused again. "Holly, do you mind me asking you something?"

Curious, she took a deep breath. "Not at all. Go ahead."

"Are you safe?" He cleared his throat, sounding uncomfortable. "I only ask because I'm aware Russell's brother is staying there in the house with you."

Something of her thoughts must have shown on her face, because Jeremy's jaw tightened and his eyes flashed. She shook her head at him and took a moment before replying to Greg. "I'm fine. Jeremy is nothing like Russell, if that's what you're asking. He speaks of you fondly. Have you welcomed him back to Blake yet?"

Now that she'd put him on the spot, Greg hemmed and hawed a moment. Finally, he informed Holly that Russell had said some pretty awful things about his younger brother and they'd leave it at that.

"Jeremy isn't like that," Holly said, her tone steely.

"There was a lot more going on with Russell than I can tell you right now. But all of his choices were his own and had nothing to do with his brother."

"I see," Greg replied, his skeptical tone informing her in fact that he did not.

"If you hear or see anything else, please keep me informed." After Gary assured her that he would, she ended the call.

"Well?" Jeremy asked. He listened intently as she relayed everything the mayor had said. When she told him the last part, about Russell turning Greg against him, his expressionless face contrasted with the pain in his eyes.

"I'm sorry," she said.

"I expected something like that," he admitted. "Though I'm having a hard time understanding why Greg believed him. Greg knew both of us growing up, even before our parents were killed. In my teenage years, I might have been trouble, but Russell always walked the straight and narrow."

"People change." She kept her voice soft. "I'm hoping Greg will be able to see that."

"Maybe someday," he agreed. "Thank you for defending me."

"It was the least I could do. After all, I know you'd do the same for me."

Heat darkened his eyes as he slowly nodded. "I would. And I have to wonder if Russell had something to do with the fire."

Stunned, she took a moment to process his words. "Russell? I don't know."

"It's possible," he persisted. "Maybe he's returned from wherever he was."

"But why would he set a fire? If he's come back and

plans to liquidate his assets to pay off his debt, it makes no sense to try and burn the house down."

"Whoever set that fire wasn't trying to do much damage," he pointed out. "Though I still can't figure out what the purpose of that might have been. Maybe to let us know he's here."

She decided to play along, even though she wasn't sure she believed any of this. "Do you think that's who I thought I saw watching me out in the garden?"

"Maybe. Probably. Especially if Thor didn't bark. He wouldn't, since he knows Russell." He sighed. "I don't know. This all sounds improbable, but to be honest, everything Russell's done seems unreal. If he really is back, and I have no reason to doubt Greg, then I wish he'd just show up and explain himself."

Though she kept her feelings to herself, just the thought of seeing Russell again made her feel queasy. While Russell battled his addiction, he'd done some awful things to her in the time they'd lived together. He'd betrayed her trust and taken advantage of her. She'd vowed no one would ever abuse her that way again. Since she'd purchased this house jointly with him, the tie wouldn't be easy to break, especially since she'd used almost every penny she'd saved so they could purchase the home with cash and own it outright. She didn't have the funds to buy him out, and she suspected he didn't either.

Either way, she hadn't begun to even be able to relax until a few months after Russell disappeared. The idea of facing him again, with his sudden rages and unstable mood swings, made her want to hop in the Land Rover and take off for parts unknown.

While she wasn't sure how to articulate this, she also knew she had to try. "I want that too," she began. "But the truth is, Russell scares me. I don't want him to ever raise his voice or his hand to me again."

There. That was the closest she'd come to telling Jeremy all of the truth about his brother. She'd given him hints, but not the entire scope of what Russell had done to her. The verbal abuse had started early on, and the physical hadn't come until later. While she could count on the fingers of one hand the number of times he'd slapped or shoved her, even once was enough.

"He won't. I won't allow it," Jeremy said. "Once, my brother understood that men don't hit women. I'll make sure he realizes that again. You don't need to be afraid."

Tongue-tied, she nodded her thanks. One glance at the strength and determination in his rugged face, and part of her exhaled in relief. She might not know this man as well as she'd like, but she understood enough about his character to realize he'd never allow anyone to hurt her. Physically or with words. Even his own brother. Especially his own brother.

While she definitely appreciated having Jeremy on her side, she couldn't help but wonder how Russell would react to having his younger brother step between him and the woman he'd come to regard as his property. Not well, she suspected. Before he'd left, his behavior had become violent and unpredictable. She couldn't live with herself if she managed to place Jeremy in danger.

"Maybe I should leave," she said, thinking out loud. "You and Russell already have a lot to mend between you. I don't want to add to that."

Jeremy froze. "You and Russell broke up before he left, right?"

Slowly, she nodded. "Yes. But that's not what I meant." Once she explained, he shook his head. "Come here," he said. Then, instead of waiting for her to come to him, he crossed the space between them and pulled her into his arms. "You're safe with me."

"Thank you," she said, managing to keep her voice level even though her head was spinning. "But even though Russell and I have been over for a long time, he's made it plain he regards me as one of his possessions. I might own half this house, but he always made me feel as if he allowed me to live here. The same with the Land Rover. He gifted that SUV to me, and my name is on the title, but he acted as if I only got to drive it due to his benevolence."

She took a deep breath. "Yes, he owns half of the house. And he's been gone, but I have just as much right to be here as he does. And I like it a lot better without him."

Admitting this out loud made her feel slightly ashamed. To counter this, she lifted her chin and looked him in the eye. "It's much quieter. Peaceful, settled, no screaming, slamming doors or dodging fists. I deserved this time after everything he put me through."

"Are you saying you think he did this for you?" he asked.

The question made her shake her head. "Everything Russell does is for himself. So no. I have no idea why he took off, though it has to have something to do with his drug dealer."

"I agree," he replied. "And I'm sorry he put you through that."

Unsure how to respond to this, she simply nodded. "Russell will return in his own good time, when he wants to. Until then, all we can do is wait. And watch our backs."

Jeremy admired Holly's honesty. She wasn't afraid to relay hard truths, despite knowing he might find them difficult to swallow.

And truth be told, she'd been gracious to allow him to stay in the house she co-owned with his brother. With Russell MIA, she'd have been within her right to toss him out on his ear. The fact that she hadn't, and had shown him only kindness, told him volumes about her character.

Tanya and her friends could spread all the conspiracy theories they wanted, but in the end, he knew they weren't true. He'd have to work things out with his brother, once Russell was found, but he had no doubt that Holly had only given him the truth.

His growing feelings for her both worried him and brought him joy. They hadn't discussed them, nor would they. At least not yet. He knew they'd have to someday, but once again, Russell's disappearance made this impossible.

Right now, he needed to focus on bringing his brother back home.

Now that Greg had confirmed the rumor that he'd seen Russell, Jeremy believed what he'd considered gossip to be truth. His brother had come back to town, or somewhere in the vicinity. But for whatever reason, he hadn't yet dared to show his face either privately or publicly. Maybe Russell had realized he needed to pay the people Gary represented, which seemed like a conclusion that the old Russell would have reached.

But if that were the case, why the skulking around, hiding out in the woods? Logic dictated that Russell make his reappearance known.

Unless he had no intention of repaying his debt. Which Jeremy knew from experience would have horrible consequences.

For the first time, Jeremy wondered exactly how much money Russell owed. As a matter of fact, why wouldn't Gary have told them the amount? If his brother would just come forward and talk to him, maybe they could work something out. After all, he and Holly could only keep Gary at bay for so long. While they weren't the ones who actually owed the money, Jeremy knew the people Gary represented wouldn't care about that.

Meanwhile, the woman he held in his arms didn't deserve any of this.

Tempted to kiss her, he stepped back instead, unable to force himself to let go.

"I'd like you to come to Mikki's with me tonight," he told her. Her eyes widened, but she didn't immediately say no.

Taking that as a small sign of encouragement, he continued. "By now, everyone knows that Russell's been seen. No one will dare accuse you of anything. Maybe they'll even apologize."

She snorted at the last sentence. "I doubt that."

Smiling, he shrugged. "But think about how nice it would be to go out in public without having to deal with any haters."

When she stepped back and crossed her arms, clearly unconvinced, he persisted. "Plus, you'd get to hang out with me."

"I hang out with you every day," she countered.

"Not in public. Think about that. I'm pretty sure Russell has no idea I'm back. If he sees us together, that might draw him out."

"I should have known you had an ulterior motive," she said. But her smile told him she took no offense. "Sure, I'll go with you tonight. I could use a drink after all this." Her smile faltered. "I'm sorry. I forgot."

What could he do but reach for her again. He pulled her in close and held her. "I meant it when I say alcohol isn't an issue with me. I choose not to drink, just to stay on the safe side. But, as I've said, I have absolutely no problem being around others who do. If you want wine or a cocktail, go for it. My club soda with a twist of lime makes me happy."

"It's a date then," she said, raising her face to his, her radiant smile back in place.

A date. He liked the sound of that. As if she knew his thoughts, her smile widened.

He kissed her then, marveling at how such a simple thing as seeing her happy made him feel buoyant inside. She kissed him back, the tenderness in her embrace letting him know she felt the same.

For the first time ever, he realized he could love this woman. The knowledge so startled him that he stepped away, breaking the embrace.

"You know, I never did get to go look for places to lease for my dog training business," he said, needing to focus on something else. He dragged his hand through his hair, hoping she didn't see through him. "Since you're not working today, do you want to go downtown with me and see what's available?"

Though the abrupt change in subject appeared to bemuse her, she rolled with it. "Sure. I know you talked to Walker at the real estate office, but I'm guessing you only discussed Russell, not properties."

"Correct." He checked his watch. "I thought I'd see what might be vacant and scout the place out before I try to negotiate a price. I don't need something right on Main Street, since my business won't be the type to depend on foot traffic."

"Okay. We can either park on Main and walk around, which would help with our visibility, or just drive until you see something you're interested in. I'll leave that up to you." She smiled again, and his chest felt tight.

"Probably use the truck at first," he managed to say.

"Okay. Give me about five minutes to get ready." And she strolled out of the room.

For a moment he couldn't breathe, couldn't move, couldn't do anything but think about how much he wanted her. While he had no idea if she felt the same, in the end it didn't matter. If he ever hoped to work things out with Russell, getting together with Holly in any way could be an insurmountable obstacle. At least until he'd talked to his brother, sleeping together couldn't happen again, and Jeremy needed to make sure it didn't.

Except he wasn't sure he wanted to stop. Not now, not ever.

A few minutes later, Holly came back into the room. Still wearing her cutoff shorts and tank top, she'd pulled her long hair into a ponytail, adding a baseball cap and sneakers. She looked like the most beautiful girl next door he'd ever seen.

"Are you ready?" she asked, stopping short when she caught sight of the no doubt fierce expression on his face. "Or have you changed your mind?"

He managed to get his act together enough to smile. "I'm good to go. Let's do this."

After promising Thor he could come next time, they left. She climbed into his truck and buckled in. Her smile once again made him feel on top of the world.

Though Blake was a small town, at different points in history, overzealous investors had either built or renovated various commercial structures. Main Street itself had four or five empty buildings, but with that prime location, rent or sale prices were higher.

The streets that fed into Main were still close enough, but less popular. Jeremy hoped to lease or purchase one of those properties. He hadn't mentioned the possibility of buying rather than renting, mostly because he hadn't run any numbers, so he wasn't sure such a thing would be doable.

Today he supposed he'd be finding out.

Riding with Holly in the front seat of his truck, he had the windows down and country music on the radio. He almost felt like a teenager again, though in reality there had been too much water under the bridge since then.

Once they reached Main, he turned left on Seventh Street. There were several small businesses here, though if one continued on, it became residential.

"I don't see anything vacant," Holly pointed out.

They continued on like this for a bit, turning on Elm, and then back up on Sixth to Main. This time they crossed over and drove up the other side. They passed a couple of empty storefronts with For Rent signs in the window, but neither of them struck Jeremy as the right thing.

"You don't even want to look?" Holly asked. "I think they might be bigger than they look from the street."

"They probably are." He shrugged and kept driving. "But I have something particular in mind."

It wasn't until he'd reached Second Street that he saw it, the For Sale or Rent sign faded from the sun. Two stories, an older brick building on the corner, with a side entrance to what at one point must have been a small warehouse.

He quickly pulled over and parked at the curb.

"The old McMillian building," he said, unable to keep the satisfaction from his voice. "When I was a teen, we used to break in here and hang out. It's going to need some work, but it has everything I want."

Smiling at his enthusiasm, she jumped out of the truck as soon as he put it in park and came around to wait for him. As soon as his feet hit the ground, she took his hand.

Surprised, then pleased, he squeezed her fingers. Together they went to the front door, trying to see through the dirty glass. The lack of light made it difficult to make out much about the interior, but unless things had changed, he knew how to get in.

Holly tried the door with no luck. "It's locked," she said.

"This way." Feeling like a daredevil kid again, he led her over to the back entrance. This door was also locked, which he'd expected. Pushing aside a thick clump of weeds, he located the familiar, rusted metal box. "It's still here," he marveled. "Hard to believe."

Twisting off the top, he exhaled with relief to see the key still inside. Taking it out, he held it out triumphantly. "Unreal."

"Maybe kids still use it," she said.

"Maybe," he replied, though he privately doubted it. When he and his friends had gotten bored with the place, they hadn't told anyone else about it. At least not that he knew of.

He fit the key into the lock and opened the back door. Before going inside, he turned and pressed a quick kiss on her mouth. "It's going to be filthy in here. And there will likely be rats and bugs."

"So?" she shrugged. "I'm sure you'll protect me." And she slipped her arm through his.

Feeling like a king, he grinned down at her.

Together, they went inside.

Spiderwebs draped like curtains in the corners, and something that might have been a rat scuttled across a dark area near the wall. He wished he'd thought to bring a flashlight, but he could use the one on his phone. Plus the dirty windows set high in the wall provided just enough light for him to realize this large space would be perfect to set up a place to work dogs.

"The front has larger windows," he said, liking how Holly kept hold of his arm and stayed close to him.

They picked their way over years of debris and went up to the front. They reached what looked like it had once been a reception area. To the left sat a decent-sized office.

"This is it," he told her. "Once I get electricity turned on and get the place cleaned up, it's exactly where I want to start my business."

"What's upstairs?" she asked. "I don't see the staircase, but I'm sure it's around here somewhere."

"It's in that back room. There's an apartment up there. I'm not sure it's safe to go up though. I'll have to get an inspection, first."

She nodded. "Have you ever been?"

"Yes. A bunch of us went up there once when we were here but got spooked and didn't stay long. I have no idea what kind of condition it might be in."

"I see."

He led her back outside, careful to lock the back door and to replace the key in its hiding place. "Let's go talk to Walker."

"Don't you want to think it over first?"

Instead of immediately responding, he wrapped his arms around her and kissed her again. "Nope. When you know, you know."

She shivered, making him wonder if she understood the double meaning behind his words. "Well, this place has clearly been empty for a long time. I have to wonder if they'd be willing to make the necessary repairs to get it up to code so you can lease it."

"I'm planning on buying it," he said. "I'm not sure who owns it, but I suspect it might be Walker. I have a feeling he might let it go for cheap."

Chapter 13

Once they got back in the truck, Holly tried again to convince Jeremy to sleep on his decision to make an offer on the building. But he wasn't having it.

"I want to talk to Walker now," he informed her, smiling so wide she couldn't help but smile back. "That place has been vacant so long, I'm sure he'll be happy to unload it. It'll be perfect for what I need. And if the upstairs living area isn't too bad, once I get it fixed up, I'll have a place to stay."

She felt a twinge at the thought of him moving out. Ridiculous, but she'd actually started to like having him around.

They drove the short distance to the Realtor's office and parked. When they went inside, Walker stood at the front counter, writing something in a notebook. He frowned when he saw Jeremy. And then raised his bushy brow at the sight of Holly.

"I don't have anything else to add to what I've already told you," Walker said. "Yes, I've heard that Russell's been spotted. I can't wait to see if he's going to be stupid enough to try and poke his head in here."

"That's not why I'm here," Jeremy told him. "I wanted

to talk to you about the empty building on the corner of Second and Elm."

"What about it?" Walker crossed his beefy arms, still scowling.

"How much is it?" Jeremy asked. "I'm guessing despite how faded the sign is, that it's still for sale. Do you know who owns it?"

Glaring at them, Walker shook head. "Like either of you don't know. The For Sale or Lease sign is old, and I should have taken it down a long time ago. I no longer represent that property or speak to the owner."

Clearly unsure how to respond to that, Jeremy glanced at Holly. As a sudden thought occurred to her, she took a step forward. "Walker, are you saying that Russell owns that building?"

Next to her, Jeremy cursed under his breath.

Something in her soft tone must have made Walker realize they truly hadn't had any idea. "Yes. He has for years. He bought it for a song from the Wilkerson estate when old man Wilkerson passed. Russell originally planned to renovate it and move his company there."

"But he didn't," Jeremy said, stating the obvious.

"No. When he started having problems, he could barely handle his employees or the space he did have. Never mind taking on major renovations. He put that old building up for sale or rent, even though he knew it would sit there vacant, the same way it had for decades. That didn't seem to bother him, so I figured he must have gotten a decent tax write-off or something."

"And then he sold his company," Holly mused.

Walker looked away. "Right."

"He must have purchased the building after I left town,

because he and I were barely making anything back in those days."

"He did," Walker agreed. "I'd say you'd been gone at least a couple years by the time his tech company really took off."

"A bunch of us used to skip school and hang out inside there," Jeremy said.

Shrugging, Walker didn't seem surprised.

"I wonder if he completely forgot about it," Holly said. "Because he certainly never mentioned it to me. You know how much Russell liked to brag about his accomplishments. I can't imagine him leaving something like this out."

Walker laughed. "I can. That property still isn't worth much, though I can say he'd get more than he paid for it if he found someone foolish enough to buy it. The likely reason he never told you is because he was probably embarrassed."

Privately, Holly doubted that. Russell's overconfident personality had seemed to make him immune to shame. And since real estate in Alaska cost a lot more than in Texas, it wouldn't have been out of character for him to want to show off the place. Because even she could see, with repairs, the property had potential.

Taking Holly's arm, Jeremy thanked him. He waited until they were both inside his truck before speaking. "I have to wonder if that's where Russell has been staying."

Thunderstruck, she stared. "What? Why would you think that? It's in the middle of town. Someone would have seen him coming and going."

"Not if he wore a disguise."

"He'd need food," she said, still not convinced. "Where would he get that?"

"He could have started stockpiling before he left," he replied.

"Eighteen months' worth?" She shook her head. "I highly doubt it. Even you have to admit that's a long shot."

"Maybe. But we didn't go upstairs. That's where the living quarters are."

"Do you want to go back?" she asked. "If we go up and check it out, will that help put your mind at ease?"

He thought for a moment before shaking his head. "No. We'll check it out another time. Let's go home and let Thor out and get ready to go to Mikki's."

While she appreciated the way he considered her dog, she would have preferred to put this to rest once and for all. Because if it turned out Russell had truly been staying in an abandoned building close to downtown, she was going to be furious. After all the accusations that had been hurled at her, the verbal abuse and amount of gossip flying around town for the last year and a half, the idea that he might have been right under their noses all along made his disappearance even less palatable.

"Do you think he might have drugs stored up there too?" she asked. "If he had a large quantity and intended to distribute them, he would have needed a larger market than Blake."

"I'd thought of that," Jeremy admitted. "Which is why I figured he must have gone to Anchorage or maybe even as far as Fairbanks or Juneau. Blake is just too small to have much of a market for that kind of thing."

"I'd think Gary and the people he works for would know that," she continued. "I didn't know about the drugs, so I assumed Russell had some remote cabin out in the wilderness."

He grimaced. "But what about food? While some people could easily live off the grid, Russell never was much of an outdoorsman."

"He must have changed after you left," she said. "Because he was always bragging about hunts he'd been on. He also loved to fish, especially salmon. I figured with that amount of skill, he'd have survived quite well on his own."

"Interesting." He finally started the truck. "I wonder who he hunted with? And usually, people who are into that sort of thing have trophies all around the house."

"I didn't think of that," she admitted. "But while I later learned Russell was an accomplished liar, why would he make up something like that? Especially since he knows how I feel about animals."

Jeremy didn't answer, just drove them back to the house. His lack of comment made her think. In the beginning of her relationship with Russell, he'd seemed overly insistent that she see him as masculine. Having prowess as a hunter would fit that scenario.

Thor greeted them both, plumed tail wagging. Holly took him out back, where he happily trotted off to take care of his business.

When she got back inside, Jeremy had disappeared into his room and closed the door behind him.

Still thinking about the day's revelations, she wondered why she'd never seen any reference to the Second Street property in any of Russell's papers. He'd always been meticulous about keeping records.

When Jeremy emerged, she mentioned it to him.

"Did he have a safe deposit box at Blake Community Bank?" he asked. "That's where most people keep important papers like deeds."

She thought for a moment. "If he did, he never mentioned it to me."

"Which means if he did, neither of us would be able to

get in to see the contents. We wouldn't be authorized, so there's nothing we can do."

Feeling a sudden need to get out of the house, she checked the time. "Too early," she said out loud. "Maybe I should take Thor for a walk."

"Too early for what?" he asked. "To go to Mikki's?"

"Yep." She shook her head at herself. "It's weird because since Russell took off, I've gotten used to staying mostly at home. Sure, I went in to work at Murphy's, but beyond that I've mostly avoided doing anything socially. Other than that time you and I went to have dinner."

"And that horrible woman tried to ruin your night." He took her arm. "Nothing like that is going to happen tonight, I promise you."

As he pulled her close and kissed her, she leaned in to his embrace. When they broke apart, they simply stood forehead to forehead, both breathing heavily.

"I'm going to go walk Thor," she finally said, taking a step back. "You're welcome to come if you'd like."

But he shook his head. "I've got some more research to do online."

"About that property?" she asked.

"Yes. That, and a few other things. And since clearly Russell doesn't know about the hidden key, at some point soon, I want to go back and see if he is staying upstairs."

Though the very idea made her heart race, she nodded. Grabbing Thor's leash, she called him. Since he knew exactly what the leash in her hand meant, he lumbered over quickly.

Clipping it to his collar, she took her dog outside, all the while trying to imagine what her life would look like if Russell returned. She couldn't imagine living there with her ex-fiancé and his brother, who happened to be the man she was falling in love with.

Confessing her growing feelings, even to herself, should have stopped her in her tracks. Instead, she and Thor kept walking. She wasn't surprised at all. The more time she spent with Jeremy, the more she realized he might be someone with whom she could be with for the rest of her life. While she'd made a huge mistake over Russell, this time her heart wasn't leading her wrong. She just knew it.

However, she wanted to take things slow, and give their burgeoning relationship more time. While she couldn't say with any amount of certainty how Jeremy felt, she suspected they were likely on the same page. Or at least she hoped so.

By the time she returned home, her mind had cleared. While she still wasn't sure what kind of criminals Russell had gotten involved with, Gary had made it clear they weren't messing around. If Russell didn't show up and either pay his debt or give them back their property, his bosses would take it out on her. And Jeremy.

She had no idea how much Russell owed them, but it had to be a substantial amount for Gary to go through so much trouble.

Thor immediately went and got a drink of water before heaving a contented sigh and curling up in his dog bed.

She found Jeremy sitting at the kitchen table, working on the laptop.

"Did you have a nice walk?" he asked, closing it. "I don't know about you, but walking or hiking outside always helps me think."

"How much money do you think Russell owes?" she asked, shocking herself. Blurting out the question hadn't been something she'd planned.

"I don't know," Jeremy answered quietly. "But it must be a lot. Probably even more than either of us could come up with, even with my settlement money."

"You're using that to start your business," she reminded him, suddenly worried that whatever Russell had gotten involved in would take Jeremy's future away.

"I know." Expression pensive, he shrugged. "I'm going to get ready to head to Mikki's."

Leaving the laptop on the table, he got up and left the room.

The temptation to open the computer and see what he'd been working on had her wavering. In the end, she walked past the table and headed down the hall toward her bedroom to get ready for her big night on the town.

Though initially she'd been looking forward to going out for dinner and a drink with Jeremy, her old, familiar mindset had her nerves quivering as they drove into Blake. She clasped her hands in her lap and stared out the window, unable to keep from imaging various potential scenarios.

Her uncharacteristic silence must have signaled her ambivalence. When Jeremy touched her arm, she started.

"Are you okay?" he asked, his tone kind.

"I'm not sure." Answering honestly, she took a shaky breath. "I guess I have no idea what to expect."

They turned onto Main Street, which meant they were nearly there. Though her stomach clenched, she kept her head up. "I've been rehearsing what to say if anyone gives me grief."

Once he'd parked, he turned to face her. "I'm sorry you had to endure all that. Russell should have done more to protect you."

Curious, she eyed him. "What do you mean?"

"Well, from my conversation with Tanya, he's let everyone believe you're staying rent free in his house, using his vehicle. He didn't mention the fact that it's half yours. Or that he gifted you the vehicle."

"I'd think the house at least would be common knowledge," she said, frowning. "Walker handled the sale, so he knows."

"But Tanya and her friends have no idea. Not only that, but she stopped short of calling you a liar. She did imply that I was gullible for believing you."

Holly snorted. "Of course she did. I'm kind of hoping she comes in here tonight. I'd really like to talk to her."

His answering grin made her laugh out loud. "I dare you," he said. "Because I'm not sure who would be more surprised, you or her."

After killing the engine, he got out and came around to the passenger side to open her door. She let him help her from the truck, glad she'd changed into a cute sundress instead of her cutoff shorts.

Holding on to Jeremy's arm, she allowed him to lead her toward the door.

When Holly had emerged wearing another short sundress, highlighting her long legs, Jeremy had caught his breath. He'd come close to sweeping her into his arms and showing her how beautiful he found her. Instead, he'd stayed put and whistled softly. "You look amazing."

She blushed and smiled. "Thank you."

Smiling back, he barely managed to get control over his arousal. He constantly marveled at how strongly she affected him. And she appeared completed unaware, which tempted him to show her.

But he'd convinced her to go out with him tonight and didn't want to do anything to jeopardize that. Holly deserved the chance to enjoy a nice night out. He wanted to see her regain her confidence and come into her own. As far as he was concerned, there wasn't another woman in the entire town who could hold a candle to her.

On the short drive to Mikki's, he had to force himself to keep his attention on the road. If he looked at Holly, with her short skirt and those shapely legs that went on forever, he'd be hard again. Walking into the bar like that would not only be uncomfortable, but it just wasn't something he wanted to do.

Meanwhile, Holly remained lost in her own thoughts, oblivious.

"It's going to be fine," he finally promised, taking her arm.

"Let's hope so," she said under her breath and moved close, linking her arm with his.

He loved the way she stayed by his side as they entered. He realized he wanted to show her off, to shout to anyone and everyone that this beautiful woman was with him. The place wasn't yet packed, though a decent-sized crowd had started to gather. He recognized many of the same people from his other two visits.

"Do you want to sit at the bar or at a table?" he asked.

"Table, please." She glanced around. "This might sound weird, but I'm not comfortable sitting with my back to the room."

Startled, he nodded. "That sounds like something I would have learned in prison," he told her, only half joking. "But I get it, believe me."

They found a table in a quiet corner. Holly snagged a chair facing the rest of the bar. "I like to see who's coming toward me. That way, there are no surprises."

Dropping into his chair, he covered her hand with his. "You've been through hell since Russell left, haven't you?"

"I tried to tell you." Looking around the room, she rolled her shoulders. "A woman jumped me one time, right after he vanished. I won't be caught like that again."

Aching for her, he wanted to chew out his brother for what he'd put her through. How Russell could have gone from claiming to love her enough to get her to leave her entire life behind to be with him, to treating her as an afterthought, infuriated him.

Mikki came over, her broad smile when she caught sight of Holly welcoming. "I'm glad to see you," she said. "Whatever you want to drink is on the house."

Holly's eyes widened. "You don't have to do that," she protested. "I'm more than happy to pay."

Shaking her head, Mikki placed her hand on Holly's shoulder. "Honey, let me do this one small thing for you. There'll be plenty of opportunities for you to buy your own drinks in the future."

Hearing this, Holly relented. "Thank you," she said softly.

Mikki smiled and went and got their drinks. A glass of white wine for Holly and a club soda with a lime for Jeremy. After she brought them, she glanced toward the door and stiffened. "Don't look now," she warned. "But Tanya just sashayed on in here."

Immediately, Holly tensed. Shooting her a sympathetic look, Mikki rushed back to the bar, where the small group of women were taking seats. As usual, Tanya had clearly taken pains to outdo them, from her expensive stiletto shoes to her tight-fitting designer jeans. Her platinum blond hair rippled in perfectly curled waves down her back.

She looked, Jeremy thought, like a woman on the prowl. Glancing across the table at Holly, once again he thought there was no competition. Holly's beauty was without artifice, a natural glow that he found far sexier.

"Great," Holly muttered. "She came with her posse. I'm thinking we should leave."

"If that's what you want to do, we can," Jeremy agreed. "But we haven't even eaten yet. I hate to let her ruin our night out."

Holly took a sip of her wine, glancing over at the group of women who now sat with their backs to the room. "I just don't want to have anything to do with her. As long as she stays over there and leaves me alone, I have no problem with staying."

He wasn't sure whether to feel relieved or panicked. He'd only spoken with Tanya once. He had no idea if she'd become confrontational once she caught sight of Holly.

Mikki apparently had similar concerns. When she returned to take their order, she planted herself squarely in between them and the group at the bar.

"I'll have a cheeseburger and fries please," Holly said, draining the rest of her wine in one gulp. "And a refill of this wine."

"You got it." Mikki turned to Jeremy, who also ordered a cheeseburger and fries.

"Thanks for being so kind," Holly said, her back ramrod straight.

"I'm just happy you didn't leave," Mikki replied, patting her on the shoulder. "If there's any hint of trouble with those women, I'll stop it before it starts," she promised. Then she walked away before either of them could comment.

He glanced at Holly, who had taken to openly watching Tanya and her friends. He wanted to tell her that the other woman hadn't seemed that bad, but then he wasn't the one who'd been tormented for the past eighteen months.

Mikki returned with Holly's wine. "Your food should be out shortly," she said.

Just then, Tanya turned to survey the room. She locked eyes with Jeremy, before spotting Holly sitting across from him. Her heavily made-up eyes narrowed.

Tensing, Jeremy got ready to put himself in between the two women. Except Mikki had also noticed and hurried over to Tanya, making sure to block her line of vision.

"That's okay," Tanya said, apparently replying loudly to something Mikki had asked. "I can talk to anyone I want."

Sensing drama, the rest of the room fell silent.

"You can't start trouble in my place," Mikki told her. "I mean it. You let them eat their dinner in peace."

With an angry flounce, Tanya turned away from them, back to face the bar.

"Crisis averted. For now." Holly sighed. "To be honest, if I wasn't so hungry, I'd leave."

"But then you'd be letting her win," he said, angry on her behalf.

"You don't understand," she replied, her voice soft. "It's not a competition. And I don't believe you can fight hate with more hate or anger with more anger. I don't care if she thinks she wins. She can have a damn trophy if that's what she wants. I just want her to leave me alone. Is that so much to ask?"

"No, it's not." He'd never respected her more. He wasn't sure he could ever have that level of willpower. The temptation to fight back, to gain the upper hand, had been ingrained in him for far too long.

Their burgers arrived, and they dug in. A few more groups of people came in and the noise level got a little louder.

Holly picked up the second half of her burger and paused

mid-bite, looking up. "What can I do for you, Tanya?" she asked, her tone cold.

Damn it. Jeremy put down his food and blotted his mouth with his napkin. "We're in the middle of our meal," he said.

"I see that." Tanya's bright red lips curved in a smile and her eyes glittered. "I just thought it might be time to clear the air, that's all."

Though Holly stiffened, she didn't respond. When Jeremy opened his mouth to speak, she gave a slight shake of her head.

"I'd like to apologize," Tanya said quietly. "Now that I know Russell's alive, my accusations were wrong. I never should have treated you the way I have. I'm sorry."

Jeremy held his breath. Whatever he'd expected Tanya to say, this wasn't it. The question was, how would Holly react?

"Thank you for that," Holly said, dipping her chin in acknowledgment. "Now, if you don't mind, I'd like to go back to my burger."

But Tanya didn't leave. "I just have one question." The urgency in her tone made Jeremy wonder. "Have you talked to Russell? I know he's okay, but when is he going to come home?"

"I haven't heard from him," Holly admitted. "Hopefully, he'll reappear soon."

Tanya's eyes filled. "I love him, you know."

"I suspected as much." Holly picked up her burger again, a clear dismissal. This time, Tanya took the hint and turned and walked away. She rejoined her friends at the bar.

Not sure what to say, Jeremy settled on nothing. He and Holly finished their meal in silence.

When he was able to catch Mikki's eye, he signaled for the check. Mikki hurried over. "Tanya paid for you both," she said, not bothering to hide her surprise. "I'm guessing she's trying to make up for being so horrible."

"Maybe so." Holly still sounded detached. She slugged back the rest of her wine, and when she stood, she appeared to be a bit unsteady on her feet.

He put his hand around her waist to help steady her. Expressionless, she glanced at him but didn't move away.

Back out at the truck, he opened her door. She climbed up inside, still without speaking. When he went around and got in, he realized tears were silently streaming down her face.

For a heartbeat, he wasn't sure how to react. Though he didn't know if she'd rebuff him or not, he reached over and pulled her in for a hug. At first, she held herself stiffly, but she finally relaxed into him, sniffling.

After a moment, she sat back, wiping at her face with the back of her hand. "Sorry about that," she murmured. "It just struck me what a mess all this has become. Alaska, Russell, Tanya, all of it."

He tried to ignore the sudden stab of hurt her words brought. "Things will get better," he promised.

"They have to." The grimness in her tone made him swallow.

She didn't speak again until they were pulling into her driveway. "One positive thing about tonight," she said. "Tanya won't be bothering me anymore."

Turning in his seat to face her, he nodded. "I'm sorry."

"Not your fault." She unclipped her seat belt and opened her door. "And you were right. I shouldn't have to spend the rest of my life avoiding her. Or anyone."

That said, she marched on into the house, not looking back to see if he followed.

Chapter 14

Though Jeremy had been nothing but kind, Holly didn't feel up to discussing her feelings with him right now. She'd seen the stricken expression he'd tried to hide when she'd rashly spoken her thoughts out loud.

She hadn't meant him. In fact, at this moment he was the one thing she didn't regret. The relationship they'd begun to form might not go anywhere, or it might become everything. It was just too soon to tell. Trying to figure out her feelings for him and how he'd fit in her life made her nervous and hopeful all at the same time.

If only there wasn't so much else going on, she'd simply like to bask in the joy of just being with him. Unfortunately, now wasn't the time for that.

Truth be told, the mental gymnastics of the past few days were exhausting. Russell had been seen, they'd learned he owned a downtown building that he'd never mentioned before, and Tanya had apologized to her. Russell might return to the house they shared ownership of, and she had to figure out whether to sell her half to him or attempt to buy him out. They damn sure wouldn't be living together, not ever again.

Though she'd gone to the kitchen to get water, Jeremy didn't follow her. Instead, he turned on the TV and sat on the couch. She liked that he didn't pressure her, instead giving her the option to talk to him or not.

Right now, slightly tipsy, she decided her best bet would be to turn in early.

As she walked past the living room, she glanced at him, intending to say good-night. Sprawled out on her couch, he'd kicked his shoes off. Though he appeared intent on whatever he was watching, the awareness instantly sparking between them had to alert him to her presence.

Slowly, he swung his head around to look at her. When he met her gaze, the heat blazing from his eyes made her stomach drop and her body clench. Her mouth went dry and her steps faltered.

"Um, good night?" She hadn't meant to turn a statement into a question.

"Good night," he replied, his sensual smile making her reconsider her options. But then he turned his attention back to his television show, a clear dismissal.

Aware she shouldn't be disappointed, she forced herself to move. When she reached the solace of her bedroom, she closed the door and sat down on the edge of her bed.

Some things were complicated. But the way Jeremy made her feel, even with a simple glance, wasn't. She got herself ready to turn in early, hoping she would have enough willpower not to wander into his bedroom in the middle of the night.

Somehow, she managed to sleep like a log, waking only to realize early morning had arrived. Sunlight streamed in through her curtains, warm and welcoming. She got up, winced when she discovered she had a twinge of a headache and hurried into the kitchen to make coffee. First, she let Thor out, standing on the back porch to watch over him. When he finished and came bounding up to her, she fed him breakfast before filling her mug and sitting at the table to drink it.

Down the hall she heard the sound of the shower starting, which meant Jeremy had gotten up. As she sipped her coffee, she briefly contemplated joining him. Just thinking about standing under the spray, water glistening on his muscular body, made her melt.

Since she knew it would warm up quite a bit later, she decided instead to take advantage of the beautiful weather. She unlocked and opened all the windows, planning to enjoy the moderate temperatures and the fresh breeze. She opened the back door too, glad for the screen mesh she'd hung there to keep the bugs out. When she got to the one over the kitchen sink, she had to get a step stool, since that one always stuck. As always, Thor followed her from room to room, his toenails clicking on the hardwood.

Pushing and tugging, she finally managed to get the window up. She wasn't sure which she became aware of first, the figure of a man standing outside, or the smell of gasoline.

She turned so fast that she nearly tumbled from the stool. Thor barked once, a warning, before he hit the screen mesh on the back door, running full out, ignoring her attempts to call him back.

Screaming for Jeremy, she jumped down and rushed outside after her beloved dog. She rounded the corner just in time to see him charging a man in a gray hoodie holding a gas can and a lit, rolled piece of newspaper.

She froze. Thor leaped, and then it all happened at once. The gas spilled and the blazing newspaper fell. Immediately, fire flared to life. The man ran.

Thor went after him, ears flat and teeth bared. Holly

yelled at him to come. The command, plus the terror in her voice brought him back.

She screamed again, from pain this time, realizing she was on fire. It hurt. Damn, it hurt bad.

Then Jeremy was there, knocking her to the ground, covering her with his body to put out the flames. Crying, gasping for air, she called Thor's name, needing to make sure he was okay.

"He's here, he's here," Jeremy soothed. But she couldn't stop sobbing until Thor pushed his cold nose under her chin and licked her face.

"It's okay," Jeremy promised, still holding her. She realized in his effort to save her, he'd gotten burned on his arms and hands.

A loud crack sounded, then a whoosh and a blast of heat. Thor barked, nudging Holly as if he wanted to herd her away.

"The house!" Yanking her up, Jeremy pulled her away from the inferno that the back part of the house had become. Immediately, he called the three-digit emergency code the town had put in place since they didn't have access to 911. While Blake only had a volunteer fire department, Holly knew they were the best hope to extinguish this blaze.

"They'll be here in a few minutes," he shouted. "For now, I'll do what I can."

Running for the house, he turned the spigot on and, despite his burned hands, began to frantically spray water on the fire.

Watching him, Holly doubled over, coughing. When she could finally breathe again, she realized her arms and hands hurt. She had numerous burns, the worst of which were on her legs and feet. She checked Thor over thoroughly too, but luckily her dog seemed uninjured.

Meanwhile, the flames roared higher and higher, eating up the wood frame of the house. Jeremy continued to try and battle the fire, but his attempts had minimal effect. The back part, which contained the guest bedroom, would be a total loss.

After what seemed like far too long, the volunteer fire department pulled up. They'd recently gotten some new high-tech fire retardant system and got to work immediately deploying it.

Jeremy dropped the hose and came over to her. "Are you all right?" he asked, his voice husky from the smoke.

She nodded, eyeing the peeling skin on the bottom of his hands. "I think so. How about you?"

"I'll survive." Glancing behind her, his jaw tightened. "The mayor is here."

When she turned, he kept his arm around her shoulders. Gaze locked on her, Greg approached. "I got a call about this fire," he said. "I've notified the state police."

"Thank you," Holly replied, leaning into Jeremy, appreciating the comfort of his solid, strong body. Pointing to her blistered legs, she then carefully lifted one of Jeremy's hands to show the mayor. "We both got burned, but I think we'll be okay. And the guy who set this took off." She petted Thor. "My dog chased him, but I called him back before he could get hurt."

"Did you get a good look at the guy?" Greg asked, looking from one to the other.

"No," Holly replied. "All I can tell you is that he was wearing a gray hoodie and had the hood pulled down to hide his face. Average height and build. Nothing unusual."

Now finally the mayor directed his gaze to Jeremy. "Where were you when all this happened?"

Though Jeremy stiffened, he replied cordially. "I was

right here. Inside the house. I came running as soon as I heard Holly screaming."

"I see."

Behind them, someone shouted. Holly turned back to look, saw they were making good progress on extinguishing the fire and exhaled. Another bout of coughing shook her. Jeremy lightly patted her on the back until she could breathe again. Thor pressed his huge body against her leg, offering his support as well.

Meanwhile, Greg shifted his weight from one foot to the other, appearing uncomfortable. "You both should know that I got a call from someone claiming they witnessed Holly starting this fire."

"What?" Holly couldn't believe it. "That's a lie. I was inside opening the windows when I saw the man with the gas can. There." She pointed at the gas can still lying on its side where it had fallen when the man had dropped it. "And where was this supposed witness anyway? The only other person out here was the guy who started the fire."

"I'm not saying I believe it," Greg continued. "In fact, I'll let the state troopers sort this all out. But I wanted you to know what I was told."

"Who called you?" Jeremy asked. "We deserve to know who's making these ludicrous accusations."

"They didn't give their name."

"Male or female?" Jeremy persisted, earning a hard look from Greg.

"Female."

"Tanya," Holly and Jeremy said, simultaneously.

"Possibly," Greg admitted. "Though now that she knows Russell's been spotted, I don't know why she'd continue to hold a grudge against you." He paused. "Plus I heard from a reputable source that she apologized to you last night at Mikki's."

"Who knows why Tanya does what she does." Holly didn't even try to keep the bitterness from her voice. "But I have no reason to want to destroy the place where I live. I own half of this house. This is the second fire. Jeremy and I were able to extinguish a smaller one a few days ago. I want whoever did this caught."

"I do too," Jeremy said, tightening his grip on her shoulders.

"We've almost got it out," one of the firefighters shouted. "Looks like a couple of rooms will have major damage. We'll know more once it's safe enough to take a look inside."

Greg walked past them, going over to inspect the smoldering structure.

"There's not only going to be smoke damage, but water damage too," Jeremy pointed out, his voice low. "I'm not even sure we'll be able to stay in this house."

Horrified, she put her fist to her mouth. "I don't have anywhere to go. A lot of the places that rent rooms or apartments won't allow a dog as big as Thor. And I won't leave him behind." She tangled her hands in her beloved pet's fur.

"Of course not," Jeremy agreed. "If worse comes to worst, we can check out the upstairs living space on that building Russell owns downtown."

"The one he might be living in? No thanks."

He flashed her a wry grin. "We don't know that. We were merely speculating. It wouldn't hurt to check it out."

Glancing once again at the home she'd come to love, her heart ached. "Maybe not. But I want to wait and see if this house is still inhabitable first."

Though his expression told her he thought that wouldn't be likely, he simply nodded.

The mayor left, lifting his hand in a wave as he walked past. Holly tried not to worry about the way he left without a more heartfelt goodbye. She'd known things were tense between him and Jeremy. Apparently, that now extended to her too.

"It looks like most of the fire is out," Jeremy said, drawing her attention back to the house. Everything appeared to be covered in wet foam, but at least the flames had been extinguished.

One of the firefighters noticed them looking and came over. "We're just about finished up. We just need to make sure there aren't any hot spots that might flare back up."

Holly nodded. "It looks really bad."

"I think there's structural damage," he said. "You really need to have it inspected. I hope you have somewhere else you can stay tonight."

Struggling not to show her despair, Holly summoned up what she hoped looked like a pleasant smile. "We were just discussing that. Thank you for all you did to try and save my house."

"You're welcome." He looked from them to the house. "My advice is to not go inside. It's not safe."

Again she thanked him. Luckily, the kitchen, garage and her art studio weren't close to the damaged part. Still, even from the outside, she could see that the water and foam appeared to be everywhere. She wasn't sure how her belongings, like furniture and clothing, could have possibly survived intact. She could only hope her artwork had managed to stay undamaged.

"Whoever did this has a lot to answer for," she said,

trying to hide her heartbreak. Sitting by her side, Thor leaned into her leg, his own way of offering comfort.

Watching Holly try to be strong only made Jeremy wish he could do something to help her. While he didn't know for sure who'd started this fire, his first suspects would be Gary and his mob of drug dealers. First suspects? Try only suspects. Gary ought to be glad he wasn't around right now. If he had been, Jeremy wasn't sure if he'd be able to restrain himself. Threats were bad enough. But doing something like this to someone who'd had nothing to do with the initial deal was an entirely new level of wrong. Not that criminals cared about that sort of thing.

Once the fire truck and volunteer firefighters left, Holly dropped her facade of strength and crumpled. It broke Jeremy's heart to see her wrap her arms around herself and fold. Luckily, he stood close enough to reach over and grab her. He pulled her close, brushing the hair away from her sooty forehead. "It's going to be okay," he promised, even though he had no idea if it would. Whatever it took, he'd do his best to help her life regain some semblance of normalcy.

Clutching him, she held on, silent but not crying either. He willed her strength, even though she was already one of the strongest women he knew. When she finally pushed herself out of his arms, she lifted her chin. "I'm going to make a few phone calls. I think the nearest building inspector is in Anchorage, so it might be a bit before I can get someone out. But I need to get on the schedule so I can see how much of this mess is salvageable."

"I think I know someone here in town," he said slowly. "Fred Stovall. He gave a talk at my high school once on career day. He was a traveling building inspector, going around to all the remote villages. He's likely retired now, but let me see if I can get his number so you can give him a call."

Her grateful smile was all the thanks he'd ever need. "That would be awesome," she said.

He pulled out his phone and sent a text to Mikki. Mikki knew everyone and would know how to reach Fred if he was still in town.

She texted back immediately to let him know that not only did Fred live just down the street from them, but he was only semiretired. He occasionally did freelance work when someone in the area needed him, only charging a small fee. And then she texted him the number, mentioning she'd heard about Holly's fire and sending her well wishes.

Forwarding Mikki's text to Holly, he repeated the rest of her message.

Holly immediately called the number. Apparently, she got voicemail. She left her name, number and the reason for her call before returning her phone to her back pocket. "Now I just hope he calls me back soon."

Aching for her, he nodded. "Now what? We've got to find a place to stay, at least for a few nights." Privately, he thought it would be much longer, but he didn't want to contribute to her despair.

She sighed. "I guess we'd better go check out that building in town," she said, meeting his gaze. "But I think we should have a plan in case it turns out that Russell is living inside."

"I agree. Maybe there's someone who wouldn't mind renting out a couple of rooms short-term."

"We'll have to ask around," she replied. "I know Kip has in the past, but usually a single room, not two. But then we don't have to stay at the same place." She took a deep breath. "And I refuse to leave Thor."

He had to admire a woman who wouldn't leave her dog.

Since he found the thought of being separated from her damn near unbearable, he changed the subject. "We'll go inside and get our things later," he said. "For now, let's go check out the place on Second Street."

"I need to grab a leash and my purse at least," she insisted. "And I want to secure it as much as I can." Which they both knew wouldn't be much.

She must have read his thoughts. "There's nothing valuable in here, really. The only thing I care about is my artwork. The studio locks, so I'm going to do that. Once we figure out where we're staying, we can get our personal belongings. Insurance will cover anything that's water damaged or smoke damaged."

Which would be most everything in the main part of the house. "Let me go with you then," he said.

"No. Please stay out here and watch Thor for me," she asked. "I promise I won't be long."

He didn't like it, but he did as she asked.

True to her word, she was in and out in less than sixty seconds. "I grabbed his leash and my purse, nothing more," she said. "Let's go."

They all piled into his truck. The huge dog sat in the passenger seat with Holly, which meant she rode smashed between him and the window. Judging by her expression, she didn't mind at all.

"Are you sure you don't want him to ride in the back?" he asked.

"In the pickup bed?" She appeared horrified at the suggestion. "Not unless I ride back there with him."

When they arrived and parked in the same spot as before, everyone piled out. While Holly clipped a leash on Thor's collar, Jeremy grabbed a flashlight from the glove box.

With the afternoon sun high overhead, the building looked even more decrepit. Looking at it, Jeremy had a moment of doubt that he'd ever be able to turn this place into his dream business. And for all that he'd said about Russell possibly living upstairs, he now seriously doubted it. The lower level had been a complete disaster. He couldn't help but think the upstairs would be the same or worse.

Locating the metal box, he extracted the key and let them both in. With the angle of the sun streaming in through the dirty front window, the amount of dirt and cobwebs, as well as litter, looked staggering. "Follow me," he said, keeping his voice low. "I'm not sure the stairs are even safe, so maybe it's best if you wait down here."

"No way," she protested. "I'm going where you go."

Slowly, he nodded. "What about Thor? Can you tie him up down here? I'd hate for him to get hurt."

"I didn't think about that," she said. "He goes where I go. If it's not safe for us, it won't be safe for him."

"Then we'll both be careful."

Since he knew it would be dark going up, he turned on his flashlight. Testing the first few steps, he found them surprisingly solid. Though that didn't mean they'd all be that way, he felt encouraged.

"Walk where I walk," he said. "I'm trying to make sure the wood is solid."

Grateful for the flashlight, he realized the first thing they'd need to do would be to get the power switched back on. Even if the place wasn't fit to live in, they'd need electricity to be able to begin any restorations.

Assuming he could do any of that without Russell's consent.

Finally, moving slowly and carefully, he reached the top of the stairs. Turning, he held out his hand to help Holly up.

Clutching Thor's leash in one hand, she gripped Jeremy's fingers in the other.

Standing on the landing, it wasn't nearly as dark due to numerous windows in each of the upstairs bedrooms. Since the windows were all closed, the heat felt stifling. The musty scent reminded him of the time Russell had brought home a box full of books that had been dried out after a flood.

"Let's go this way," he decided, whispering for no reason.

"I'll be right behind you," she whispered back. Though she moved quietly, Thor's toenails clicked on the wooden floor.

He took a left, keeping his flashlight on since he didn't want to be surprised by any small creatures. The first bedroom sat empty. Shredded curtains hung limply on each side of a single window. He saw nothing but ruined hardwood floors half-covered by dirty carpet. No furniture remained.

The second room looked virtually identical. They also checked out a full bathroom, complete with a claw-footed tub, which surprisingly seemed mostly intact despite the layers of years of grime.

"I think this is the only upstairs bathroom," he said, still keeping his voice to a whisper.

The dust inside or the smoke she'd inhaled earlier made her cough again. She stopped for a moment, clearly trying to keep the sound to a minimum but failing. "Sorry," she said, when she could speak again. "This stifling mugginess doesn't help."

He agreed. The more he saw of this place, the more he realized that no one had been in here in years.

Next, they found the kitchen with most of the appliances in place, though he couldn't tell if they were in work-ing condition. The same layer of dust covered everything, along with the array of spiderwebs and what appeared to be rodent or bat dung.

He decided not to mention bats. He hadn't even thought of them and right now didn't want to risk shining his flash-light up at the ceiling. The last thing he wanted to do was freak Holly out.

"I'm guessing the main bedroom must be on the other side," she said, oblivious to his thoughts. "If Russell were to be staying anywhere, I think that'd be the room."

"I'm beginning to think no one is staying here," he told her. "I don't see any footprints or signs of anyone being here recently."

"Not to mention the dirt and dust and heat," she said, agreeing with him. "But we might as well check out the rest of this before we go."

Resisting the urge to check his watch, since he knew they had to find some place to stay, he continued on.

A small living area contained a lumpy old couch, an end table with a lamp and a coffee table. He even thought he spotted an area rug, though it was difficult to tell with all the dirt.

On the other side of that, they found the last bedroom.

When they first stepped into the largest of the three bed-rooms, the four windows appeared to have been cleaned, at least a little. While still grimy and smudged, they weren't caked with dirt like the others were. He shined his flash-light to the floor but still couldn't see any footprints.

"Furniture," Holly breathed, stepping inside and turn-ing slowly. A large, four-poster bed sat between two of the windows, and an ancient box fan had been placed between the bed and the doorway.

Thor tugged on the leash, wanting to explore. "Not yet, boy," she said, keeping a tight hold on him. "I don't want you surprising any small creatures."

"The bed is made up," Jeremy observed. "Though I don't think that's recent. And that fan looks pretty old. It might have been left here by whoever used to own the place."

"I don't know." Holly shot him a doubtful glance. "None of the other rooms had even a single stick of furniture."

"The thought of pulling back the sheets to check the bed…" He let the sentence go unfinished. "Who knows what might have taken up residence under there."

Though she'd taken a step forward, his comment made her stop and shudder. "I didn't think of that," she said. "But I tend to disagree that no one has been staying here. Look at this. But if it's Russell, we wouldn't want to either."

Relieved, he nodded. "Not a chance in hell. And if we're going to find someplace else to stay until the house is okay, we'd better get busy."

But she made no move to hurry toward the exit. Instead, she and Thor walked around the bed to a nightstand. "This lamp," she breathed. "It's beautiful." She peered closer. "And the lampshade seems clean."

As she lifted the lamp to examine it better, she brushed her fingers over the switch to turn it on. To his shock, it lit up immediately.

"There's electricity," she breathed. "That changes everything."

Jeremy froze, resisting the urge to spin around and bellow out his brother's name. Because there could only be one reason for this old building to have power. It had become Russell's lair.

"Now I'm expecting Russell to show up at any moment," Holly said, sounding nervous. "I really don't want to be around a desperate man who might be using. Especially not here. No one would hear us if anything happened."

Jeremy eyed Thor, who sat at Holly's feet, his tongue lolling. "He seems relaxed," he pointed out. "I think he'd warn us if we were in any sort of danger."

"Maybe." Still, she kept looking around, her gaze darting from place to place. "Thor doesn't really like Russell, so I definitely think he'd let me know."

"He would." He spoke with more confidence than he felt. "There's only one way up here. My truck is parked right outside. I have a feeling Russell doesn't want to see us any more than we want to see him."

She nodded and took several deep breaths. "I'm sure you're right. While I can't help but feel we'll have that confrontation soon, I don't think it will be here. He hasn't stayed hidden this long by being caught unaware."

Chapter 15

Trying to calm her racing heart and sudden case of nerves, Holly focused on their surroundings.

Despite the obvious filth everywhere else, now that they had light, the spacious main bedroom appeared relatively clean. Sure, a thin layer of dust covered everything, but it wasn't nearly as filthy as the rest of the living quarters.

While Jeremy stood rooted in place, Holly turned on both lamps and the fan, then opened all the windows.

"It'll be much better with a nice breeze coming through," she said. "And I have to wonder, once we take a look with the lights on, if we'll see the rest of this place is cleaner than it appeared. I now think it's possible Russell might be staying here after all."

"Maybe." He opened the closet. "It's empty." Next, he pulled out a drawer in the oversize dresser. "No clothes in here either."

"He might be keeping his personal belongings on him at all times," she said. "It would make it a lot easier if he had to make a quick getaway."

"You suddenly seem well-versed in how to hide out without a trace," he observed, eyeing her closely. "Is there something you forgot to share with me?"

This comment made her laugh. "I watch a lot of true

crime shows. And based on what I've seen so far, I think this is where Russell's been hiding out."

Judging by his expression, he wasn't convinced. "But what about the bathroom?" he argued. "No way has anyone been using that. Same with the kitchen."

"Maybe he just needed a place to sleep." She shrugged. "I'm not sure. But if he's not staying here, since there's electricity, as long as there's running water, I can clean the other two areas. It'll work for us as a temporary place to live until we can come up with something else."

As long as Russell didn't suddenly materialize, accusing them of intruding on his secret hiding place. She'd rather live in a tent in her own backyard than deal with that.

"I don't know," Jeremy said, as if reading her thoughts. "I think we should look into exploring some other options."

"Agreed. But if we don't find concrete proof of Russell's presence, I still think this might work."

He looked around again. "This is really rough."

"Yes, it is," she replied. "But I've stayed in worse, and I'm betting you have as well. Let's go see if there's running water before we make any decisions."

That said, she hurried down the hallway to check, with him right behind her.

In the bathroom, she flicked on the light. Just like in the big bedroom, the room wasn't nearly as filthy as it had appeared in the dark. The instant she turned the faucet in the sink, clear water came out. "Wow," she said, slightly surprised. "I honestly didn't expect that. I guess I should have."

Walking over to the bathtub, she checked those faucets too. "It's even hot! Someone has to be staying here." And by someone, she meant Russell.

"I agree. I suppose we need to see if there's food in the

224 *Alaskan Disappearance*

refrigerator," Jeremy said, sounding more resigned than excited. "That would be definitive proof."

Together they went down the hall to the small kitchen. Holly flicked on the light, blinking at the sudden brightness. The heavy layer of filth covering the stove told her it either wasn't operational or simply hadn't been used.

Meanwhile, Jeremy opened the fridge. "It's empty," he said, stepping aside so she could see. "But cold."

Which made no sense. "Why go through the trouble of making sure the utilities are turned on but not keep food on hand?"

"Let's check the cupboards." He began opening up cabinets, one by one. "All empty. No dishes or plates, or canned goods."

She checked under the sink and pulled out a few of the drawers. "Absolutely nothing."

"You sound disappointed."

"Maybe." She shrugged. "Only because it would have been a tidy way to solve a long, ongoing mystery."

"I wonder if Russell had everything turned on before he left and then forgot about it," he mused. "Maybe he'd planned to start renovations before all the trouble started."

Looking up at him, admiring the way his sheer size filled the room, making everything seem smaller, she sighed. If ever a man could make her feel protected and safe, Jeremy did. She wished she could figure out a way to tell him without sounding sappy.

"Holly?" he asked. "Are you all right?"

She blinked, realizing she'd gotten lost in her thoughts. "I'm fine," she replied, momentarily struggling to remember what they'd been discussing. "About the utilities being on for the last eighteen-plus months. If that were the case, I'd think I would have seen a bill. And believe me,

I haven't. Until Walker told us, I wasn't even aware Russell owned this place."

Jeremy frowned. "He probably has them set up on automatic payments somewhere."

Since that made sense, she nodded. "Then what do you think? Should we stay here, at least until my house is made livable?"

He looked around again, still considering. "I think it's good to have this option," he finally said. "But first, we need to go back to your place and take another look. I'm thinking we could check it out a bit more thoroughly. Maybe it's not as bad as the firefighters said."

Giving in to impulse, she crossed the space between them and wrapped her arms around his waist. "Optimism and desperation make strange bedfellows," she said.

To his credit, he didn't ask her what she meant. Instead, he hugged her back.

They stood that way for a moment, just holding on to each other. She wished she could share all the thoughts that rushed through her head. Yes, she wanted him again, that was a constant. But she wanted more than just sex. More than what she'd pictured as her future with his brother, only to learn her fantasies didn't resemble reality at all.

But with Jeremy, she wanted it all. Shared sunrises and sunsets. Renovating old buildings like this one, working side by side. When he opened his dog training business, she wanted to help him. Not training dogs, obviously, since she had no idea how, but taking care of the administrative work.

In short, she wanted to be his partner. For the rest of her life.

Tears stung her eyes, and her throat ached. Suddenly afraid, she stepped back and turned away, pretending to be checking out the kitchen yet again. "I wonder if this stove works at all." As if she cared.

If he noticed the slight tremor in her voice, he didn't show it. "Let's get out of here," he said. "I really want to go back to your place and see what we can salvage."

"I agree. We should do that. It's time to grab some clothes and other personal belongings, if we can find enough that weren't too damaged."

"Exactly." Gaze warm, he took her arm. "Let's turn off the lights and go."

They were both quiet on the short drive back to the house. Holly, because she needed more time to think. And Jeremy must have felt the same. He didn't turn up the radio or even make an attempt at small talk. They simply rode home in silence.

Was Russell staying in that building? If so, how had he managed to go eighteen whole months without anyone seeing him?

As they pulled onto her street and she caught sight of her house, her breath caught. Someone had put yellow crime scene tape around her front and side yard, which was interesting since the police had not yet made it out this way.

"Who do you think did that?" she asked. "The mayor?"

"Probably," Jeremy replied, echoing her thoughts. "Maybe it'll make any intruders think twice before breaking in."

Hopping out of the truck, she sighed. "I wish them luck. Anything even remotely worth stealing likely has water and smoke damage."

Thor tugged on the leash, wanting to go home. "We've got to wait, big boy. Come on, let's go through the gate into the backyard." At least there, she could see how much of the house appeared relatively undamaged.

Jeremy followed as she and Thor went out back. Once there, she unclipped the lead, smiling slightly as her dog bounded off.

As she turned to face the house, Jeremy slipped his arm around her shoulders. "From here, you can't even tell there was a fire."

Studying the blue painted wood, she realized he was right. The house looked the same as it always did. No smoke or water damage was visible from the back side. "Maybe it'll be safe to go in if we use the back door," she said.

"Would you mind if I go first?"

Eyeing him, she slowly nodded. She liked that he asked, instead of simply pushing his way past her.

"Is it even locked?" he asked, aware of her habits.

She grimaced. "I don't know. When I came inside to secure my studio, I didn't even think about the back door. Probably not."

"Come on then." He tried the doorknob, which turned easily. As he stepped inside, she called Thor to her. The dog immediately responded, rushing over to sit in front of her.

"I'm so amazed that you trained him yourself?" Jeremy said, "Like I've told you before, you've done a great job."

"Thank you. It was a labor of love." She gave Thor a head scratch and praise. "He's the best. Smart and eager to please. We still practice at least once a week."

"That's amazing. Most people don't have that level of dedication."

She grinned. "Only because I'm surprisingly good at it," she said. "Who knows, maybe once you get your business up and running, instead of working part-time for Kip at the general store, I might be able to help you."

The intensity in his gaze made her smile falter. "What?"

she asked, wondering if she'd been too pushy. After all, she'd made some rather large assumptions.

"I didn't think it was possible to love you more," he muttered. "Then you go and say something like that."

He *loved* her? Had she heard correctly? She waited breathlessly for him to say more, maybe expand on his statement.

But he didn't. In fact, if he realized the magnitude of what he'd just revealed, he didn't show it. Instead, he'd already turned back around and taken a step into her kitchen.

Keeping Thor close to her side, she took a deep breath and followed.

Since they'd had to turn the power off, it took a minute for Jeremy's eyes to get used to the dimness inside. He heard Holly and Thor come in right behind him but didn't turn back to look. He couldn't believe he'd slipped up and used the *L* word so casually. He could only hope she hadn't heard. Judging by her lack of reaction, he figured that likely was the case.

The smell hit him first, clogging his throat and making his eyes water. Smoke and dampness combined to make for a cloying scent. Since she'd already opened the window above the sink, he left the back door open so they'd have more fresh air.

Though she coughed a few times, Holly didn't comment on the odor. Instead, she stood still while he shined his light around the kitchen.

"Everything in here looks just the same," she said, relief coloring her voice. "Maybe there's smoke damage, but it's difficult to tell without the lights."

"I think the first thing we need to do is empty the fridge

and get everything over to the empty one on Second Street," he said, carefully avoiding making eye contact.

"What about Russell? He might be staying there."

"He might," Jeremy agreed. "Or he might have at one time. I don't think he is now. And if he shows up, good. It's time we all had a heart-to-heart talk, face-to-face."

Plus, they had nowhere else to go. Holly knew that as well as he did.

She thought for a moment and then nodded. "I agree."

"Good. Then let's save as much food as we can. There's no sense in letting all of it spoil."

"You're right. I didn't even think of that," she replied. "I've got a few ice chests in the garage. Let me go get them, and we'll fill them up."

"I'll do it," he said, stepping in front of her. "We don't know what kind of shape the garage might be in. Let me go and see." He flicked on his flashlight and then, without waiting for an answer, opened the door to the garage.

Sweeping the area with his light, he saw her Land Rover appeared untouched. He located three ice chests stacked up against the back wall. There were two large ones and one small one. Grabbing them, he hauled them back into the kitchen. "There's probably still enough ice in the ice maker to keep everything cold," he said.

"I bet there is. And since I just stocked up on meat, I'm really glad you thought of this." She glanced toward the garage door. "How'd my SUV look?"

"As far as I could tell from a quick glance, it's fine."

"That's good." Clearly relieved, she nodded. "We'll need to start it up and take it with us. I've got to have transportation of my own."

"Yes, you do. And there's more room for Thor."

As always when he mentioned her dog, she smiled. "That's true. There's not a lot of space in your truck."

Struck momentarily dumb by her beauty, he looked at the ice chests instead.

"I'll empty the fridge and freezer," he told her. "As much as I can, anyway. Why don't you go check out your art studio? Do you have a flashlight in here somewhere?"

"I'll just use my phone," she said.

He nodded. Thor regarded him steadily, his eyes shining in the dim light. Once she'd turned on her phone flashlight, she headed off to her studio, Thor right on her heels.

He started with the freezer, packing up all the frozen meat and fish. She also had several bags of frozen vegetables, french fries and some ice cream bars. He packed all of this up, dumped some of the ice from the ice maker on top and then started on the refrigerator.

Once he'd completely filled all three ice chests, he went to check out nonperishable food in the cabinets. He'd noticed Holly stored her plastic grocery bags in a box at the bottom of the pantry. Grabbing several, he packed up every bit of food he could. He even managed to locate a handheld manual can opener.

This done, he decided to check out his bedroom. He figured not much of his meagre belongings would be salvageable since that room had burned pretty badly. When he got there, he realized he was right. Stunned at the devastation, he stood in what remained of the doorway and stared.

If he'd thought the aroma of charred wood, fire retardant and water had been bad before, this was worse. Even with the gaping hole on the exterior wall where the fire had burned through. Eyes watering, he saw that most of the furniture appeared to be a total loss. And though his closet door had remained closed, he'd bet that most of his clothing would be too heavily smoke damaged to be of any use.

In fact, he didn't see a single thing in this room worth saving. Luckily, he didn't own a lot, but it made him sad to lose what little he had. But they were just material things and could be replaced. Holly and Thor were safe, and that's all that mattered.

Retreating to the kitchen, he sat at the table to wait for Holly. He still wasn't sure about staying at the Second Street building, but he supposed it would do temporarily. Unless Russell were to show up.

If he were to run into Russell right now and the two of them were to look each other in the eyes, face-to-face, Jeremy wasn't even sure his brother would recognize him. Or vice versa.

The decade that had passed had brought a lot of changes. Jeremy had grown from a lanky, sullen teenager into a muscular man, but his physical appearance had only been part of his transformation.

He'd traveled a long road, from being put out on his own at such a young age, to figuring out how to support himself by working as a busboy, a cashier and a waiter, all at different places, concurrently. Not only had he overcome his addiction, but he'd found a new fulfillment helping others deal with theirs.

Then the drug bust gone wrong and three years spent locked behind bars. He put that time to good use, struggling against bitterness, and had not only earned his GED but had gotten certified as a dog trainer as well.

He was proud of the man he'd become. And he'd been excited to share his transformation with his older brother.

Only to learn Russell had apparently skied a downward slope into a free-falling spiral. Jeremy wondered if his brother would shy away if he offered to help.

But Russell's whereabouts remained a mystery.

The building on Second Street with electricity and water turned on had surprised Jeremy. Holly too. At first they'd both suspected that Russell had been living there. But by the time they'd finished searching for any kind of concrete proof, Jeremy had convinced himself that was not the case.

He wasn't sure what Holly thought. When she'd started getting emotional while they'd been standing in the kitchen, he'd been puzzled as to the reason why. It had occurred to him she might be worried about seeing Russell again. The swift and strong flash of jealousy that had accompanied this thought had nearly bowled him over.

In the short time he'd known her, he thought they'd formed a connection. Now he had to wonder if it might be all one-sided. She certainly hadn't responded when he'd let the *L* word slip. He could only hope it was because she simply hadn't heard him.

"Guess what?" Waving her flashlight around like a beacon, Holly emerged from her art studio, beaming. "Nothing was damaged. All of my inventory is fine. I've locked the door, so if anyone breaks into the house when we're not here, it should be safe."

As she hurried over to him, he started to stand. Instead, she put both hands on his shoulders and kissed him. Surprised and aroused, he opened his mouth, trying to remain passive even though he wanted to take control.

She lingered over the kiss, passionate, smoldering and exploratory. When she finally lifted her head, they locked gazes. His senses reeled. Sensual and emotional. Almost as if she were giving him back his declaration of love without actually speaking it out loud.

Stepping back, she held out her hand. "Let's go."

After using the manual pull to open the garage door, she started the Land Rover to make sure it ran and backed it into the driveway. They loaded the ice chests in the back, and the grocery bags full of canned goods and perishables into the back of his pickup.

Despite the physical labor, his body still buzzed from her kiss.

Now that they'd loaded up both her Land Rover and the back of his pickup with whatever personal items they'd been able to salvage, they were ready to drive back to the Second Street property that would be their new, temporary home. Holly had even grabbed a bunch of cleaning supplies, vowing to get that floor into tip-top shape.

"Are you ready?" he asked.

"I am." She smiled back.

Rounding the corner together, hand in hand, both Jeremy and Holly stopped when they saw the black Mercedes-Benz parked in front of the house. Next to them, Thor growled low in his throat.

"Damn it. We shouldn't have come back here," Jeremy muttered.

"We had to grab some of our things," Holly replied. "I'm hoping once he sees the result of what he did to us, he'll move on and leave us alone."

Jeremy doubted that. The fire had been set to intimidate them. Gary would want to make damn sure his tactic had worked.

They stood side by side in the driveway, while Gary got out of his car and strode toward them. "What happened here?" he asked, frowning.

"Like you don't know," Jeremy replied. "Setting the house on fire was bad enough. What else do you want?"

Gary stopped in his tracks. "I had nothing to do with this. Believe me, if I did I'd definitely let you know. I came by to see if you had my money ready."

Holly laughed and laughed, the sound bordering on hysteria. Expressionless, Gary stared at her, arms crossed. Jeremy had to clench his hands into fists to keep from punching him.

Finally, Holly stopped, the sound trailing off into hiccupping sounds. She glared at Gary. "I don't know why you think I would be able to cover Russell's debt. I'm barely scraping by as it is. And now this." Waving her hands at the ruin of what used to be her home, she shook her head.

Still Gary didn't move.

Jeremy found himself taking a step toward the other man. "Tell me something," he said. "I'm not sure why you haven't mentioned this, because how can we repay a debt without knowing the amount? How much does Russell owe you?"

"I figured you knew," Gary said, frowning as he looked from Holly to Jeremy. "Or at least *she* should know. She's been living with him."

"I don't have any idea," Holly said. "I wasn't aware of any of this. So how much is it?"

"A few thousand shy of a quarter of a million dollars," Gary replied, his tone as smooth as if they were discussing the weather. "And that debt needs to be settled now."

Holly gasped.

"Or what?" Jeremy decided he'd had enough. "You can't get blood from a stone. Sure, you can kill us. But that isn't going to get you paid. We don't know where Russell is."

"Then I guess you'd better find him." Gary smirked. "Or you might find yourself wishing you were dead. There are quite a few businesses in this Podunk town. Murphy's General Store and Mikki's, to name a few. I know you consider yourselves friends with the people who run them. It'd be a shame if something happened to them or their buildings."

"You son of a—" Jeremy lunged for him. Only Holly's quick grab at his arm stopped him.

"I thought so." Spinning on his heel, Gary strode back to his car. When he reached it, he turned once again and faced them. "Ticktock. Your time is running out. You'd better figure out a way to find Russell or come up with the money yourselves. Or people you care about will pay."

With that, he got in his car and drove away.

"He can't do that," Holly protested, her voice breaking. "Can he?"

Since they both knew the answer, Jeremy didn't respond. "We've got to find Russell," he said. "Though I doubt he has $250,000 sitting around, there's still the possibility that he might have some of it left."

"Or maybe he can return the drugs," Holly said. "Though to be honest, I don't understand why he would even attempt to distribute drugs. I mean, I suspected he was using. But that's a far cry from selling them."

"True. And he couldn't do that in a place as small as Blake. He'd have to have been working in a bigger city, like Anchorage."

"I don't know," she said. "Russell became an awful person, it's true. He struggled with addiction and his own kind of mental illness. But I think he'd draw the line at becoming a drug dealer. How do we even know what Gary is saying is true?"

"That's just it," he replied. "We don't. But we also have little to no choice but to believe him."

"What about going after the people above him?" she

asked, her voice as fierce as her expression. "Maybe they'll be willing to listen to reason."

As appalling as he found that idea, he could tell she also had no clue why doing that would make things worse. They'd be lucky to walk out of that alive.

"Oh, Holly." He loved her innocence. And he wished she never had to lose it. But he suspected by the time all of this was over, Holly would understand how truly awful the other side of humanity could be.

He'd do just about anything to keep that from happening.

"Well?" she pressed.

"The kind of people Gary works for don't do negotiations. They shoot first and ask questions later." He took a deep breath, recognizing the stubborn set of her chin. "The good thing is, Gary won't be able to find us."

"At least not until word gets out where we're staying," she said. "You know how fast gossip travels around here."

He watched while Holly and Thor got into the Land Rover. Once he started his pickup, they followed. Just in case, he constantly checked his rearview mirror to make sure they weren't being followed.

To his relief, he didn't see a single other vehicle. Slowly, his heart rate returned to normal. Maybe this would work out after all.

When they turned onto Second Street, he scanned the area again. No other cars or trucks were parked on the block, since all the buildings nearby were deserted and/or boarded up. Pulling up into the alley, he backed up as close as he could get to the rear door. Holly did the same.

As they unloaded and carried stuff in, Thor sat down just outside the back door, watching them. "He's guarding us," Holly commented, smiling fondly at her dog. "I'm guessing he can tell that I'm slightly nervous about the possibility of running into Russell."

About to admit the same, he changed his mind. Worrying wouldn't change anything, so all they could do was hope for the best.

Once all the food had been transferred to the refrigerator or freezer, they unpacked all the other kitchen items. Holly had brought paper plates and plastic utensils, as well as some of her pots and pans.

As she got ready to carry her suitcase of clothes upstairs, she froze. "I just realized there's only one bed."

Chapter 16

They stared at each other. Holly figured that, although Jeremy knew the gentlemanly thing to do would be to offer to find somewhere else to sleep, there weren't any other beds. And no way did she intend to have him make a bed on the floor.

"We'll have to share," she said slowly, watching his face. "I hope that's okay with you. I know Thor will do a great job of protecting us."

At the mention of his name, her big beautiful dog wagged his tail. "See," she pointed. "He's ready."

To her relief, Jeremy finally cracked a smile. "Thank you. The only downside is that arrangement might make it difficult to get a lot of sleep."

Laughing, she flicked on the switch that lit up the stairway. In addition to clothes and towels and bed linens, she'd also brought her vacuum, broom and mop. If they were going to be living in this place, she planned to make darn sure she got and kept it clean. She'd have it feeling like home in no time.

Like home. All her life, she'd heard people say it wasn't the place you lived that mattered, it was the people you lived with. She'd certainly hoped this would turn out to be true when she'd taken a huge leap of faith and moved all the way to Alaska to be with Russell. But despite jointly purchasing his house—a place she loved—she hadn't felt at home until a few months after Russell had left. And even then, she'd been conscious of an ache inside, as though something might be missing.

Somehow, by his mere presence, Jeremy had taken that ache away. While she wasn't sure where their relationship might be going, she knew everything would be better with him by her side.

"Are you okay?" Expression concerned, Jeremy touched her shoulder. "You seemed lost in thought."

Suddenly bashful, she ducked her head. "I'm fine," she said. "Now I'd better get the rest of this stuff put away."

"Let me help." He grabbed several bags and a large box and followed her up the stairs.

By the time the two of them, working in unison, had finished scrubbing and cleaning the top floor, Holly felt a pleasant sort of exhaustion. She and Jeremy met in the kitchen, grinning at each other.

"Looks like a different place," Jeremy said. And then he kissed her.

She melted into his embrace, giving as well as receiving. As usual, as soon as their mouths met, passion ignited. Fire, heat and that familiar raw tingling of sensual awareness.

Hands all over each other, stripping their clothes off as they went, they barely made it to the bedroom. Once there, they fell onto the bed, devouring each other. When release came, explosive and pure, they lay curled in each other's arms until their heartbeats slowed.

"I'm glad I changed out the sheets and comforter," she commented, her voice as lazy as she felt.

"Me too." He kissed the top of her head.

Later, Jeremy went over to Mikki's to grab takeout for

their dinner. Then, since they had no television to watch, he produced a pack of cards he'd borrowed from Mikki, and they played several rounds of poker while sitting on the lumpy couch. She made Jeremy inspect it earlier, just to make sure there were no critters living inside.

To her delight and Jeremy's feigned frustration, she learned she had a knack for the game of poker.

"It's a good thing we're not playing for money," she teased.

"Next time, we should play strip poker," he teased right back. "Though the way this is going, I'd be sitting here naked while you stayed fully clothed."

She hadn't had this much fun in ages. It seemed oddly freeing, to be staying in an unfamiliar space and feel so much at home.

As the evening went on, when she caught herself yawning, Jeremy got up and held out his hand. "Let's turn in," he said.

Gladly, she slipped her fingers into his and went with him into the bedroom. After changing, they got in between the clean sheets and fell asleep nestled against each other.

When morning came, she woke slowly, coming to full awareness of her location and the large man still sleeping beside her.

Moving carefully, she slipped out from under his arm. Her dog raised his head to watch her, but he laid back down when she gave him the hand signal to stay.

Leaving Jeremy asleep in the bed, with Thor sound asleep in his favorite dog bed at the foot, Holly decided to run down to Mikki's and grab some donuts. She started coffee brewing, decided she'd get a cup when she returned instead of waiting, and grabbed her car keys and her purse.

She took the steps two at a time, feeling better than she

had since the fire. After she had coffee and donuts, she planned to file a claim with her insurance company so she could get that process started.

Rushing on her way out the back door, Holly collided with someone coming up the front steps, nearly knocking him down. As it was, she rocked back so hard she stumbled. About to begin apologizing, the words died in her throat as she realized Gary stood there, a pistol in his hand.

"Back inside," he ordered, gesturing with his weapon. "Your time has just run out."

Instead of moving, she tried staring him down. "How'd you find us?"

He smirked. "Word travels fast around here. The two of you shacking up in some abandoned building is all anyone is talking about. I stopped in at Mikki's for donuts and coffee and listened to the conversations people were having."

Though she supposed she should have known, she had no idea how anyone else would have found out. The area had been completely deserted when they'd arrived. Someone had to have driven by, gone up the alley and noticed their vehicles parked in the back lot. The only person who might have done something like that was Walker, checking out the place Jeremy had been interested in and that Russell owned.

"Now get back inside," Gary ordered.

Still, she didn't move. She knew she had to stall, to figure out some way to alert Jeremy. If he could catch Gary by surprise and take him down, they might be able to come up with some sort of plan to get out of this.

"If you shoot us, that won't do anything to get you your money," she said. "Neither of us have it. We also don't have any idea where Russell is hiding out."

"Inside, now," he barked, pointing his pistol at her. "You

and your ex-con boyfriend are going to be how I draw Russell out into the open. Now move."

This time, she did as he asked.

Once inside, he blinked at the mess. "How the hell are you living here?" Before she could answer, he shook his head. "Tell Russell's brother to show himself."

Since he hadn't gone around the corner to see the staircase, she feigned confusion. "He was right here. I don't know where he got off to."

Evidently her bad attempt at acting didn't fool him. He yanked her to him, and then with his arm around her throat, he pressed the gun against her temple. "Tell him to get out here or I'm going to kill you right now."

Absolute terror weakened her knees. Until this very instant, she'd been able to convince herself that nothing bad would happen. After all, she'd had nothing to do with Russell's illegal business dealings. Why should she have to pay just because he'd crossed the wrong people? Any reasonable person would understand she wasn't involved.

Clearly, Gary wasn't reasonable. Just desperate.

She opened her mouth to call for Jeremy but couldn't push out any sound. Gary tightened his grip, choking her. Struggling, the edges of her vision turned gray and then black. About to slip into unconsciousness, she couldn't manage anything more than a gurgle.

"Drop the gun, Gary," a familiar voice said from behind them.

Arm still around her neck, Gary spun them around. But at least he loosened his grip, enabling her to breathe again.

Panting, struggling to suck in great gulps of air, she could barely focus on the blurred image of a man facing them. Her ex-fiancé. And he too held a pistol.

"Russell," Gary said, satisfaction oozing from his voice.

"You came a lot quicker than I expected. Someone must have alerted you that I was asking around at Mikki's about Holly."

"Not really." Despite the obvious threat, Russell didn't sound alarmed. "This is my building. I figured out pretty quickly she was staying here after the house fire. I actually came to talk to her, not you."

"You didn't expect to find me instead," Gary said, laughing. "And now that you have, it's time to pay up."

Meanwhile, now that she could breathe and see again, Holly debated how she might best escape. A quick twist and an elbow in the ribs might work, but she had to consider that this man had a gun and wouldn't be afraid to use it.

"Let her go," Russell repeated. "You and I can settle this man-to-man. She doesn't need to be involved."

"Not going to happen." Gary snarled. "She's my ace in the hole." He tightened his grip once more, though not as much as before. "Now pay me what you owe or this woman is going to die."

Rolling over, Jeremy reached for Holly only to discover she'd gone. He pushed up on his elbows just as Thor put his massive front paws on the bed and nudged Jeremy with his nose.

"What's wrong, boy?" Jeremy asked. Thor whined, glancing toward the doorway. And that's when Jeremy heard voices downstairs.

Getting up quietly, he pulled on his pants and T-shirt and stepped into his shoes. Then he and Thor moved quietly to the landing. The acoustics were much better there. Listening, he could make out Gary telling someone to pay up or Holly would die.

Someone? A second later, his suspicions were confirmed. Russell spoke again. "Hurt one hair on her head and I'll drop you," he said. Which meant Russell must be armed too. And Jeremy knew from past experience that his brother had excellent aim. He'd won awards for his marksmanship back in the day.

Head swimming, when he reached the midpoint landing, Jeremy gave Thor the hand signal for "stay" and continued creeping down the stairs. How had his brother managed to reappear at the exact same moment Gary had shown up to threaten Holly?

"I've been watching you," Russell continued. "I don't get why you've been harassing her or my brother. They have absolutely nothing to do with the deal you and I made."

Gary snarled something unintelligible.

"I said *let Holly go!*" Russell ordered. *"Now!"*

Heart in his throat, Jeremy crept closer. If anything happened to Holly, he'd be gutted. And she must be absolutely terrified.

When he reached the bottom, he weighed his options. He might or might not have the element of surprise on his side, depending on which way Gary was facing. That could be good or it might be disastrous. He didn't want to startle a man with his finger on the trigger, especially if that barrel was pressed against Holly's head.

"I said let her go," Russell repeated. "Harming her won't do anything to get you paid."

"Do you have my money?" Gary demanded. "If you care about this woman at all, you'd better show it to me right now. Otherwise, you'll have to live with being responsible for her death."

Heart pounding, Jeremy quietly moved closer. He glanced back once. Thor, bless his obedient heart, watched him from the "stay" position.

And then Holly screamed.

Jeremy started forward.

A blur rushed past him. Thor, breaking the "stay" command and using all of his brute strength and power to save his Holly.

The dog leaped. Caught by surprise, Gary went down. The gun went off. Still screaming, Holly fell. Had she been hit?

Both Russell and Jeremy moved at the same time. Both went to grab Gary, who scrabbled to get his pistol, which had apparently been knocked away.

Russell reached the other man first, knocking him to the floor. "Get something to tie him up with," he told Jeremy.

About to do as Russell asked, Jeremy turned and called for Holly. He'd seen her fall. "Were you hit?"

"No." She was sitting up, her arms wrapped around Thor. "I'm okay."

Rushing to the kitchen to look for something to use to tie up Gary, all Jeremy could locate was a box of heavy-duty trash bags. Russell had flipped him over and forced Gary's arms behind his back, kneeling on top of him to keep him down. Jeremy got out the trash bags and used several of those to secure Gary's wrists and ankles. Once he felt certain the other man's restraints were secure, Jeremy went to check on Holly.

As he approached, Holly and Thor both looked up. The big dog appeared to be as close as he could get to sitting in her lap. She kissed the top of Thor's head, and he responded by licking her face. "I was so worried he got shot," she said. "But I've checked him out and don't see any injuries."

"Russell?" Holly asked, looking past Jeremy to his brother. After restraining Gary, Russell had started to stand but instead remained on his knees.

"Do you need help getting up?" Jeremy asked, walking toward his brother and extending his hand.

Wincing, Russell tried to wave him away.

And then Jeremy saw it. The blood staining his brother's shirt, blooming red on his shoulder.

"We should call for an air ambulance," Jeremy said, suddenly terrified. With the closest hospital in Anchorage, the quickest way to get an emergency patient there was by air.

"No need," Russell insisted. "The bullet just grazed me. I just need to clean it up and bandage it and I'll be fine."

"Let me take a look at it," Jeremy said. While in prison, he'd learned how to quickly and safely take care of most wounds.

Kneeling down beside his older brother, he marveled at how, despite the years that had passed, Russell still looked the same. Sure, he had a few more lines in his face, and he wore his hair longer than Jeremy had ever seen it, but Jeremy would have recognized him in a crowd.

Gently, he helped Russell remove his bloodstained shirt.

"Let me get a wet washcloth to clean it," Holly said, pushing to her feet and heading upstairs. She returned a minute later. "I also packed a box of adhesive bandages and some antibiotic ointment. You just never know."

She knelt down by them both and gently began dabbing at Russell's wound. Despite the amount of blood, once she'd got that cleaned off, Jeremy could see Russell had been correct. The bullet had grazed him and had taken out a chunk of skin, but that was all.

None of the bandages were big enough to cover the entire thing, so Holly used several, overlapping them.

Meanwhile, Gary watched them silently, his narrow gaze shooting daggers. Finally, just as Holly finished up with

Russell, Gary spoke. "All I want is what's owed. You don't understand. If I don't get the money, they'll kill me."

This, Jeremy knew to be true. He'd heard and seen enough in prison to believe the stories the other inmates told.

"Are you able to pay him?" Jeremy asked his brother.

"Not all of it." Russell hung his head. "I went away to get clean. I stashed most of the drugs in the forest, but I was wasted when I did, and now I can't find them."

"At least you didn't sell them," Holly said.

"If he had, maybe he could repay his debt," Gary pointed out. "Seriously. What are you people going to do about that?"

Searching his brother's face, Jeremy saw no sign of impairment. His pupils were normal size and his gaze unclouded. "How much of what you owe do you have?" he asked.

"Not much." Slowly, Russell shook his head. "I used every cent I had to put myself into the best rehab I could find. That's where I've been most of this time. Down in the lower forty-eight. Arizona, to be specific. I spent six months there, and when I got out, I stayed another six to make sure I could stay clean." He looked down. "And I've been back here, searching for the other six."

Jeremy nodded. While he personally knew how difficult kicking addiction could be, Russell had been both verbally and physical abusive to the woman Jeremy now loved. He couldn't help but notice the way Holly stayed back, away from them, though she watched Russell closely. Russell owed her an apology, though even that might not be enough. For now, Jeremy would give it time.

"Now, what about you? What are you doing here?" Russell asked, clutching at Jeremy's arm. "I didn't think you'd ever be coming back."

"Well, I did." He glanced back at Holly, wishing he had her by his side.

"Damn, my shoulder hurts." Russell grimaced, then eyed Holly. "Are you going to call the police?"

Holly didn't immediately answer. "I'm not sure," she finally said, meeting Jeremy's gaze.

"Please don't," Gary interjected. "There's no need to get law enforcement involved."

"He has a point," Russell said. "If you call them, Gary and I are both going to be arrested." He spoke slowly, his voice raspy. "And I don't think Jeremy wants to be involved in any way, shape or form with anything that even slightly has to do with a drug deal."

Jeremy nodded. While he hadn't thought that far ahead, he knew how easy it was to get railroaded into a conviction even without being guilty. Then, as his brother's words registered, he wondered if Russell had been keeping up with him all these years.

"Worse," Gary added, "once the people I work for find out you sold them out, we're as good as dead." He looked around, making eye contact with each and every one of them. "All of you."

"The problem is," Jeremy said, "none of us have a quarter of a million just sitting around." Inwardly wincing, he tried to keep his voice as expressionless as his face. Because he actually did. That just about summed up half of the total amount he had in the bank from his reparation payment. He sighed. If they couldn't work something else out, he'd offer it up. But since he'd planned to use that to start his business, doing so would put those plans completely in the gutter.

Gary looked at Russell. "Unless you can somehow manage to remember where you left all those drugs. I'm sure they'd take them back in lieu of payment."

"I've tried." Russell groaned. "That's what I've been doing nonstop ever since I got out of rehab. Searching every wooded area near the river. Which is a lot. Even worse, I put them inside a half-fallen tree trunk. Do you know how many of those are out there?"

Everyone fell silent. Personally, Jeremy hoped the drugs were never found. Not only did he not want to take a chance on being caught with something like that, but he knew far too many people who'd relapsed fresh out of rehab. He didn't want that to happen to his brother.

"There's got to be some way work this out." Gary stared Russell down. "I've been looking for you for a long time. I can only stall them for so long."

"We tried that," Jeremy reminded him. "But not only have you been threatening us, you set Holly's house on fire."

Russell groaned. "I wondered about that. How did you think doing something like that would get you paid faster? At least before, we could have sold the house. My half would have more than repaid you."

"And you were the one sending threatening texts and watching me when I was out in the yard, weren't you?" Holly asked, her arms crossed.

"What does it matter? I need the money now," Gary barked. "You don't understand. Since I brought you in, my life is on the line too."

Suppressing a sudden surge of anger, Jeremy took a deep breath. He had a pretty good idea of how Gary had roped Russell in. After all, he'd seen it happen over and over to people he considered his friends. People he'd helped get sober. There had always been some friendly, helpful drug dealer there in the beginning. Offering free samples and then, once they got hooked, turning them into mules or distributors to help feed their addiction.

"This building," he asked Russell. "What do you think it's worth?" He'd done some online research, and a retail commercial property like this one would sell for well above what Russell owed. At least in Alaska. It might not be worth much, compared to other, more renovated properties in larger towns, but it would be enough.

"Oh, it would more than cover that," Russell said. "But finding a buyer would take time. Even though I did some renovations and brought it up to code for electricity and plumbing, as you can see, it still needs a lot of work."

"We don't have time," Gary interjected. Both men ignored him.

"Just give me a number," Jeremy insisted. He glanced at Holly. She gave him a small nod of approval. Clearly, she'd figured out what he had planned.

Russell frowned. "I don't know."

"If you were going to sell it today, for cash, what would be your price?" Since he'd been planning to buy the building anyway, he might be able to make something work.

"Why?" Russell countered. "Do you have a buyer?"

"I might. Depends on the price."

"Two hundred and fifty thousand," Russell said. "Cheap enough to make it go quickly. That way, I can pay Gary and make him, and all of this, go away forever."

"Done." Jeremy held out his hand. Heart pounding, he waited to see if his brother would shake.

Russell's eyes widened. "You?"

When Jeremy nodded, Russell grabbed his hand and

they shook. "Looks like you own this building now. I'll have the paperwork drawn up tomorrow."

Later, after Jeremy had gone to the bank and gotten a cashier's check, he paid Gary. Gary studied the check as if he wasn't sure it was real. Once he was satisfied that he had collected the correct amount, he grinned. "Thank you. I'd say it was a pleasure doing business with you, but it hasn't been."

Silent and expressionless, they all watched him go.

"I wish I could call the police and get him arrested," Holly muttered. "He's a serious creep."

Without thinking, Jeremy went to her and pulled her into his arms. "You'll never have to see him again."

"Ahem." Russell cleared his throat. "Are you two together now?"

Arms still around each other, together they turned to face him. "We are," Holly answered. "And since I think you two have a lot to talk about, I'm going to take myself upstairs and get to work cleaning."

"About that." Russell grimaced. "Jeremy and I do need to talk, but not just yet. There are a few other things I've got to straighten out first. Is that okay with you?" he asked Jeremy.

"As long as you don't disappear on me again, we have plenty of time to fill each other in on what's happened over the last ten years," Jeremy replied. "I'd like to catch up as soon as possible."

"Me too." Russell sighed. "Before anything else, I owe you an apology for the way I treated you. You were just a confused, angry teenager. I should have tried to help you, not tossed you out on your ear."

Though he'd been waiting to hear his brother say this for what felt like forever, Jeremy only acknowledged this with a dip of his chin. "Thank you."

Holly looked from one to the other. Her expression combined distaste with a kind of fear that made Jeremy want to promise her he'd protect her. No one would ever hurt her again while he was around.

"I should go," she said. Before she could start for the stairs, he pulled her close again and kissed her cheek. "Wait," he murmured in her ear, gratified when she shivered.

"One more thing," Russell continued, oblivious. "I actually have been staying here off and on. It might be a bit awkward now."

With his arms still around her, Jeremy and Holly both turned. Holly met his gaze, and he gave an almost imperceptible nod.

"There are two empty bedrooms upstairs," Holly offered, trying to conceal her reluctance and failing. "I guess if you got an air mattress or something, you could use one of those."

Russell shook his head. "No way. I've done enough to make your life difficult." Briefly, he bowed his head. "I'm sorry for the way I treated you, Holly. You gave up everything to be with me, and I broke every promise that I ever made. Sure, the drugs turned me into someone I didn't recognize, but there's no excuse for what I put you through."

Clearly not sure if she wanted to offer absolution, she crossed her arms and said nothing. Jeremy didn't blame her. While he and Russell had a lot of discussing to do to clear things up between them, Holly had to find her own path forward. Whether she could forgive his brother or not would be solely her decision.

Hopefully, they'd all manage to work out some kind of peace between them. He hoped to have both his brother and Holly as part of his life going forward.

"I'll make things up to you," Russell continued, a thread of desperation creeping into his voice. "Both of you."

It was the first time he acknowledged he and Jeremy had issues to resolve as well. Jeremy took a deep breath. Holly squeezed his waist, letting him know she understood how he felt.

"How long have you two been together?" Russell asked, looking from one to the other.

Holly stiffened.

"Not long enough," Jeremy said, smiling. At his light-hearted comment, Holly relaxed and leaned into him.

"I'm glad you found each other." Russell shifted his weight, wincing slightly from the wound in his shoulder. "Since I don't have a phone at the moment, would you mind if I borrowed one of yours so I can call Tanya? I have a lot of explaining to do to her as well, but I think she might let me stay with her. I just can't remember her number."

"I have it." Jeremy passed over his phone to him. "I saved it in my contacts in case I ever needed to call her. All you need to do is press Send."

Then, while Russell called his former and possibly current girlfriend, Jeremy took Holly's arm and the two of them headed upstairs. Thor trotted along right behind them.

Once they were alone, Holly took a deep, shaky breath. "This is a lot," she admitted. "I think I need time to process it all."

He nodded. "Do you want me to leave?"

"Of course not." She turned in his arms so they were facing each other. "I'm just wondering where we're going to go from here."

"The two of us? Or you, me and Russell?"

Moving closer, she brushed her mouth against his. "You

and I. Russell's on his own. Hopefully Tanya will take him in."

The press of her lips made him shudder with desire. He fought the urge to deepen the kiss, since they both knew where that would lead.

Instead, he pulled back slightly, gaze locked on hers.

"I already told you how I feel about you," he said, his heart hammering in his chest. "I know you heard me."

A half smile teased her mouth. Slowly, she shook her head. "You're going to have to do better than that. Just tossing a few words offhandedly isn't much of a declaration."

"Do you want me to shout it from the rooftops?" he asked, more than half-serious.

"Maybe." She shrugged. "But more likely not. Words are one thing. Actions are something completely different."

She wanted actions. He'd give her actions. Hell, he'd give her both.

Reclaiming her mouth, he kissed her with all the pent-up longing and hunger inside him. When they finally broke apart, they were both shaking.

"Holly, we have something special going on between us. You know it as well as I do."

"I do," she murmured. The tenderness in her gaze made his gut clench. Then she repeated the words he'd said when he'd found this building. "When you know, you know."

That right there, those five words, summed up every emotion he'd been feeling since the first time he'd looked into her beautiful blue eyes. Pressing his forehead into hers, he repeated them back to her. "When you know, you know."

Thor barked and nudged them apart, tail wagging happily. They both looked at him, smiling. "He gets it too," Holly said.

Jeremy truly believed the dog did.

Chapter 17

Three months later

"Today's the final walk-through," Holly said, touching Jeremy's shoulder and allowing her hand to linger. "If all goes well, we should close on the house tomorrow."

Jeremy jumped to his feet and kissed her. Smiling, she kissed him back, before regretfully pushing him away and shaking her head. "No distractions," she told him, the mock severity of her tone not fooling him in the slightest. "You shouldn't want any either, especially since you know I need the money to get everything ready in my part of the store-front."

He nodded. "We're just lucky the insurance came through on the house."

"That too," she agreed. "But you know as well as I do that offering the incentive of working on this commercial building as well made the construction crew work faster on completing the repairs."

Which hadn't been as bad as they'd initially feared. The fire had done some damage, and the water and smoke had done more, but in this part of the country everyone knew they had to get construction work done before the first snow fell. Things tended to shut down after that.

The repair crew had worked fast, taking advantage of the long days and moderate temperatures. Within two months, the house looked like new. Maybe even better. If not for the fact that Russell still owned half, Holly might have considered staying there.

Except she wanted to make a fresh start. A clean break, especially since the situation with Russell had been anything but.

With Russell's agreement, they'd put the house on the market the first week of September. It had gone under contract five days later.

After today, Holly would officially be homeless. She didn't mind. She'd been staying with Jeremy on the top floor of the Second Street building anyway.

"Are you going to have to talk to Russell at the closing?" Jeremy asked. He knew she'd been avoiding his brother, and he couldn't blame her. They both knew Russell had a lot to answer for, and he hadn't gone out of his way to try to mend the fences he'd destroyed.

"No," she answered. "The Realtor from Anchorage said he'd be signing separately."

If Jeremy was disappointed, he hid it well. He simply nodded and got back to painting baseboards.

To Holly's dismay, the reconciliation Jeremy had longed for had never come. After he and Russell had signed the paperwork transferring the deed of the Second Street building to Jeremy, Russell had taken off with vague promises to keep in touch.

He'd also been scarce around town. While gossip would seem to indicate that he'd been staying with Tanya, he might as well have gone back to wherever he'd been staying in the woods. No one had seen or talked to him, nor had he made any amends or attempts to right the wrongs he'd done.

For herself, Holly didn't really care if she never saw Russell again. But for Jeremy, she wanted the two brothers to forge some kind of relationship.

The past three months had passed in a blur. She'd stayed busy, whether overseeing the repairs on her old house or helping Jeremy get his business up and running. They'd decided on a simple name—Jeremy Elliot's Dog Training—and a sign had been installed two weeks ago.

The work on converting the building had also gone quickly, even more so since Jeremy and Holly had pitched in and done some of it themselves. It helped that the electrical and plumbing had already been updated by Russell years ago. Building walls, staining concrete, replacing windows and cleaning had made the entire structure unrecognizable.

Holly absolutely loved the place. She'd moved all of her things from the house to upstairs, and had even negotiated with Jeremy to use part of the storefront as her own art gallery and studio. They'd walled off that portion, though they'd share the same front entrance, and she'd also chosen a simple name—Holly's Art.

Business had been slow here in town, but she'd always gotten the bulk of her orders from online sales. Though once she'd longed to be accepted by the townspeople, these days she'd been both too busy and too happy to worry much about that.

She and Jeremy had become more than friends and lovers—they'd morphed into partners too. In every sense of the word. Though they hadn't had any serious discussions about making things permanent, she'd matured enough to understand that this kind of decision took time. They'd get there eventually; of that, she had no doubt.

Right now, they were blissfully happy. They had each

other, and Thor. She had her art and the added blessing of helping the man she loved make his dreams come true.

At his request, she'd gone with Jeremy to Anchorage, where they'd visited not only Anchorage Animal Care and Control, but also the SPCA and the Humane Society. Jeremy had been looking for a particular kind of dog, taking into account not only breed, but temperament and age.

They'd chosen two dogs to start with, both male. One appeared to be a Belgian Malinois mix and the other a Lab mix.

They were young and friendly and got along not only with each other, but with Thor too. Jeremy had begun the long process of training them, with the eventual goal of making them search dogs, whether for SAR units or police departments. He'd explained to her how valuable a well-trained dog like this could be and how his reputation would be built one animal at a time.

Though Walker had been the real estate agent at Holly's insistence, he'd refused to communicate with Russell except through her or Jeremy. Which she'd done via text message, since Russell refused to pick up the phone. Since Walker also had a retired attorney friend who acted as a title officer, the closing had been held at the small-town bank. Holly signed, was told money would be sent by wire transfer into her account and left the keys. The new owners, a retired couple from Anchorage who'd wanted a simpler life, would move in immediately.

After leaving the bank, Holly's phone rang. "Kip," she said, answering. "I hope you remembered I'm off work today."

"I did, I did." Kip sounded bemused. "But I wondered if you'd heard from Mikki yet. She asked me to help her gather up the entire town for some sort of meeting at her place tonight. Six o'clock. I wasn't sure if she was going to call you or not."

"This is the first I've heard of that," Holly said, surprised. "What's this meeting about? Has someone gone missing?"

"I'm not sure." But the hint of satisfaction she heard in his voice told her he knew more than he was letting on. "I just know Mikki specifically requested you and Jeremy attend."

Just then, her phone beeped, indicating another call. She told Kip she'd try to go and then clicked over.

"Holly?" Jeremy sounded as confused as she felt. "Mikki just told me she's having a town meeting at six and that if we value her friendship, we have to go."

"Kip said something similar," she said. "I guess it won't hurt to pop in there." She'd been making an effort to get out more. Since Russell's reappearance, no one had confronted her, but no one had apologized either. It was what it was.

"We can grab a bite to eat too." Jeremy added, clearly trying to sweeten the deal. He more than anyone understood how uneasy she still felt going out in public. Too much ugliness had made her wary. But her innate optimism kept telling her the past would fade with time.

The scars on her heart might take a bit longer to heal.

When she got back to the Second Street building, a place she'd come to think of as home, she found Thor supervising as Jeremy worked with one of the new dogs, the Lab mix they were calling Loki. They'd named the other one Walter.

Thor greeted her, and together they watched as Jeremy put Loki through his paces, which consisted of foundation work of basic obedience. The quiet competence and respect between man and dog made her breath catch.

The One, she thought. And went upstairs to get ready for the big town meeting later.

After showering and changing, they made sure all three dogs were fed and taken outside. Thor stayed in their living quarters while they were gone, while Loki and Walter remained in the kennel area downstairs.

"Are you ready?" Jeremy asked, the warmth in his gaze kindling an answering heat inside her.

"I am." She allowed herself to drink in the sight of him, all the way from his boots and worn jeans, to his fitted T-shirt and muscular arms. As always, desire flared. When their eyes met, she swallowed hard and looked away.

"Later," he promised, letting her know he felt the same. "We need to be early if we want to have any chance of finding parking."

"Or we could simply walk," she replied. "It's just a few blocks, and the weather is still nice."

They linked hands and went outside, where both their vehicles waited. "Are you sure?" he asked. Though the night air had turned a little chilly, it still felt comfortable.

"Why not? You know the cold and snow are coming soon. We might as well enjoy this bit of autumn while we can. Plus, we've got time."

Hand in hand, they strolled up to Main Street. Despite being fifteen minutes early, it seemed as if every parking spot on Main had been taken.

"See?" She nudged him. "Walking was a good idea."

He pulled her to him and kissed her. "Yes, it was."

Once they reached Mikki's, they could barely get inside the door. Small groups of people stood outside, talking and laughing. As always, Holly felt a little self-conscious, and she could tell when someone noticed her, but no one said anything or even directed any hostile stares her way. A definite improvement, though she wondered if she'd ever feel as if she belonged.

Inside, rows of folding chairs had been set up. Mikki must have been watching for them, because she shouldered her way through the crowd to get to them. "Welcome!" she said, hugging first Holly and then Jeremy. "I've saved you a couple of seats in the front row. Follow me."

Though they exchanged bemused looks, they did as Mikki directed. She showed them to two chairs front and center. "VIP treatment for you tonight," she said, smiling. She left them with a wave and went to greet someone else.

A podium with a microphone had been set up on the small stage where local bands often performed.

Now Holly felt even more nervous. Still, she sat down, glad to have Jeremy next to her. "This is concerning," she said. "What do you think this is about?"

Jeremy kissed her cheek, clearly not caring who saw. "I think we're about to find out. Don't worry. I have a feeling it's all going to be fine."

A few minutes later, Mikki stepped up to the mic and asked everyone to please be seated. She waited, drumming her fingers on the top of the wooden podium, while everyone found chairs. As usual when they had a town meeting, there were never enough seats, and an overflow standing-room-only area soon filled up as well.

"We called this meeting for several reasons," she said. "First up, one of our former residents, Gary Acosta, was found dead this morning in Anchorage. Right now, his death is being considered a homicide. The Anchorage Police Department has reached out to his family, but they also ask if anyone knows anything about his murder to please contact them."

Several people began talking at once, demanding more

information. Mikki dealt with this the best she could, though mostly she kept repeating the need to contact the Anchorage Police Department.

Though Holly had instinctively straightened at the news, a quick glance at Jeremy showed he appeared unconcerned. When he noticed her look, he shrugged. "I have no idea," he said, pitching his voice low. "It was likely some of the dangerous people he worked for."

And had nothing to do with Holly, Jeremy or even Russell. As horrible as it might seem, Gary's death also meant she no longer had to worry about him reappearing for any reason.

"Moving on," Mikki finally declared. "Someone else would like to address all of you." She turned and gestured. Russell stood and made his way to the podium.

The place went utterly silent. So quiet, Holly could hear Jeremy's quick intake of breath. As Mikki took a seat, Russell looked out over the packed room. When he located Holly and Jeremy, he nodded.

"I wanted to speak to everyone today," Russell began. He looked better than he had in a long time. Clean, sober and healthy, his eyes were clear and his voice strong. "All of you are aware of my disappearance. I understand that all kinds of rumors were circulating around. The vast majority of them were untrue."

When he locked his eyes on Holly, she fought the urge to squirm in her seat. Luckily, he next looked at Jeremy.

"Some of you might know that I became addicted to drugs. While that does not entirely excuse my behavior prior to my leaving, I'd like you to take that into consideration." He took a deep breath, his gaze once again sweeping the room.

"I did some awful things to many, many people. Most of

them I'd once considered my friends. I abused their friendship and their trust. For that, please know that I am deeply sorry."

No one spoke.

"And to my younger brother, Jeremy," Russell continued. "Together we held strong after losing our parents. But when you needed me, I failed you. Instead of offering you help, I turned my back on you. I regret sending you out alone into the world at the young age of sixteen. I vow to make it up to you somehow, if you'll allow me to."

Staring hard at his brother, Jeremy slowly nodded. Holly knew how much he hated having his personal baggage made public, but she also suspected he understood Russell's need to make community amends. Hopefully, he'd follow through with his promise to forge a new relationship with his younger brother.

Several people in the audience had begun talking and whispering. Russell waited until it had once again grown quiet before speaking.

"But there is no one I wronged more than the woman sitting next to my brother in the front row. Holly Davis. I not only got you to upend your life and move from Texas all the way up here, but I lied to you and I abused you. Both verbally and physically. What I did to you is beyond appalling, and I am deeply ashamed. I know that I can never make it up to you, but I will forever regret the way I treated you. You're a good woman, Holly. You deserve more than anyone to find happiness and love."

Touched, she slowly nodded. While she wasn't quite ready to offer him forgiveness, she hoped to be able to do so someday. Because she understood all too well how bitterness and resentment could fester inside.

"Now that I've bared my soul," Russell said, once again

looking around the crowd. "From what I hear, there are several of you who owe Holly an apology. If you're brave enough, then I suggest you come up here and do so. You'll feel a lot better, I promise."

With that, Russell took a seat next to Mikki.

At first, no one stirred. People began to talk, whispering and muttering amongst themselves.

Now Holly fidgeted. She didn't need or want a public apology. She had no desire to dwell on the past. Instead, she chose to move forward. One thing she'd learned during her time in Alaska was that actions always spoke louder than words.

The sound of high heels clicking on wood had everyone turning. Tanya, wearing jeans and heels and a white cotton button-up shirt, walked up to the stage. Rumor had it that she and Russell had tried to work things out but, in the absence of Russell's desire to party, had failed.

"I too would like to tell Holly I'm sorry," Tanya said, staring directly at her. "Over jealousy and lies, I made your life a living hell. I'm very sorry. And to all my friends, all the nonsense I told you about Holly being responsible for Russell's disappearance was bull. By now, I'm sure you're aware. If you tormented Holly because of me, you also owe her an apology."

That said, Tanya spun around and went back to her seat.

One by one, various people stood. Though no one else made their way to the podium, several voiced their apologies. By now, Holly wished the floor would open up and swallow her. But she kept her back straight and her chin up, managing to nod graciously as each individual spoke.

Finally, Mikki regained the microphone. "If that's everyone, then I think we can safely say this meeting is—"

"Wait!" Jeremy stood. "I have something to say."

Holding out his hand, once Holly took it, he pulled her to her feet. Together they went up to the podium. Fingers linked with his, a feeling of calm confidence settled over her. The magnitude of what had just happened washed over her, making her realize she might just have a place in this town after all.

"Many of you have expressed your desire to make amends for the way you've treated this woman," Jeremy said, his deep voice carrying out over the room. "And there have been numerous others who have been there for her all along. You know who you are. And your friendship, loyalty and trust is deeply appreciated."

When he squeezed Holly's hand, she thought he might stop there, but he continued. "As you may or may not be aware, Holly is a phenomenal artist. She'll be opening her own gallery, showcasing and selling her work, in the old McMillian building on Second Street. She'll be having a grand opening soon, and I hope you'll attend and support her. Thank you."

Turning to her, he squeezed her fingers with one hand. Covering the mic with the other, he quietly asked her if she had anything she wanted to say.

Overwhelmed and inexplicably near tears, she shook her head no.

"Okay, then." Speaking into the mic, he said what Mikki had been about to say a moment ago. "This meeting is adjourned. The kitchen and the bar are open. Everyone go get something to eat and drink."

Later, after snagging a seat at the bar and ordering burgers, Holly and Jeremy struggled to eat uninterrupted. So many people stopped by to either wish them well or let Holly know that they planned to be at her gallery opening. She couldn't help but notice Jeremy hadn't mentioned his dog training business, so she made sure to do that, offering her support.

Finally, when they'd had their meal, they ducked out of Mikki's, which remained packed. A band had started playing and several couples had made their way onto the dance floor. Holly and Jeremy had looked at each other, briefly tempted, but in the end they decided to go.

Outside, dusk had turned to darkness and the stars shone like diamonds in the black velvet sky. Fingers still entwined, they walked slowly through the quiet streets of their town.

"Thank you for doing that," Holly finally said. "I appreciate you supporting my gallery."

"Anything for the woman I love," Jeremy replied. He used the word so easily, so casually, that at first she wasn't sure how to react. After all, he'd done that once before, on the day they'd gone to see how badly the fire had damaged her house.

"No response?" he asked, stopping and turning to face her. "I'm beginning to think I might be alone in how I feel."

A quiet happiness bubbled inside of her. "I don't think you believe that," she said, resuming the walk. "After all we've been through together. You know how I feel. Actions speak louder than words."

"True," he conceded. "But it'd be nice to hear you say it anyway."

They crossed another street, now just a block from home. As they walked, she thought about what she wanted to say, and how to best speak it, but in the end she could only give him the simple phrase that fit her emotions.

She waited until they'd reached the corner directly across from their building. Stopping, she turned to face him, reaching for his other hand. "I love you too, Jeremy Elliot. More than words could ever convey."

They kissed then, a warm and soulful kiss, full of passion. "See? That wasn't so difficult, was it?" Jeremy teased, smiling. The love and happiness shining from his brown eyes made her all warm and melty inside.

"Let's go inside," she replied, her answering smile full of promise. "And I'll show you."

Laughing, he sprinted for the back door, tugging her along with him. Once inside, she proceeded to show him exactly how she felt.

* * * * *

HARLEQUIN
Reader Service

Enjoyed your book?

Try the perfect subscription for Romance readers and get more great books like this delivered right to your door.

See why over 10+ million readers have tried Harlequin Reader Service.

Start with a Free Welcome Collection with free books and a gift—valued over $20.

Choose any series in print or ebook.
See website for details and order today:

TryReaderService.com/subscriptions